SPELL
BOUND

Also by Gretchen Rue

Something Wicked

SPELL BOUND

Gretchen Rue

HEAD
of ZEUS

An Aria Book

First published in the United States in 2023 by Crooked Lane Books,
an imprint of The Quick Brown Fox & Company LLC.

First published in the UK in 2024 by Head of Zeus,
part of Bloomsbury Publishing Plc

9 7 5 3 1 2 4 6 8

A catalogue record for this book is available from the British Library.

ISBN (PB): 9781035904280
ISBN (E): 9781035904310

Cover design: Meg Shepherd/Head of Zeus

Printed and bound in Great Britain by
CPI Group (UK) Ltd, Croydon CR0 4YY

Head of Zeus
First Floor East
5–8 Hardwick Street
London EC1R 4RG

WWW.HEADOFZEUS.COM

For my mother, Jo-Anne.
My first fan, my biggest fan,
the best person I know.

Chapter One

"**D**ead people have the best books."

I looked down at the newspaper that had been placed in front of me, then up at the woman who had put it there. Imogen Prater, the only other full-time employee who worked at the little bookstore–slash–tea shop that I owned, was staring down at me expectantly, her brown eyes gleaming.

Imogen was usually pretty stoic, rarely wearing her expressions so keenly on her face, so I leaned back on my stool and picked up the newspaper she had slapped down.

"I'm sorry, did you say *dead people?*"

She nodded eagerly, reaching over the top of the page to tap an area of specific interest. "Look, there's going to be a massive estate sale at the old Weatherly mansion in Barneswood. The former owner was apparently a massive bibliophile. Phoebe, I bet there are thousands of books in the library."

I read the item she was pointing to, which did indeed advertise a large estate sale and auction happening the next day. I then glanced past Imogen to the bookstore behind her. While the shelves still appeared to be full and we had several boxes of extra stock in the basement we could use to top them off—not to mention the new releases that arrived weekly—I had to admit that our bargain bin was looking a little barren. And the idea of going to an estate sale to scout for books was pretty enticing.

It had been about seven months since I'd inherited the Earl's Study from my aunt Eudora and moved to the small town of Raven Creek to take over the business and start my life from scratch. Divorced, without a home or a sense of direction, I had mourned my aunt's passing, but was also grateful to her for the opportunity she'd given me.

I had a new home—a beautiful Victorian mansion, no less—and a thriving business to run. Between that and Bob, the fat orange tabby cat she'd left behind, Eudora had given me everything I needed to start fresh and feel fulfilled. Of course, my introduction to life in Raven Creek hadn't gone totally smoothly.

My first week in town, someone had ended up dead behind my shop, and I'd gotten myself on the wrong side of the town busybody, Dierdre Miller. Seven months later, no one else had died, thankfully, but Dierdre still wasn't terribly fond of me.

Being more settled into my place in the little town also meant I no longer felt too guilty about taking a day off work at the shop or making big decisions on behalf of the business. It was *my* business, after all.

"It says here it starts at eleven. I'm supposed to work the morning shift tomorrow . . ." I worked the morning shift almost every day, as Imogen wasn't an early bird, and Eudora had always been the one to open the shop. I wasn't much of a morning person either, but I'd learned to enjoy the quiet time the mornings offered me. I would go for a run, weather permitting, then load Bob up into the most ludicrous cat backpack I'd ever seen, and we would bike over to the shop together.

Charlie Bravebird at the pet store had sold me on the backpack when I'd admitted that I wanted to keep bringing Bob to work with me but hated wasting gas and hurting the environment by driving such a short distance. I didn't want to walk with Bob's carrier, though, even if we lived fairly close. The backpack looked like something out of a sci-fi movie, with little bubble windows Bob could see out of and breathing holes to give him air. And much to my surprise, he loved it.

Every morning, once he finished scarfing down breakfast, he would go to the front door and sit next to the backpack, letting out a plaintive "Mrow?" as he waited for me to get ready.

Over the winter we'd eschewed the bike in favor of a warm car, but now that spring was turning into summer and the weather was delightful when it wasn't raining, we biked.

Currently, Bob was curled up in one of the big leather armchairs next to the fireplace, dozing. In the other chair was old Mr. Loughery, who came in every day for tea and to read his latest used-book purchase. When he finished the book—he was currently reading a Laura Lippman mystery—he'd trade it back in for store credit and start the process all over again. He had done this pretty much since Eudora opened the shop. I liked the comfort of the routine. Plus Mr. Loughery gave good feedback about new test recipes from my little kitchen.

We didn't make a lot of food at the Earl's Study, as it wasn't a restaurant, but we liked to supplement the pastries we brought in daily from the Sugarplum Fairy next door with ones we made ourselves. Our Earl Grey Tea Shortbread was hugely popular, and I'd started adding homemade sourdough toasts to the menu a few times a week. Sometimes we did avocado toast with eggs on top; other times I'd do a ricotta toast with figs and honey. No matter what was on the menu, it always disappeared by the time the lunch rush died down.

I looked from Mr. Loughery, who was currently asleep, snoring softly, back to Imogen. "If I open up shop tomorrow, do you think you could come in for nine instead of ten? That would give me enough time to get to Barneswood before the sale starts."

"Bless you for not asking me to get here for seven," Imogen laughed, brushing her long black braids over her shoulder. She changed the color in them on a semiregular basis, augmenting the black hair of the braids with fun statement pieces. Right now she was sporting electric blue, which managed to give her dark skin an almost golden undertone. "You've got yourself a deal."

"Obviously, I'll give you overtime for the extra hour," I added, as if she still might need convincing.

Imogen scoffed. "Thank you, but it's not exactly a hardship to come in for an extra hour."

"We can call Daphne to help you for the lunch rush. I know she's always looking for more hours than just her weekend shifts." I wished I could give the girl more time on a regular basis, but the shop was rarely busy enough to justify the added wages, and while we were doing well, we weren't doing *so* well that I could manage another full-time staffer.

It was a small town, after all, and while tourist traffic was beginning to pick up now that winter was over, I still liked to keep the budget tight to balance out the off-season slow times where it was mostly just locals coming in to collect special orders or stock up in case they got snowed in.

Being "snowed in" in the Pacific Northwest didn't look the way it did in the Midwest, by any means, but it rankled me sometimes that people made fun of our responses to ice storms. I'm sorry, but have you ever tried driving a car up a sharply inclined hill when the road is a literal sheet of ice? Try *walking* up it. Impossible.

I cut out the notice from the paper and went to the office to slip it into my wallet. I had a relatively decent idea of where the sale was, and I'd driven to Barneswood a few times since I'd moved to Raven Creek, but just in case I got lost, I wanted to have the details handy.

Looked like I was going on a store-sponsored shopping spree. I had to admit I was more than a little excited.

Chapter Two

The next day dawned bright and cheerful. After the long winter with its gloomy mornings, it was such a relief in May to have the sun come up before I did. I turned on the coffeemaker and fed Bob his favorite wet food before lacing up my running shoes and heading out the door for my morning jog.

It was just before six, and I went only about three miles, which gave me enough time to run home and have a quick shower before meeting Amy at the Sugarplum Fairy around seven. She was there a lot earlier than that prepping breads and pastries for the day, but seven was plenty early enough for me.

The morning run had become a part of my ritual, and while it had often been too cold or otherwise difficult to do it over the winter, I tried to get one in whenever I could. The morning air today was crisp, still holding the tiniest hints of winter's chill, and I was glad I'd decided to wear my long-sleeved running jacket.

While the forecast for the rest of the day was sunny and warm, we weren't quite at that point yet, and I didn't want to catch a cold. My long, nearly black hair swayed back and forth in its high ponytail as I ran, and my running playlist pounded out a beat that matched my footfalls. There's nothing quite like a little Destiny's Child on a spring morning to put some extra bounce in your step.

I completed my short loop, waving to early-morning dog parents who had to let their fur-children out before the workday began. I remembered the dogs' names but rarely the people's. Eugene was the little corgi whose owner was a middle-aged woman with a graying pixie cut, and Goliath was the towering Great Dane who belonged to a tall, slender man with thick black glasses and a neatly trimmed goatee. I saw them both like clockwork every morning, and we waved in mutual early-bird greeting but rarely stopped to chat.

There were a handful of other regulars I sometimes saw: a Chihuahua named Tank, and three golden retrievers named Sandra, Ruth, and Sonia, which made me chuckle every time their owner called them inside. Naming your dogs after female Supreme Court justices was absolutely fabulous, and I often wondered what the older woman with her coiled gray perm had done for a living, because she certainly appeared to be retired now.

After my three-mile loop was complete, I jogged back up my front steps and paused on the top board as it let out a loud creak.

Since I knew I hadn't suddenly put on any extra weight, I didn't think the board was protesting that. I stepped backward, then onto the board again, and sure enough, it groaned and sagged under me.

I let out a loud sigh. Auntie Eudora's house was glorious, truly a beautiful thing to behold, looking for all the world like somewhere the Addams family would feel at home if they decided to go on vacation. But it was also very old, and in my aunt's later years, she hadn't been able to do as much maintenance on it as she had when she was young and spry.

I'd been trying to ignore a lot of the necessary upkeep over the winter, but evidently the months of wet snow and ice had taken a bit of a toll on the front porch and steps.

Cautiously I moved around the porch, testing out several of the graying boards, and found quite a few places that bowed under my weight.

Replacing them was going to have to go to the top of my to-do list.

I wondered vaguely if I might be able to bribe Rich and Leo—with a case of good local craft beer and some delicious pizza from Tony's Pizzeria—into providing a little elbow grease and getting the job done.

When I'd visited Raven Creek as a kid and stayed with Eudora, I'd befriended two local boys, Leo and Ricky, and we'd been fast friends for about as long as it was cool for boys and girls to be buddies at that age, and then as teens we'd drifted apart. My family moved to Chicago, and I'd stopped coming to visit as frequently. But Leo and Rich had remained close to Eudora, and she had put them to work quite often in their teen years helping with upkeep on the old house. Maybe it was time to get them back into the habit.

After I'd come back to town, I'd reconnected with the boys, who were now fully grown men, obviously, and while it had initially felt as if something might be blossoming between me and Rich, we'd put things on an extended hold almost immediately. We were both freshly divorced, and starting a new romance seemed like a recipe for disaster.

Leo, I suspected, might like to ask me out, but he was shy and hadn't taken the plunge yet. While he wasn't my normal type—he was a big bear of a man, tall and heavy, with a big beard—I thought I would say yes.

Well, I'd give them a call when I got back from Barneswood to see what their weekend plans were. Didn't make sense to put off the inevitable with the porch, and I could probably pick up some lumber on my way home today. Raven Creek had only a small hardware store, but Barneswood had a proper lumberyard.

I checked my watch, then ducked into the house quickly to grab a tape measure from the kitchen junk drawer. I couldn't exactly buy lumber if I didn't know what I needed. Back out on the porch, I realized just how major of a job it would be to get the whole porch completed and decided beer and pizza wouldn't cut it for something of that scale. But we could probably get the entrance boards replaced over the weekend so I didn't accidentally put my foot through them coming home after a run.

I did a quick measurement of the area I thought was most vital to tackle, including the front steps themselves, and jotted the numbers down on my phone. By the time I finished, I had only about five minutes for a quick shower, which wasn't nearly enough for the water to heat up properly, and I was grateful to my past self for setting out my clothes the day before so I didn't need to think about it.

While the weather was turning toward summery, it was still cool enough in the mornings and evenings to justify long sleeves. But in the Earl's Study, we had the fireplace going, and the heat from the ovens as I baked bread and cookies also kept me pretty toasty. I opted for a pair of nice jeans, my comfiest black loafers—standing all day meant smart footwear ruled over cute, and who knew what the estate sale situation would be like—a light-gray T-shirt with an Alphonse Mucha art print on the front with shiny gold highlights accenting it in places so I glittered in the right light, and a cinnamon-colored long cardigan that fell to my knees. The cardigan had actually belonged to Eudora and was one of several items of her clothing I had salvaged from her closets to keep for myself. The rest had been donated to a local thrift store, but I was impressed by some of Eudora's clothing choices and loved that she had favored high-quality wardrobe staples that felt timeless enough to easily blend into my existing wardrobe.

Between the cardigan and the T, I was set for any kind of weather that might come my way.

Bob was waiting for me at the front door when I finished getting dressed, his orange tail swishing back and forth and his big yellow-green eyes watching me carefully. He had noticed that his backpack wasn't at the door waiting, and the judgment in his expression was as clear as day.

"Mreow," he trilled.

"Don't look at me like that. You're still coming; we're just taking the car today. Though I probably should leave you at home rather than force poor Imogen to deal with that stare all day."

He slow-blinked at me and made a little *mrr* sound, which I knew meant he didn't believe I'd leave him behind and that Imogen loved spending time in his company because he was a perfect gentleman with her.

When I'd first taken ownership of Eudora's estate, no one had told me there was a cat involved in the package. He'd just been waiting on the porch for me when I arrived. Leo told me later that Eudora had asked him to come by periodically to feed the cat before I arrived, and Leo had been *very* generous with Bob at mealtimes. The ginger menace had been quite the chonk when I'd met him. He was still a big boy but definitely a bit healthier now.

He didn't appreciate the little diet I'd put him on, but the vet had insisted he could stand to lose about five pounds for his long-term health. I'd heard the same thing from my own doctor a time or two, especially right after my divorce when my diet had consisted largely of my good friends Ben, Jerry, and Tim.

Since we weren't biking to the store today, a carrier felt unnecessary. Bob wasn't the type of cat to make a break for it the second I opened the door, so I slung my purse over my shoulder, made sure my keys were in hand, and hefted him up.

"Mrrroowwww," he said dramatically, tail swishing a bit harder now.

"It's this or the travel cage, so the choice is yours, pal."

He started to purr.

"That's what I thought."

Less than ten minutes later we were unlocking the back door to the Earl's Study, and Bob made a beeline for his favorite chair, leaving Mr. Loughery's vacant as always. He gave a huge stretch, then curled himself into a tight orange ball.

Typical.

I stashed my purse in the office and headed for the front door. It was a delightful treat to have the Sugarplum Fairy right next door. It was a charming little bakery with pink and white accents and adorable Parisian café tables outside, and her customers almost always found their way into my own store or vice versa.

Who didn't love books and lattes together, or tea and pastries? While our offerings did overlap with those of the bakery, there was no rivalry. Amy didn't do a lunch special and we did, and we mostly served her pastries at our shop, while she carried a selection of our most popular loose-leaf teas at her place. It was a symbiotic relationship that seemed to work well for everyone.

And I loved to have an excuse to visit her every morning for a perfect chocolate hazelnut latte. She offered other flavors on a seasonal rotating basis, but I was a sucker for that sweet morning treat and rarely changed my standing order.

Before I headed into Amy's shop, I took a moment to soak in the peaceful morning stillness on Main Street. While Raven Creek wasn't a bustling metropolis by any means, the main streets would certainly get busier as the day wore on. Between locals and an ever-present supply of tourists, we saw a lot of foot traffic around town.

For months it had been dark when I got to work, so I rarely got to appreciate the beauty of my new hometown, and this was going to be my first time experiencing spring and summer here as an adult.

The sun was rising through the tall pines and turning the mountains in the background a gray-pink hue that made the whole thing look like a fake Hollywood backdrop. Birds sang merrily, and the smell of fresh bread wafted out from Amy's place.

I smiled to myself and gave a contented sigh, feeling a sense of calm that one can experience only when they know they're home. And that's what Raven Creek felt like to me now. Maybe more than anywhere else I'd lived since I was a child.

Though it was only seven in the morning, Amy's OPEN sign was on, and the lights blazed inside. Bakeries needed to keep early hours, and Amy closed when she sold out. She arrived every day at about three to start the loaves baking for her morning pickups and deliveries, and by six thirty she was open for walk-in traffic.

Not that there was a heck of a lot of it at this hour.

I was the only person in the shop, and she emerged from the back with a big smile. My white order boxes were already neatly stacked on the counter behind her, waiting for my arrival.

"The usual?" she grinned, plucking an empty pink coffee cup from the stack.

I held out a reusable mug I'd brought from home. "Imogen keeps lecturing me on my carbon footprint, so I ordered these." I showed the mug to her. It was mint green, and in bronze script it showed off the Earl's Study logo, the same one as on the big wooden sign hanging over our door. "I'm getting some frosted ones for summer that are a bit bigger so people can see the pretty colors of the iced tea. What do you think?"

Amy took the lightweight plastic cup, which looked identical to a paper one except that it could be washed and reused over and over.

"This is really cool, Phoebe. Do you mind sending me the information on where you ordered from? I'd love to get some of these for the shop."

"Of course." I grabbed the notepad that sat on her counter and jotted down the name of the website I'd used. "They do great deals for bulk orders, and you can get samples first so you know it looks good. I'm going to offer a discount to anyone who brings their own cup in."

"I love that." She went to the sink next to the coffeemaker and gave my cup a quick swish in the hot water, then started to make my usual latte.

I scanned the jars of loose-leaf tea on top of her pastry cabinets. "You're looking a bit low on the Lemon Meringue Pie blend. Do you want me to pop by a bit later with some more?"

"That would be awesome. Thank you." Amy and I didn't have a traditional customer relationship. We swapped goods back and forth; I gave her whatever tea she wanted, and she gave me her pastries so cheap they were basically free. It had worked for her and Eudora and continued to work now.

What Amy *didn't* know, and I often wanted to tell her, was that she was also actually my tenant. Shortly after arriving in Raven Creek, thanks to the dead man who had unexpectedly shown up behind my shop, I had learned that I didn't own just the Earl's Study. Eudora had owned the deeds to half the businesses on Main Street.

Rather than using the rental income for her own benefit, she'd promised the previous owner to use the money only for the betterment of the town. I let things stay much the same now that I was the owner. I hadn't told anyone the truth about my landlord status, because I suspected they would treat me differently if they knew I was an on-paper millionaire.

The money wasn't really *mine*, though. I ran it through a secondary business with the help of some lawyers, and they would just come to me when something in town needed attention. The properties were kept pristine, rent was never raised, and over Christmas we had better decorations than any larger city in a fifty-mile radius.

It was weird to technically own the Sugarplum Fairy, but I was glad to know I had the power to keep Amy and other business owners from ever needing to worry about being able to keep their businesses open.

Raven Creek was small, and it needed the cute little boutique shops all around town to draw tourist attention. We were known for our great hiking and bird-watching, not to mention the charming European vibes the local architecture radiated, but it was the people and businesses that made visitors keep coming back.

Plus, Amy already knew my *other* biggest secret, and that was more than enough. If someone could call it a secret.

The bookstore and the fat cat weren't the only things that had been part of my inheritance.

After Eudora died, I'd also learned that she was a witch.

And so was I.

Chapter Three

There had been a long-standing joke in Raven Creek about Eudora being a witch. Even when I'd visited as a child, other kids had treated Lane End House like the home of a wicked witch.

They'd challenge each other to go knock on the door and run away, something I had learned to my annoyance was still happening after Eudora died, and it freaked me out every single time someone did it.

I'd written off those rumors as silly childish nonsense, but what I couldn't have known at the time was that while the children were scaring each other with stories of the house and the witch who lived within, their parents were turning up at her shop to buy her *special* tea blends. The ones we kept in the back rather than out on display.

Eudora had a special gift for spells of intention, I'd learned from my friend Honey, who owned the shop New Moon. Her special magical gift was being able to help others get what they most wanted. It was a uniquely selfless gift, because it worked only to benefit others and not Eudora herself.

She took that gift and poured it, metaphorically, into the teas she made. People who drank her love teas, her money teas, or any of the other special blends she put together were sure to have positive results. She really wanted what was best for people.

I could do the same, but with less potency. I'd learned, thanks to unexpected trial and error, that I was especially gifted in probability magic. Meaning in certain situations I could *literally* stop time and change the course of things already set in motion. It wasn't exactly something I could control, though I was working on trying. It was the kind of gift that sprang up at unexpected times and let me help strangers who had tripped before they fell to the ground. In one very exciting encounter I hoped never to repeat, I'd been able to step out of the path of a moving bullet.

It was a very cool gift to have, but I wished I had a bit more say in when it popped up.

As for more general witchy skills, I had been visiting New Moon every other week since I'd discovered the truth about myself to drink tea—or sometimes wine—with Honey, the owner and a fellow witch, and practice some basic skills I had at my disposal. Most witches had one or two things they were naturally better at, but every witch had more general magical abilities.

Unfortunately, none of my witchy gifts were much use when it came time to do things like fix my porch or mow the lawn. I *could* turn off my lights from bed with the snap of a finger, though, which was a pretty nifty development.

Honey tried to make me feel better about my lackluster witchy skill set, reminding me that most witches discovered their power at around puberty and I'd been something of a late bloomer. I'd had less time to learn and develop, which meant I hadn't been able to sharply hone all the basics just yet.

I'd get there; it just took time.

I was thinking about how helpful magic would be as I balanced two large pastry boxes, my to-go coffee cup, and my store keys. I glanced down as I worked through my daily struggle, wondering why I had never developed a better system than this, and spotted Bob sitting on the inside window ledge, staring up at me with his big unblinking eyes.

If only I could train the cat to open doors.

No, scratch that; I'd never know a moment's peace if he knew how to get outside on his own. What was it with cats and the outdoors? Inside it was nice and cozy; there was free food and comfy places to sleep. Yet so many of them acted like they were prisoners.

Bob wasn't like that, but he definitely kept an eye on the door whenever I went anywhere without him. He probably would have been okay outside on his own; it wasn't a busy area, especially up the hill by my house, and I didn't think there were too many potential predators in the woods behind Lane End House, but it made *me* feel better to have him inside.

I wrestled the door open, the bell over the frame chiming happily as if to congratulate me, and then managed to get all the way to the tea service counter as Bob weaved himself around my ankles with each step.

"If I didn't know better, I'd think you were trying to kill me," I chided him. "But joke's on you, pal; you're not in my will yet."

He purred loudly, then wandered back toward the bookstore side of the shop and his waiting chair, where there was now a little Bob-shaped divot in the leather. Even the weekly old ladies in the Knit and Sip crew left Bob's chair open for him as they got together around the fire to knit, gossip, and drink steaming pots filled with tea. We had a stack of other chairs in the back we pulled out for Friday, and Bob was able to sit with the women undisturbed.

Over the winter, several of the ladies had made him little holiday sweaters, which was just about the cutest thing I'd ever seen. Bob didn't love them and wriggled mightily whenever I tried to put one on, but I'd made sure to get photos of him in all four of them and given them as cards to the women for Christmas. They'd been delighted.

I put all the pastries out on the long white serving plates we used in the glass-fronted cooler, making sure the pretty strawberry tarts and rainbow-colored macarons were prominently displayed on the top shelf. I left an open space for our signature Earl Grey shortbread and headed into the small kitchen to get started on that, as well as the daily loaves of sourdough.

The sourdough at the Earl's Study was from a starter Eudora had made when she was about my age, which meant it had been an active starter for longer than I'd been alive. Sourdough was a fascinating creature, like a live animal you needed to care for and respect, and I made sure ours got fed twice a day at the shop.

Since we'd started doing lunch specials at the store, I'd had to increase the number of loaves we made regularly. We used to be able to get away with two, but now we were up to four, and we still ran out by the time the lunch rush ended.

I had four big proving bowls on the counter, each covered in a well-dusted dish towel and left to sit out overnight to rise. Two of them were standard, run-of-the-mill sourdough, one was a cracked black pepper and rosemary, and the other was a new recipe I was playing with that had big chunks of cheddar cheese in it as well as chopped bits of jalapeño. I'd been experimenting with it, trying both fresh jalapeño and then pickled, but I'd found the most success with the latter, since the pickled version didn't wrinkle up and get leathery during the baking process.

Normally I tried to do a savory loaf and a sweet loaf, but we were going all savory today. The plain breads could be used for something with more of a dessert flair. I did have lofty notions of trying a peanut butter and chocolate chunk variation next week.

Something about the tartness of sourdough and the slightly bitter sweetness of dark chocolate played really well together. My main concern was figuring out the best way to get the peanut butter into the mixture. Should I just swirl it into the dough? Perhaps I could try spreading some out on parchment paper and freezing it, then mixing the frozen pieces into the dough, which might be a little cleaner to work with.

As I thought about sweeter bread options, I started to think about all the fresh produce that would soon be easily accessible to me and how I could use it. Washington had some of the best local produce you could buy in the country, everything from apples to peaches to pears. The spring and summer bounty was going to give me a lot to work with. Perhaps a cherry chocolate chunk loaf? Dried cherries served as the base for our Cherry Pie Chai tea, so I definitely had some kicking around.

I had been so busy dreaming up new kinds of bread to make that the first batch of shortbread was already finished. I took out hot trays of baked cookies and left them on a rack to cool, then put the first two loaves of bread into the oven. They looked fine, but I'd been watching videos online in which much more skilled bakers than me would wrap their loaves in twine and use a lame—a razor with a handle designed specifically to artfully slice bread dough—to cut intricate patterns into the surface. Part of me wanted to try something that elaborate, but I also knew we didn't sell our bread by the full loaf, so all that effort would be for my own benefit. And maybe Instagram's.

With my handy-dandy timer clipped to my apron and my not-so-fancy loaves baking, I did a walk-through of the shop to make sure everything was in good order for the day ahead.

It was just habit at this point, because I knew Imogen would always leave the place spotless, and any books she didn't get around to putting on the shelves would be neatly stacked on our rolling library cart. Right now, there were only a dozen or so on it.

I straightened out the new display of reusable cups on the tea counter and made sure our little freebie bin of Earl's Study stickers was stocked. I'd been playing around with different marketing, making sure the shop had a distinctive look and recognizable branding. We had a firm schedule for the store's Instagram page, something that Daphne excelled at. She'd also been trying to convince me that short-form video apps like TikTok were a huge draw for customers, but since we didn't have an online storefront, I was hesitant to take the plunge.

That was another one of my long-term goals. Eudora had been perfectly happy with the foot traffic the store generated, and we did plenty of that, but I'd been scouring the websites of other indie bookstores, and lots of them had online order systems that would allow customers to order and have items shipped to them.

It would mean extra work, and we'd need to talk about the logistics of packing and shipping, but it might be enough to give Daphne full-time hours if it took off. But there were expenses involved, not to mention the arduous task of creating a complete online inventory. Right now, none of the store's used books were cataloged by title. We just put price stickers on them and entered the prices manually into the register. It made things a lot easier when we decided to move old stock into the bargain bins—just slap an orange sticker over the price on the back and you were done.

But I had wheels in motion and was hoping to get the whole store digitized before fall rolled back around. It was going to be a big project, and we'd need to close for a few days to get it done, but it was probably worth it in the long run, and might boost our sales over the winter months when fewer people were coming in off the street.

Heck, we could put the tea shop inventory online as well and start shipping that.

I wondered if there were any regulations regarding mailing tea out so people didn't think I was sneakily running some kind of drug operation.

Glancing over at Bob, I thought about the *other* project I was in the process of getting started, and that was bringing in adoptable cats to live at the store. I'd spoken to the shelter director in Barneswood about it over a month ago, and they seemed open to the idea of offering up some of the adoptable animals who had been in the shelter longest to come stay in the store.

We couldn't leave them out loose like Bob, but I had plans to build a nice kennel wall for them near the fireplace. The idea was that people who came in and browsed would be lured in by the cute animals and the homey environment, see Bob sitting by the fire, and realize that they also wanted to have a cat at home to sit with when they read books.

Bob got so much love and attention from customers; I could only imagine all the other cats we could help find homes.

That plan, too, was not something I could launch overnight. I had the thumbs-up from the shelter and had a space for the kennels—we'd moved one of the smaller bookshelves to a different area—and Leo had even offered to help me build them. Now I just needed the go-ahead from the town council, because evidently having *my* cat in the store and having adoptable cats were very different things, and I'd had to apply for a zoning adjustment.

Considering I owned the building and all the surrounding buildings, there was no one who could complain about it. I made sure everything was a safe distance from where we made and served food. The kennels were literally as far from the tea shop as you could get without being inside the Sugarplum Fairy. My work was done; I just needed to wait for official approval before we could get things under way, and that was taking forever.

Bureaucracy was no joke, even in small towns. Maybe especially in small towns. It didn't help me at all that Dierdre Miller was on the council, and probably the entire reason my paperwork was being held up.

You accuse a woman of murder *one time* and she holds a grudge forever.

There was a meeting scheduled this week where new business could be brought up, and I was hoping if I pitched my idea in public, they would expedite the process.

Admittedly, I also just enjoyed the open-floor town council meetings that happened once a month. I had thought the meetings in *Gilmore Girls* were a bit silly until I started to go to the ones in Raven Creek and suddenly realized that yes, small towns really could be just a little over-the-top sometimes.

The fitness tracker on my wrist buzzed, telling me two things: one, I'd barely moved since getting into the shop that morning, and two, it was ten minutes to eight, meaning the shop would be opening soon.

I loaded the now-cooled tray of shortbread cookies onto their display plate, and the front cabinet was now filled to the brim and ready for the morning ahead. I picked a big canister of Honeycrisp Apple and Honeysuckle tea from the shelf and emptied a quarter of a cup into a clear glass mason jar, then put the canister and jar onto the front counter with a *Tea of the Day* sign.

Iced tea season was coming, and I was going to have to assess Eudora's blends to see which would be the best served cold. I'd pretty much mastered making her existing recipes when things needed to be restocked, but I still wasn't brave enough to play around with my own blends.

At some point I would have to try *something* new, because the Earl's Study was well-known for its unique blends, and Eudora always loved to do seasonal recipes around major holidays. We'd already gone through one Christmas where I had stuck with the tried and true favorites, but I had a feeling people were going to want something different this year.

I was still so intimidated by the idea of trying my own thing that I kept it as the lowest checkbox on my to-do list. What was funny about my reticence over making new tea blends was that I had no issues at all trying creative and fun things with the food menu, as demonstrated by our rotating lunch offerings. But tea had been Eudora's *thing*, her niche, and she'd spent decades traveling the globe to learn everything she could about tea.

I just knew what I liked when it came to the flavor and how to steep the perfect cup or pot for my customers. Creating something new was going to be a daunting task. I wanted to make Eudora proud.

The morning flew by faster than expected. I had a dozen boxes dropped off from a major publishing house and spent the first hour of my day unboxing them and organizing them on the library cart in some semblance of order. I liked to tackle the new-release wall myself, typically, but maybe I'd leave that job up to Imogen today.

Speaking of my brilliant and wonderful full-timer, she waltzed in right at nine, as promised. I'd initially thought I would duck out as soon as she arrived, but the boxes were almost done, so I finished off the last of the sorting as she handled the few walk-ins we had who'd stopped by for a morning tea or pastry. Not a lot of book sales first thing in the morning, but the traffic habits would switch in the afternoon after the lunch rush died down.

"Daphne is going to be here at eleven thirty," I reminded Imogen. "Keep her around as long as you need. If she wants to stay until six so you can leave at five, I'm totally okay with that."

"Stop worrying so much," Imogen said. "We'll see how the day goes, and Daphne and I will decide from there, okay? You just go and enjoy the sale. I promise you we'll keep the ship afloat here without any problems, okay?"

I let out a little breath I hadn't noticed I'd been holding. She knew me too well if she'd realized I was having a bit of a hard time giving up any level of control. She and Daphne had both worked here with Eudora and were perfectly capable of running things in my absence. After all, they both had experience operating the place alone. I had nothing to worry about.

"I'll try to be back by six to pick up Bob, but if I'm not, just leave the light on in the bookstore so he doesn't think I've forgotten him. I'll get him on my way home. I think he'll be happier spending the day here than at home, which was why I brought him along."

"Of course. At this point I think Mr. Loughery would be upset to not have his buddy riding shotgun for the day." She laughed, and like clockwork, Mr. Loughery came through the door, wearing an old tweed jacket with leather patches on the elbows and a plaid newsboy cap, which he took off and tipped in our direction.

"Good morning, ladies. Hope this fine morning is treating you both well."

"The usual?" I asked. In almost seven months he hadn't once ordered something different, but I tried not to make assumptions about people. Who knew, maybe one day he'd come in and order a matcha?

I snorted quietly to myself at that idea. No, Irish Breakfast it was. Always Irish Breakfast.

"If it's not too much trouble." He plopped a five-dollar bill on the counter. We would keep him in hot tea for the rest of the day, but after my first week of observing his habits, I'd insisted he stop paying me by the cup. Five dollars for a whole day of tea was probably undervaluing my goods, but it didn't feel right letting him give me almost twenty dollars over the course of an eight-hour day. He would pay for any food he got, which happened only every few days. I pretended I didn't see that he usually brought a sandwich from home.

He had to be over eighty, and I knew that meant he was probably on a fixed income. A bit of free tea and access to the best seat in the house seemed like a reasonable way to let him spend his days. Sometimes he'd chat with the other regulars, but mostly he read for a couple hours, then fell asleep for a couple more.

"Morning, Bob," Mr. Loughery said to my cat, settling into the chair opposite him. "You're looking very orange today."

"I'll get his tea," Imogen said. "You need to get going or you'll miss the start of the sale. Bring us back something fun."

"Fun or not, I just hope we can bulk out the used-book shelves a bit more for summer."

"Get out of here. I promise you, nothing bad is going to happen. You worry too much."

Maybe.

Or maybe I worried precisely as much as I should.

Chapter Four

The drive to Barneswood was lovely. Now that summer was on its way, the trees were all lush with leaves in a dozen different verdant shades, and the blue sky was bedecked with fluffy white clouds.

Because we were in the Pacific Northwest, I knew better than to expect bright clear days like this all the time. Rain was the norm more often than not, but it simply helped with the greenery.

I'd arrived in Raven Creek in mid-October, which meant I was very familiar with the chilly, snow-frosted winter season and the gray, rainy spring. Summer was the time I remembered best, though. Those were the months I had more frequently come out to visit Eudora when I was younger, and so my best childhood memories had a Raven Creek summer as their backdrop.

The smell of damp greenery was so phenomenal I had to roll my windows down as I drove out of town and hit the highway going south. A warm, peaty scent clung to the air, with the background aroma of sun-kissed linen and the first flowers of summer just opening their cheerful faces.

Today was going to be a great day. I could feel it.

I was about twenty minutes away from Raven Creek when I got the first sign that my prediction for the morning might not come true.

"Mreow?"

No.

No, it couldn't be. I was imagining things; I had fallen asleep to a cat purring on my head one too many times, and it was messing up my brain chemistry and making me hear cats where there weren't any.

"Brr?" In my rearview I watched an orange head pop out of my bag of bags, the reusable grocery totes I kept in the car for when I got food or went thrifting. I'd brought extras along today in case I needed something to haul my new books home in.

Now a fat orange cat was staring out of the bags at me, squinting his green eyes into the bright light of midmorning.

I immediately pulled the car off to the shoulder of the road, thankful I wasn't on a busy city freeway but rather an underused highway between small towns. There were no other cars on the road right then, but the last thing I wanted to do was risk an accidental swerve into the opposite lane.

Putting the car into park, I swiveled around in my seat to get a good look at the back seat, just to confirm that my brain wasn't playing miserable tricks on me.

"Bob, are you kidding me?"

The cat had somehow managed to stow away, sneaking into the car at some point between when I'd left the shop and headed out on my trip. The last time I'd seen him he was snoring away contentedly on the leather chair next to Mr. Loughery. I knew I'd been a bit scatterbrained getting myself loaded into the car and onto the road, making sure I had everything I needed, but it seemed truly impossible that a very large cat could have snuck in without me noticing.

Then a mental picture of me running back into the store with the back doors to both the shop and the car wide open as I retrieved my purse flashed into my mind, and I knew that the little jerk had seized his opportunity.

"Oh, buddy, you're killing me." I glanced at my watch, knowing even before I looked there was simply no way I'd be able to get him back to the store and hightail it all the way to Barneswood again before the sale started. We were so close to the estate at this point it truly didn't make any sense to retrace my steps. "You're just going to have to hang out in the car for a little bit."

This probably made me a Grade A terrible cat mom, but it wasn't too hot out, and I could crack a window. Once I saw what was being offered in terms of books at the sale, I could go back to the car and sit with him until it was time for my lot to come around. If there was anything worth bidding on. And if I ended up not wanting anything, we would turn around and head right home.

I used this to justify pulling back onto the road and heading onward to Barneswood, trying not to let that nagging voice in the back of my head convince me I was doing the wrong thing. After all, clearly Bob had wanted a bit of open-road adventure, and who was I to deny him?

I cracked the back window ever so slightly, and he jumped out of the bag of bags, clambering over to put his nose up to the open air. He blinked a few times, then let out a little sneeze.

"Bless you."

"Brrow," he trilled back at me.

He made no move to come into the front seat, instead plopping down right behind the passenger seat so I could look at him if I glanced over my shoulder. How very *Driving Miss Daisy*, except I was Driving Mr. Bob.

About fifteen minutes later my GPS told me, "Your destination is on the left." And sure enough, there was a big wrought-iron gate on the left side of the highway, about five minutes away from Barneswood.

Weatherly Manor was printed in iron letters in a big arch over the gate, and I felt like I was pulling into either a gothic horror novel or Professor X's mansion from *X-Men*. Either way I could already tell I was going to be completely out of place in my cardigan and jeans.

Oh well. Wouldn't be the first time I'd stuck out like a sore thumb.

It took over a minute to drive through the overlapping trees, which formed a thick canopy and blotted out some of the bright midmorning sun. When I emerged from their coverage, an enormous mansion was waiting at the end of the circular drive. While there hadn't been any markers on the road to indicate this was the right place to go, a banner stand outside the front door read *Estate Sale*. Obviously, whoever was running this had done similar events in the past. It looked very fancy and professional.

I parked the car in the shadiest area I could find and opened all four windows a tiny crack to allow fresh air in. Upon rifling through my purse, I found a container of cat treats I must have thrown in to bring to the shop with me, then subsequently forgotten about.

Tossing a handful of Seafood Sensation Snax to Bob, I said, "Please be good. I won't be gone long."

He stared at me, as if wondering how stupid I was to believe that a cat would behave just because he was asked nicely. He yawned, then started to chow down on the treats. I had to believe he was going to be okay, because otherwise I'd just spend the whole afternoon worrying. He was a cat, the car wouldn't overheat or freeze, and now that he was stuffed with fishy calorie bombs, he wasn't going to starve.

I got out of the car, locking it behind me, and jogged in the direction of the mansion, where there were a number of other cars parked outside already. Some were especially fancy. I noted a Jaguar and an Audi in the mix, which made me feel even more like I was going to stand out as a poor townie.

Was I going to need to invest in a pantsuit for these events in the future?

As someone who used to work in a corporate world, I had no intention of ever going back to the stuffy, pressed-dress-shirt ways of my past. But I supposed if blending in would help me occasionally, maybe I could dig up some outfits from the back of my closet.

Though I wasn't entirely sure I still owned anything that screamed *business casual*.

Bounding up the steps of the mansion's front entry, I was surprised to find the foyer completely empty when I walked in. I'd expected the place to be bustling, but instead I had to follow the quiet murmur of voices to a pair of closed double doors at the back. Another banner sign here indicated I was in the right place.

I slid open the big doors, and the voices within fell to an instant hush as about a dozen faces turned to look at me.

My cheeks immediately felt flaming hot, and I wished they wouldn't stare. I wasn't even late. I gave a polite wave and picked up a glossy-looking printed pamphlet about the size of a magazine that had the mansion emblazoned on the front. As I flipped through, I saw that it was a detailed listing of all the items up for auction today.

They varied from simple kitchenware to antique furniture and even a few fancy cars. Inside the room I had entered, tables were laid out to display smaller items that were available to purchase directly— collectibles, including a huge lot of old baseball cards, and various bits of jewelry and men's accessories, such as vintage Tiffany cuff links, still in their original box, and a number of bejeweled tie pins.

I hadn't looked into the reason for the estate sale before coming but was now wondering if it was impolite of me to not know why all these goods were for sale at auction. It appeared to be mostly men's items, but there was a decent enough mix of women's goods as well, indicating these were the accumulated goods of a marriage. Was the husband downsizing, or had they both passed away, leaving the family to get rid of things they had no interest in?

Maybe there weren't any children to inherit and so the estate was being liquidated.

There were a lot of options, and none of them was more obvious than any other. It just seemed surprising that all these nice things were for sale and not going to someone else in the family, the way Aunt Eudora's things had come to me.

It felt a bit sad, honestly.

I walked slowly around the room and inside another area that had likely been a dining room, based on the layout and existing furniture. More goodies awaited me here, and I couldn't help but fall into the trap of leaning in and looking at different pieces of art and pretty baubles that I most definitely could not afford and didn't need.

Someone cleared their throat behind me, and I turned around so see a pretty, if severe-looking, woman standing behind me. Her dark hair was pulled back into a tight bun at the base of her neck, and not a single flyaway was present. Her skin was flawless, if a bit on the pale side, and her red lipstick might as well have been applied with a razor, the lines were so precise.

She pushed her black-rimmed glasses up on her nose and gave me a once-over. This morning I'd been fairly certain I looked cute, but based on how she was looking at me now, I might be a bit too librarian-chic for the event. Was she about to kick me out?

My stomach churned at the thought.

"Good morning. My name is Madeline Morrow. I'm running the sale today." She offered me a slim, dainty hand. When I shook it, I was shocked by the viselike grip of her squeeze. I got the feeling Madeline was probably in a male-dominated industry and accustomed to matching the intensity of her male colleagues. But that was just a guess based on my currently crushed metacarpals.

"I'm Phoebe Winchester. Very impressive setup you've got here. I, uh, like your banner signs?" I offered meekly.

"Oh. Thank you. What brings you to the event today? Anything specific caught your eye? I'd be more than happy to give you a look at some of the more specialized items that are part of the auction. Unless you're just looking at the *à la carte* pieces."

Ah, so that's what this was. She wasn't here because she thought I was a fraud; she was here to help boost the bidding by letting people inspect their chosen objects. That would probably work well for things like the cars and larger furniture.

"Actually, yes. I'm the owner of a little shop in Raven Creek called the Earl's Study." I paused, in case she was familiar with it, but no flicker of recognition passed over her perfectly made-up face. "We have a bookstore, and I was hoping to see the books that are included in the auction to determine if they'd be a good fit for us."

Based on my quick perusal through the auction brochure, I knew the books were being sold in two lots. One was antiques, which I didn't think I could afford, nor did I think we'd recoup our costs on it—the Earl's Study didn't do a lot of business with older books—but the second lot had been described as "pleasure reading," which I suspected was a polite way to indicate it was mostly mass-market or trade fiction. That might be a lot more our speed.

That said, if the owners of the estate had been big World War II history buffs or anything similarly dry, I didn't see much point in spending money on books that would sit on shelves at the store and wind up in the bargain bin in a few months.

"Oh, of course. I can take you to the library." Madeline snapped her fingers in the direction of a younger woman with frizzy red hair and an explosion of freckles across her nose and cheeks. "Franny, do you mind keeping an eye on things for a few minutes while I show Ms. Winchester here the library?"

Poor Franny's expression said the absolute last thing in the world she wanted to do was take the lead on things, but she glanced up from her iPad long enough to both look terrified *and* give a nod.

"She's new," Madeline explained coolly as we left the main auction area. "Just graduated from college and is really keen to get into the estate sale business, but between you and me, I don't think she really has what it takes."

"Is it a fairly difficult industry to get into?" I asked, genuinely curious. I had a hard time envisioning home auctions being a cut-throat business, but this was also my first time attending one. Especially one that was a unique blend of auction and basic estate sale.

"Yes, very, and if you don't have the killer instinct, well, you're not going to go very far."

I didn't know Franny, nor did I have the faintest sense of how good or bad she was at her job, but given how stressed-out the red-head had appeared and how dismissive her boss was being over her performance, I had to wonder if perhaps Franny wasn't the issue. Maybe Madeline was just hard to work with.

I'd known Madeline less than five minutes but had already gotten the idea that she was *never* called Maddie, and probably fell asleep in a neatly pressed pantsuit.

She struck me as exacting and more than a little scary.

I followed her up a wide set of stairs to the second floor of the mansion and realized that the people gathered downstairs were only some of the amassed attendees of this event. It appeared that at least a dozen more would-be buyers were wandering in and out of rooms on the second level. Some were sipping what looked to be champagne from tall glasses, while others had napkins in their hands with cute little mini pies and other tasty morsels.

While I personally thought eleven in the morning was a wee bit early to be popping bubbly, I certainly wouldn't say no to whatever the other guests were munching on. I'd forgotten to eat breakfast this morning—something I did with alarming frequency, considering I sold food at my shop—and my stomach was beginning to rumble.

Madeline guided me into another room with wood double doors, though this time the doors were opened wide, and I noted a few other people within. I stopped paying any attention to the people, however, when the scope of the library itself revealed itself to us.

"Oh, wow." I felt a bit silly for staring at it like a slack-jawed simpleton, but *wow* was the only appropriate thing I could say. Belle from *Beauty and the Beast* would want to marry this room. It was floor-to-ceiling bookshelves, painted bright white, which made the room look light and airy. The shelves were positively groaning under the weight of hundreds and hundreds of books.

After the initial shock of how big the room was, a second realization hit: there were *too* many books. There was no way I could possibly afford to bid on all of these, let alone haul them all back to Raven Creek in my little compact car. I didn't know what I'd been expecting, but this wasn't it.

"This is the antique collection." Madeline waved her hand around, as if I could possibly have missed all the leather-bound editions and the sweet smell of paper that lingered in the air. I wanted to open all the books around me and press my nose into their aging yellow pages and just take a big sniff.

I'd read somewhere that the reason old books had such a distinctive smell was because the organic ingredients making them up were breaking down over time; in other words, they smelled that way because they were slowly dying. There was something both incredibly creepy and also a little romantic about that.

"I assume if you're planning to use the books for retail, you were more inclined towards the . . . popular fiction collection." Madeline said this like popular fiction was beneath her and she would never be caught dead with a romance or mystery novel in her hands. But she was also right.

"Yeah. These are gorgeous but not really the style of our target demographic."

"Mmm," was all she said. "This way."

We passed through a door toward the back of the room and into a *second* library. This house was truly a magical sight to behold. I was pretty spoiled by having bookshelves around me all day, but that was a store—it was supposed to be packed to the rafters. I'd thought Eudora's sitting room had been impressive in terms of books, but she had nothing on this place.

The second library was cozier, with lower ceilings and the original wood all still in place, making it darker but also warmer. Two huge overstuffed green armchairs, angled inward, sat side by side near the large window. A small table stood between them, a stack of books still sitting on it as if waiting for their owner to come pick them up and start reading them again.

In here, the books were all newer, though some were obviously still fairly old. Battered paperbacks occupied all the lower shelves, and neatly organized hardcovers filled the top shelves. There were still hundreds of books, but I could see that these ones all had names and titles I was familiar with. More importantly, they were books my customers would be interested in. There were Agatha Christies by the dozen, along with more current mystery writers like Michael Connelly and Sue Grafton (Mr. Loughery would be thrilled), and I could make out row after row of brightly colored romance novel spines.

The mix was eclectic, with a great assortment of mysteries, thrillers, romances, and popular literary fiction. I could make it pay for itself in no time, provided no one outbid me or drove the cost up too much.

"This is great. Between us, do you know if many of the buyers here have their eye on this?"

Her smile was more like one thin line of lips curved up ever so slightly on each side, like the human version of the unsure emoji. "From what I've heard being discussed, the focus appears to be much more on the other collection. We have a couple rare-book buyers here who are quite keen to get some of the books the Weatherlys had collected over the years. Some are worth a great deal."

"I'm sure." I was scanning the shelves, trying to figure out if I'd have to rent a U-Haul to get all this stuff back to my shop. Daphne and Imogen would need to come help me unload it. Maybe Rich and Leo could be bribed as well.

If I did get the collection, bringing it all in and getting it sorted between the shelves and basement storage would be an enormous undertaking, but it also might make for a perfect excuse to close the store and complete my online inventory.

I loved it when the stars aligned.

"Thanks so much for your help," I told Madeline.

"A pleasure." Her phone rang, a classical piano song, and she gave me another tight smile before excusing herself from the room. I was so absorbed by walking around with my head tilted sideways to read the titles that I almost missed the sound of her voice coming back into the second library.

She had stepped into a small alcove, not the larger library, and though I felt guilty for overhearing her conversation, it was sort of hard to miss, given her raised voice.

"No. *No.* That wasn't our agreement at all. Now you listen to me, we had an understanding, and you can't go back on that now." A pause. I stepped closer to the alcove door, and she began to speak again. Her tone was angrier than before. "You're *where*? No, that's absolutely out of the question. You have to go immediately." Another beat. "Don't you dare threaten me. I *made* you. No, this isn't over. You're going to be sorry."

I realized the phone call was coming to an end and scrambled across the room so she wouldn't catch me eavesdropping, but Madeline never reentered the room.

A moment later I peeked my head into the alcove, and she was gone.

Chapter Five

Fancy estate sales offered incredible snacks, but the worst tea I'd ever had in my life.

I was back in my car, still parked under the protective shade of the tree, and Bob was sitting next to me in the passenger seat, carefully sniffing a salmon puff I had placed there for his consumption. He did not look convinced by the offering.

"It's good," I promised him, and popped one of the flaky, creamy treats into my own mouth.

I had loaded up a napkin with anything that looked worth trying and grabbed a small plastic cup of iced tea before coming back to the car. The auction itself was set to start in about ten minutes, and I'd need to head back in so I didn't risk missing out on the lot I wanted, but I felt bad leaving Bob unattended for too long.

The windows were still all faintly cracked, letting in the slightest breeze and keeping the car a very comfortable temperature. I had finished off the iced tea quickly and knew from the first sip it had been oversteeped and oversweetened. Sweetened iced tea was not a crime; it could be very good as long as the base tea was prepared right. But this was clearly an attempt at a sweet tea that had failed miserably on almost every count.

For one, they'd mixed lemon with a black tea base, and then they hadn't bothered using any kind of fruit to lighten the flavor. It was just . . . cold, bitter tea with some sugar in it.

Scratch that, *lots* of sugar in it.

I rolled my window down all the way and poured the remaining tea out, sad to waste it but genuinely unable to stomach a single swallow more. It certainly gave me a really good idea of what *not* to do when I started my iced tea offerings this summer.

The Earl's Study's teas would all include a fruit mix of some kind, whether fresh peaches, raspberries, or strawberries—muddled so their flavor could really shine through—or sliced cucumber with fresh garden mint. Heck, there was nothing wrong with classic lemon slices. Whatever we used would help bring out the flavor of the teas I selected.

Imagining muddled strawberries with Eudora's Strawberry Shortcake tea, with some natural local honey blended in, was enough to make my mouth water. Yeah, we could definitely do better than this.

Rolling the window back most of the way, I noticed Bob had finally started to scarf down his seafood treat, which made me happy. I left his cup of water in the drink holder and gave him one last vigorous pat on the head, scratching behind his ears and then at the little spot at the base of his tail he loved so much. He was purring loudly when I exited the car.

"I'll be back in a bit, bud. And I'll probably be broke, so it's going to be ramen for me and the cheap salmon pâté for you for the next six months." Who was I kidding? He loved the cheap canned food. He wasn't nearly as fancy about his eating habits as I sometimes pretended to be.

A quick glance at my fitness tracker told me I was borderline late for the beginning of the auction.

Hustling across the big driveway, hoping the hurried steps would count for something on my tracker, I made my way back into the big doors just in time to smack directly into someone on their way out.

It was Franny, the assistant, her freckled face red like she had just been crying.

"Oh, I'm so sorry," I said instinctively, then seeing how upset she was, I added, "Hey, are you okay?"

"Fine," she muttered hastily, before disappearing down the steps and out among the parked cars.

How interesting. I hoped it was nothing too serious, but I also didn't actually *know* Franny, so I wasn't going to go running after her to offer her comfort. I didn't want to stick my nose in someone else's business.

The grand room I'd walked through earlier was now set with chairs in neat rows, and it was much more apparent how many people had come to this auction. When we were spaced out through the house, it hadn't seemed as if there were too many, but all together there were close to thirty of us.

I eyeballed the other guests, wondering if any of them were keen on buying up my would-be stock or if, like Madeline had implied, they were a bit too hoity-toity for that. Everyone seemed to be dressed expensively, making me think a bunch of used paperbacks wouldn't appeal to them.

My lot was the twentieth one, which meant sitting through quite a bit of back-and-forth bidding on other items. The first couple of times, it was interesting to watch a handful of people try to get the best of each other over pieces of jewelry or antiques. The prices they were bidding were astronomical, making my stomach churn with anxiety.

Just how much would they want for the books if single jewels were going for thousands of dollars?

Once I got used to the process, my gaze started to drift around the room, eyeing up any other interesting buyers. The place was pretty full, but a few people stood out to me for reasons I couldn't explain. A couple in their midthirties stood back near the exit, behind all the chairs, and I glanced at them a few times throughout the auction proceedings. At one point after about twenty minutes, only the woman remained. Though I hadn't heard the doors jostle when the man left, they were now slightly ajar.

There was another man who seemed to be here alone, sitting in the back row on the opposite side of the aisle from me. He hadn't bid on a single thing and didn't seem primed to start anytime soon, with his sunglasses still on and his arms folded across his chest. I briefly thought he might be asleep until he crossed his legs at the knee, and I stopped staring.

A few seats over to my left, close to the wall, was a girl who was maybe twenty if that, her sweater sleeves pulled down around her knuckles and her knees bouncing nervously. She checked her phone a few times but didn't make a move to bid on any of the early lots. I hadn't expected to see someone her age at an event like this, which seemed geared more toward a stuffy older crowd. I considered leaning over to say something to her, but then the auctioneer announced lot twenty was up and I perked up in my seat. It was my time to shine. I hoped.

The bidding started at five hundred dollars, which made my throat immediately go bone-dry, but he had detailed that the lot was roughly two thousand mass-market and trade paperbacks and seven hundred hardcovers. I didn't have to do the mental math to know I could afford to go as high as about twenty-five hundred dollars and easily recoup my money, and probably quickly too. The lot also, I'd learned with great delight, included the packaging and delivery of the boxes right to the store.

Still, with five hundred as a starting point, how high could it go?

I lifted my hand to bid, and the auctioneer pointed to me. "We've got five hundred, do I hear seven fifty?"

"Seven fifty," said a spiffy-looking man from the front row.

"Seven fifty, do I hear one thousand?"

Oh my goodness, they weren't messing around with how quickly this was escalating. "One thousand." I tried to look casual about it as I lifted my hand, but I'd drawn the attention of the man in the front row.

"Fifteen hundred," he said. The woman sitting beside him gave his knee a very gentle squeeze, something I might not have noticed normally, but the chairs were spaced just so, and the firm set of her jaw told me she wasn't amused.

"Two thousand," I said, my voice briefly catching in my throat.

"I hear two thousand, do I have twenty-five hundred?" The auctioneer glanced around the room and at my competitor, and I tried not to follow his gaze. If someone bid twenty-five hundred, I simply couldn't go higher. "Going once. Twice. Sold to the lovely lady in the back row."

Me? I glanced behind me as if to be sure there wasn't a secret row that had been added while I was bidding, but no, he meant me. I was overjoyed, but only for a moment, because as I glanced behind me, through the gap that had been left in the great room doors, I saw something small, orange, and furry walk past with his tail held high.

Oh no.

Chapter Six

*N*o *no no no no.*

I tried to act calm as I slid out of my seat, like I was merely done with this section of the auction and perhaps needed to take a trip to the ladies' room or get more of that terrible iced tea.

Instead, I needed to go recapture my horrible, sneaky cat, who had somehow gotten himself out of the car and into the house. I briefly wondered if perhaps the family who had lived here might have had a cat, but I could picture them only with a big, fluffy, flat-faced cat that cost thousands, not a precocious ginger tabby who was clearly up to no good.

I did understand cats well enough at this point to know that they were *generally* up to no good, but I had sort of hoped mine was the exception rather than the example of the rule.

I slipped through the open door at the back of the room, as everyone else was more focused on the auction and the bids flying over the antique book collection I had no interest in. Guess Madeline really understood her crowd, because it was valued at over ten thousand dollars before I'd even left the room.

Come to think of it, the one person I *hadn't* seen while in the auction was Madeline herself. Maybe she'd used that opportunity to take a break and let the auctioneer handle things, since she'd obviously been going nonstop showing potential bidders around the estate. I'd want a reprieve from those towering stilettos too.

Still, she'd struck me as a person who wanted control over every aspect of the auction. I would have imagined she would be overseeing the bidding, giving her an opportunity to see who had bought what. I could picture her writing thank-you cards and planning lot deliveries as things went on. Her not being there felt a bit wrong.

But again, it was my first estate auction ever; I didn't know what was typical or expected. I just hoped Bob wouldn't run into the prim woman and that I might be able to get him out of here before anyone knew he'd been inside.

As soon as I thought I was out of earshot of the auction room and that the auctioneer's ongoing monologue of prices and bids would drown me out, I stage-whispered, "*Bob. Bob, get over here this instant.*" Like he was a petulant child and I was his overbearing mother.

In fairness, that felt like the truth some days.

"Brreow?" came a small, trilling voice from upstairs.

Oh no, he'd already gotten upstairs.

I took a quick look around to make sure no one would see me, and that there weren't suddenly security guards who would tackle me for going the wrong way. Then I had to remind myself that despite how fancy this house was, it wasn't a museum, and I'd been allowed upstairs previously.

Also, there were no security guards.

Jogging up the stairs, I followed him in the direction I'd heard his little voice come from. "Bob?"

"Mrow."

He was definitely somewhere in the library. At least he'd had the common sense to go in the direction of what was familiar: books. I just hoped I could scoop him up before he decided to start sharpening his claws on any antiques worth tens of thousands of dollars.

When I stepped into the main part of the library, I immediately saw a dozen dark paw prints leading in my direction from the library annex where my new collection of books was housed. "Oh, Bob, did you get into a plant?" I sighed, knowing I'd need to clean this up ASAP before someone saw it.

The cat in question was sitting at my feet, his orange tail flicking, and I immediately grabbed him and held him to my chest.

His paws quickly left marks on my pale-colored shirt, and it was only then I realized it wasn't dirt or mud on his paws.

It was blood.

My heart dropped into my stomach, and I slowly followed the direction his prints had come from. The redness of them was much more apparent in the bright-white annex room, but his prints continued farther, into the little alcove where I'd heard Madeline on her phone call.

Bob was kneading his paws into my chest and purring loudly, enjoying being held, even as my pulse hammered. My mouth had gone desert-dry.

There, in the small alcove, was someone lying very still, a pool of blood forming around them. My immediate instinct was to check for a pulse, but I knew checking wouldn't be necessary. This person was obviously already gone.

Then I saw the sky-high stiletto pumps on her feet and the dark hair pulled back into its severe bun.

Someone had murdered Madeline Morrow.

Chapter Seven

I was still clinging to Bob when the detective arrived, and it took me a few slow blinks to realize she wasn't a stranger.

Detective Patsy Martin must have helped out with major crimes across several local small towns, as we certainly didn't supply enough excitement in Raven Creek to keep her occupied.

She'd shaved her hair extra short since the last time I'd seen her, and it gave her bone structure an opportunity to shine. Her dark skin was as flawless as it had been before, and stupidly I thought I should ask her what moisturizer she used. But she wasn't here to talk to me about skin care.

"We meet again, Ms. Winchester." Her voice was warm enough that it didn't immediately put my guard up. "And I see you've brought another familiar face. Hello, Bob." She had met Bob after a particularly eventful evening at the bookstore, and given that those circumstances had also involved arresting a murderer, I was impressed she remembered the cat.

"No offense meant by this, Detective, but I wish it had been a lot longer between meetings."

"Yes, I have to admit I don't usually like to see the same people more than once at a crime scene, as I'm sure you can appreciate." She gave me a long, assessing look, then smiled softly and took a seat in one of the chairs beside me. "Can you tell me what happened?"

I quickly recounted the tale of going looking for Bob, finding the paw prints, and following them to Madeline Morrow's body. As I spoke, Detective Martin called over a uniformed officer, who took a few photos of Bob's paws and my bloody shirt, and a crime scene technician, who took samples from both Bob and me as well.

"Now, I know you're not totally unfamiliar with how all this works, Phoebe, but I want to impress upon you how serious this situation is. While I appreciate you being so forthcoming with us, I'd also very much appreciate it if you didn't take any sudden vacations or leave the area anytime in the next little while."

"Am I . . ." I could barely form the words as I hugged Bob closer to my chest. "Am I a suspect?"

Again she smiled, but it wasn't as warm this time around. "We'll be asking everyone here today the same things."

I noticed that wasn't exactly a no. It was hard to blame her. I was the one who had found the body, after all.

"Oh, and one more thing, Ms. Winchester."

"Yes?"

"I'd really appreciate it if you could leave that shirt with us. If you don't have anything else to change into, I think we might have a police fund raiser shirt in one of the cruisers you could use." When I must have visibly blanched, she added, "We just need to make sure it's only Madeline's blood on you, you understand."

While I tried to assure myself this was all in the name of finding Madeline's killer, I couldn't help but feel there was a discerning eye pointed right at me, thinking perhaps I was responsible.

I *was* covered in blood, after all, which didn't exactly scream *inno-cent*. But it was blood in the shape of adorable cat paw prints rather than anything remotely resembling an attack. I watched *Dateline*, and I knew I didn't look like someone who had just finished murdering another person. I hoped the detective could see that as well.

When someone had been murdered behind my shop shortly after I arrived in Raven Creek, they'd never pointed a finger at me, which had been an enormous relief. This time, I'd been a lot closer to the dead body when the cops showed up, and I supposed it was second nature for the police to mistrust anyone standing over a corpse.

Again, hard to blame them.

I snuggled Bob a bit closer, wanting nothing more than to get back to Lane End House and take a hot bath in Eudora's old claw-foot tub. There were so many bubbles in my future.

Detective Martin asked a few more questions, none of which were particularly suggestive that she thought I was guilty of anything, until she said, "We'd like it if you came in to the station in Barneswood. It doesn't have to be today—I know you've had quite a shock, and you probably want to take Bob home. But, Phoebe, we do need to get your fingerprints and ask you a few more questions about today. Maybe if you sleep on it, you might remember something else."

"My fingerprints?"

"It's just standard procedure. We'll be getting them from everyone else here today as well." She gestured around the room to where the other attendees had been broken down into smaller groups and were being questioned by either uniformed officers or Detective Martin's male partner, whom I hadn't met yet. He must have been in his early forties, but he had the kind of face that looked much younger. She'd introduced him to the crowd when they'd arrived as Detective Kwan Kim, but I hadn't spoken to him after that. "We just need to be able to rule out anyone's prints as we go through the place."

Again, my extensive love of all things true crime should have made this apparent, but it's hard to remember what you know when you're in the middle of a murder investigation.

"I'll call the station in the morning to make an appointment. Can I bring the shirt in then as well? I don't have anything to change into right now." Too late, I realized this might seem as if I wanted to hide something as I remembered she had just offered to give me a shirt.

"I'm afraid we really do need that shirt today. Officer Houghton can take you to the cruiser and get you something to change into, and he'll watch Bob while you change. Look, Phoebe, we appreciate you calling this in and all your information today. I know we'll speak again tomorrow, but if you think of anything between now and then that you think might be especially relevant, please don't hesitate to give me a call. My cell number is on the back." She handed me a card with her name neatly printed on the front.

"I will."

I had a million questions of my own, most of them involving how Madeline had died and how long they thought she'd been up there while the auction was happening on the main floor. Who had been the last person to see her, and who could have wanted her dead so badly they would kill her around that many potential witnesses?

But I didn't ask Detective Martin any of those questions. Instead, I slipped my purse over my shoulder, held my cat tightly to me, and followed Officer Houghton out of the room. The officer chatted with me as we walked to his cruiser, but I barely heard a word. All I could think about was Madeline's body.

Someone at the auction today had been a killer, and I wanted to know who.

* * *

The drive home to Raven Creek was a quiet one. I couldn't be bothered to turn on the radio, and Bob seemed to recognize that now was not the time to chatter at me. He sat silently in the passenger seat, where I'd placed a promotional shirt from my old job that I'd found in the trunk. Guess I hadn't needed the freebie from the cops after all.

I was going to need to give Bob a bath as soon as we got home. The blood on his paws was mostly dried now, but I didn't want him having to clean it off himself.

Absent-mindedly I reached across and gave him a scratch behind the ears. None of this was his fault. If anything, I should be proud of him for finding Madeline's body; otherwise, who knew how long she would have lain upstairs undiscovered.

Plus he was a cat. There was no way for me to retroactively scold him for leaving the car and wandering into the mansion. He wasn't going to understand.

About forty-five minutes later I pulled up to the front of Lane End House and turned the car off. My cell phone pinged—a message from Imogen. *Daphne says she's closing up and can't find Bob. We didn't see him all day.*

I couldn't believe it was already almost six. Between all the waiting around at the estate sale and all the time spent talking to Detective Martin, the afternoon had completely evaporated.

He's with me. Snuck into the car before I left.

Little devil, she replied. *I'll let Daphne know not to worry. See you tomorrow.*

Oh gosh, tomorrow. Tomorrow I'd need to show up to the store and act like everything was fine and normal, bake some cookies, sell some tea, and plan a time to go have my fingerprints taken at a police station.

Since Detective Martin worked out of several different small towns, I was going to ask her if I could just stop at the small station here in Raven Creek for the prints. I knew it wasn't the same thing as going back to Barneswood, but I wasn't sure I had it in me to drive forty-five minutes each way for something I didn't even want to do.

I picked up Bob and grabbed my purse, then headed inside with both. In typical Bob fashion, he began yowling at me the second his feet were on the floor, his tail twitching in the air.

At least some things were unchanged.

Hanging my purse on the banister, I followed Bob into the kitchen, where I tortured him further by giving him a quick bath in the sink, concentrating on his paws—which he made sure to tell me he hated having touched—and the few specks of blood dotted along his white belly. Once he was clean, and furious, I made him his dinner, a can of wet food and a top-up of the dry, and set both dishes on the floor. He had a big cat bed on the flagstone hearth of the fireplace that connected the kitchen with the big dining room on the other side of the wall. Initially he'd just lain on the stone, but when it was apparent that was where he would spend much of his free time, especially during winter, I was coaxed into upgrading his cushion.

There was a small pet shop in town, and it was becoming a real danger for my wallet, because I kept finding reasons to buy new things for Bob. Bob, on the other hand, chose to ignore most of the expensive toys I bought him and loved to play with the twist ties I used on my produce and bulk items from the grocery store.

Go figure.

After Bob had his meal, I knew it was time to feed myself. I might not be in much of a mood to eat, but life went on, and as traumatizing as my afternoon had been, I still had responsibilities in *my* life that weren't going anywhere. Much to my chagrin, I found myself wondering what was going to happen with the books I'd bid on. As far as I could tell, the arrangement was binding, and the auctioneer had collected my information before leaving so that someone other than Madeline could contact me about making a payment.

It felt surreal that after all of that, I was still getting all those books.

I put my new police half-marathon fund raiser shirt in the laundry and changed into pajamas before I grabbed a serving of frozen lasagna out of the fridge, thankful I'd had the foresight to put it there before leaving this morning, knowing I'd be hungry and lazy when I got home. Morning Phoebe was, at times, something of a genius.

As the microwave spun, I pulled a small notebook out of the junk drawer and plopped down at the antique wood country kitchen table. I wrote *Madeline Morrow* at the top along with a big question mark.

At the time Detective Martin had questioned me, I'd still been mostly in shock, but now that I'd had more time to sit with things, little bits of the day were starting to come back to me, and I wanted to write them down before I forgot again.

Franny, I wrote. *Left crying*. What time had that been? *Around 2pm*. That's when I'd wandered back inside for the start of the auction. Madeline hadn't been terribly fond of Franny and had alluded that perhaps the younger woman wasn't long for the job.

Maybe she'd been fired and she'd snapped, killing Madeline and then fleeing the scene. People killed for much less. I was sure someone with the auction company would have mentioned Franny to the detectives, but likely none of them had seen her leave in tears.

I made a quick list of everyone I remembered seeing and anyone who stuck out. But it was admittedly a pretty short list. While there'd been a lot of people at the auction, almost everyone had stayed in the auction room the whole time, which I had to assume was when

Madeline had been killed. The best time to do it would have been when everyone in the house had been gathered elsewhere.

Phone call, I wrote.

Madeline's stressful and angry phone call in the alcove was certainly worth mentioning to the police. While I hadn't heard who she was talking to, the whole conversation had sounded vaguely threatening. Perhaps whoever was on the other end of the line hadn't been too keen on being threatened?

What kind of argument was worth killing someone over?

Chapter Eight

The next morning Bob was extra aloof as I got out of bed. I suspected this was in large part because he was still mad about me washing his paws and belly the previous evening and was going to give me the cold shoulder. At least until it was breakfast time.

I considered skipping my run but decided the combination of fresh air and some time to think might be good for me after such an unusual day.

The run was great in terms of getting some nice spring air into my lungs, but even with time for nothing but thinking, it wasn't any clearer who among the guests at the auction could have been capable of murder.

I wished I'd paid better attention to everyone when we'd all been in the same room so that I might have noticed those who were missing. Because I'd gone to hang out with Bob in the car, I hadn't gotten much of an opportunity to see everyone's face or even really chat with anyone besides Madeline. A few people had been memorable to me, but there'd been so many other people in the room whom I'd barely registered.

Franny's hurried exit still stuck out as a good jumping-off point for the investigation, but something nagged at me. If I called

Detective Martin and pointed her in Franny's direction and it turned out the poor girl was just upset over something totally unrelated to the murder, suddenly she'd have the extra stress of being a murder suspect.

Considering I could feel the weight of suspicion on me even now, I didn't want to do that to anyone else if they were innocent. I wondered if I might be able to chat with Franny somehow and get an idea of what had set her off. If I thought she was being sketchy or got a sense she might be involved, it would be easy to call the cops immediately after that.

I just felt bad for her. Madeline had obviously not liked her or thought much of her abilities, but was that enough to suggest she might kill her boss?

By the time I got home, I didn't have any clear suspects, but I at least knew my next steps. I was going to call the company Madeline and Franny worked for and see if I could chat with the latter, maybe offer to meet her for a nice cup of tea.

I also wondered if there was a way I might be able to find out more about the other attendees. Detective Martin must have a working list or something to go off.

Or maybe you should just leave this to the experts, I told myself. Detective Martin was good at her job, but I didn't like the idea of being a suspect. If I could do a little digging on my own based on some of my observations, I could point the police in the right direction. Was that so bad? They hadn't been at the auction for the whole day like I had, and there was a chance I'd seen or heard something important without even realizing it.

The nagging voice of logic told me to leave it be, just give Detective Martin the notes I had jotted down last night and let her do her job, but another voice, one I had come to distinctly recognize as Aunt Eudora's, told me to keep digging.

As I jogged up the steps of my house, another idea struck me. *Magic.*

Of course. Why hadn't that occurred to me sooner? If magic could help me make recipes that made people more honest and Eudora could blend teas to help people fall in love, there *must* be a magical way to help me remember more of what I'd seen at the auction, maybe point me in the right direction of where to start looking.

I made a mental note to call Honey, my witchy mentor, and ask her if that was something we could do. There was still so much I didn't know about my witchy side that I often forgot I had magical abilities and should learn how to use them.

With a new excited bounce in my step, I fed Bob—who was speaking to me again—and got myself ready for the day. I briefly considered leaving him at home, but it seemed cruel to punish him for something he had little control over, so I grabbed the bubble backpack and set it next to the door to see if he'd hop in. Like every day since I'd bought it, he crammed his orange tabby self into the bag and stared out the dome window, looking for all the world like he was about to go on a voyage into space, or twenty thousand leagues under the sea. It was truly delightful, even if it made people look at me funny on the street.

I zipped him in and grabbed my purse, then locked the house up behind us. As I made my way onto the porch, the wood under my feet gave a particularly loud creak, and the feel of it was much closer to stepping on a sponge than a nice sturdy piece of pine. Again, I made a note that I was going to need to ask for some help with fixing the boards, because one of these days they might just crumble to dust underneath me.

The weather today was stunning, warm but with the slightest edge of late-spring crispness on the breeze making everything smell fresh and alive. Bob was an extra weight on my back as I cycled toward Main Street, but it was a comfortable, familiar sort of weight that I was glad of.

I cycled slowly, mostly so as not to push my luck with Bob's patience in the bag—he hated going too fast and would yowl the whole way if he disapproved of my speed—but also so I could take in some of the spring decorations coming to life in town.

Now that the risk of frigid overnight lows was behind us, the town's beautification committee had set about putting out the flowers that would brighten up the town through spring and summer. Hanging baskets adorned every other lamppost on the busier streets, and huge wooden barrels sawed in half had appeared on the sidewalks overnight. The barrels were teeming with freshly planted marigolds and petunias, and the whole of Main Street looked like something out of a storybook.

In no time at all I was pulling up in front of the Earl's Study and locking my bike to the rack between my shop and Amy's. I honestly could have just left the bike unattended all day and it probably wouldn't go anywhere, but it was hard to shake a big-city mentality that told me anything I left lying around would get stolen in five seconds flat.

I was pretty sure half the people in Raven Creek kept their doors unlocked at night. I wasn't one of them, but I could also appreciate why those who took the risk weren't terribly worried. I'd lived in Chicago and Seattle before this, so there was no way you'd ever catch me leaving a house door open.

I left Bob inside the shop, making sure the zipper was undone so he could get out at his own pace, then headed next door to collect the morning baking. The moment I walked through the doors of the Sugarplum Fairy, Amy was waiting. Her normally perfectly styled white-blonde bob was pulled back into little pigtails today, and she wore a pink bandana over the top of the rest of her hair.

"You look great," I told her.

"Me?" She flushed. "I must look like an absolute mess. One of our ovens stopped working this morning when I got in, so I'm trying to get the bread all finished for my daily deliveries. What a nightmare. Someone is supposed to come fix it, but they can't be here until after ten, so I'm just sweating up a storm in here trying to make it work."

"Oh, Amy, you should have called me. My oven isn't industrial by any means, but I can help. Give me a couple trays to take over with me and I'll get some stuff done."

She looked as if she might cry. "But Phoebe, you have your own baking to do."

"Which one of us is a bakery, and which of us can just say *sorry, no shortbread today*?" I put my hands on my hips, letting her know I wasn't messing around. "I'll have *loads* of time to bake and cool the sourdough before lunch. Now give me some trays."

It had not escaped my notice that despite the sparser-than-usual stock in her display cases, my two morning to-go boxes were still set aside waiting for me. She could have easily told me that my order couldn't be filled, but she'd prioritized my pastries over filling up for her own customers.

The woman was a saint.

Her lower lip trembled, but she steeled herself, giving her foot a stomp with her pink Croc shoes scuffing against the tile floor. I think she was trying to fight her desire to cry in relief.

"I can handle the breads here if you could take some cookies and squares?"

"Load me up." I was grateful that I'd left my purse back at the shop, so it was one fewer thing to juggle.

Amy ducked back into the kitchen and returned with three carefully stacked cookie sheets. "I'll come right behind you with some brownies and blondies. If you can handle these over the morning, I think I'll be able to catch up." I didn't bother to tell her a third time that it would be my pleasure, as she had already gotten the point, but she followed me out the door with two big trays of beautifully decorated squares.

As we approached the Earl's Study, the door directly beside the store opened up and Rich Lofting walked out, still wearing his pajamas: a rumpled navy Henley shirt and matching plaid pants. He was picking up the newspaper from his front stoop and stopped when he saw us coming.

"I don't think I requested breakfast delivery, but I sure won't complain."

He was so handsome that even with his dark hair mussed from his pillow and stubble dotting his cheeks and chin, my heart skipped a beat to see him. When he smiled, a little dimple appeared on one cheek, and I found myself grinning like an idiot back at him.

"Well, if you're already here, you might as well help," Amy declared, handing him the two trays she was carrying. She used her newly free hands to grab my keys and unlock the front door of the store.

Rich, who hadn't yet fully processed his role in all of this, followed me into the store and went, "Uhhh?"

I replied, "In the kitchen."

The kitchen, of course, was much too small for two people to stand in together. I deposited my three trays onto the counter, and the moment I turned around, Rich was right behind me. The only thing keeping us from touching was two big trays of brownies.

I paused just long enough to stare into his eyes, the color of liquid honey, or a glass filled with whiskey, then took the trays out of his hands. "Thank you."

"I'm still not entirely sure I'm awake."

"Do a lot of your dreams feature you helping me carry baked goods?"

The corner of his mouth tipped up in a smirk. "Maybe."

That was enough for me to break eye contact as my cheeks turned red hot and I had to look down at the brownies. "Well, I'm glad you were up. Why *are* you up, come to think of it?"

Rich's job as a private investigator meant he kept unusual hours and normally worked through the night. It was a rare thing to see him up before eight in the morning. Though usually when I saw him, he was wearing nicely tailored clothes and had recently brushed his hair, none of which was true right now.

Now he looked much more like the rough-and-tumble kid I'd known during my childhood summers here, and it was nice to know that kid was still in there somewhere.

"Have to meet some clients a bit on the early side and wanted to make sure I had time to make myself presentable." He glanced down. "More presentable than this, anyway."

"I think you look good." *Oh my god, Phoebe, shut up.*

"Well, you'd be too nice to tell me I looked bad, so I'm not sure I believe you, but thanks. Looking pretty good yourself this morning. Nothing like a woman carrying cookies to make seven AM a bit less terrible."

"And I can't even offer you one."

He smirked again. "You'll find a way to make it up to me."

For a guy who had agreed that taking it slow was the best approach for two newly divorced people, he sure was flirting enough to set my hair on fire.

"'Scuse me," came Amy's voice as she handed Rich another tray. She then held out a sheet of paper to me, which a quick glance told me had the temperature and bake times for all the items I'd taken from her shop. It was also the perfect excuse for Rich to extract himself from the kitchen after depositing the last tray on my counter.

Before he could get all the way to the front door and completely escape this situation, however, I called after him. "Hey, Rich?"

He turned around. It should have been illegal for someone to look that good while still wearing their pajamas, and my heart did another little flip-flop when he smiled back at me. "What's up, Phoebs?"

Oh gosh, a nickname. I was done. I was a puddle on the floor.

"Do you think I could come by after work?"

Both of Amy's brows shot up, practically into her hairline, as she swiveled her attention between me and Rich like we were either a tennis match or her new favorite soap opera and she was just dying to see what happened next. Rich cocked his head to the side, glancing first at Amy, then back at me, and I realized how awkward I'd just made everything.

"Professionally. I might need your help with something." Why it hadn't occurred to me until we were wedged together in the kitchen that knowing a private investigator might help me when it came to finding Franny and some of the other guests at the auction yesterday was beyond me. But in fairness, whenever I was in close proximity to Rich, I tended to forget my own name, so how could I be expected to remember what he did for a living?

This seemed to relieve him and disappoint Amy in equal measure.

"Oh, sure. You're off at four usually, right?" He went to check his watch before realizing he wasn't currently wearing one. "I should be home around six if all goes well tonight. I'll let you know if anything holds me up. Are you going to the town council meeting tonight?"

I'd almost forgotten about the meeting in all of the other drama I'd found myself embroiled in. But there was no drama quite like town council drama, and I had no intention of missing my opportunity to get them to hear me out about my shelter.

"If you think I'd be missing another no-holds-barred fight between Dierdre and Mayor Collins about whether or not we should repaint the covered bridges, you are out of your mind. Meeting starts at seven and you said you're off at six? Why don't we plan to meet at Peach's?" I suggested. "I mean, you've gotta eat, right? We can talk business, then walk over to the meeting after."

Sweet Peach's was the local diner, where we'd gone on what some might consider our first date. It was also where I'd discovered that I had magical powers almost entirely by accident. I had managed to avoid any further magical slipups there in visits afterward, but it had also been seven months since I'd gone with Rich. I didn't want to push him into anything he wasn't ready for, and I really *did* need his professional help, so I was hoping Amy's excited expression wouldn't put him off the suggestion.

"Sure, that sounds great. Six o'clock at Peach's. Unless someone decides to cheat on their wife between now and then." He laughed and gave a little shrug, knowing full well how ridiculous his job could seem to others.

As soon as he was gone, Amy's gaze pivoted to me, and she gave me a knowing smirk. "Ohhhh, someone's got a daaaaate."

I pushed her toward the door. "Didn't you hear me say *professional*? I need his PI skills, that's it. And no one finishes up their date at a town council meeting."

"Mm-hmm, sure." She nodded several times and gave me an exaggerated wink as she opened the front door. "I'll tease you more about it later. Call me as those come out of the oven, and I'll come grab them from you. I can't thank you enough, Phoebe, seriously. You're a lifesaver."

"It's nothing. I'm glad I could help."

With her gone, I quickly reviewed the list she'd given me so I could plan what would be best to bake together so we didn't waste a moment of time or oven warmth. With the cookies in first, since they'd take the shortest time, I prepped my own sourdough loaves so they'd be ready to go into the oven as soon as Amy's stuff was done. It would be tight timing, but I was positive I could get both Amy's goods and my own loaves done before lunch started.

My investigation into Madeline's murder was going to have to take a literal back burner, because my entire morning was soon consumed by baking.

Chapter Nine

Busy days are always the best in a business, because time just flies before you have a chance to get bored. It helped that the news of the murder in Barneswood had been slow to make its rounds to Raven Creek and that no one had yet made the connection that I had been involved.

Soon enough they'd piece it all together, and curious townspeople would be at my door asking questions, but at least they usually bought some tea when they did that, so I wasn't going to complain too much.

Imogen, however, had put two and two together right away, and the moment she came through the door at ten she was a whirlwind of braids, energy, and questions.

Thankfully, with Amy's baking keeping me busy and the shop surprisingly bustling, she didn't get a chance to ask too much before I was whisked off to another customer or another tray of brownies. A lot of people were disappointed by the lack of Earl Grey shortbread, which was something of a relief to me, because it meant people enjoyed my cookies. I promised it would be back the next day.

We powered through the lunch rush, but I could tell Imogen was just dying to start her interrogation. By the time the last of our lunch hour toasts were gone and we were sold out of pastry, I sighed and said, "Before you start, let me make us each a cup of tea."

.   I knew Imogen well enough to know she didn't care if I made her the tea or not, but she watched impatiently as I took a tin of Lemon Meringue Pie off the shelf and carefully spooned it into compostable tea bags. The heavenly scent of dried lemon rind wafted out of the canister, and the little flecks of dried marigold petal reminded me of the new flowers outside. I boiled the water, then watched Imogen tap her toe against the front desk as I poured the nearly boiling water over the bags and set a cup down in front of each of us.

I glanced at the clock so I wouldn't let the cups overstep, then said, "Okay, I know you're about to burst. Just ask."

"*Finally,*" she breathed. She pulled up the stool behind the cash counter as I cleared some dirty plates from the little café tables and waited for our tea to be ready. "So, I read there was a death at the auction last night. My first question: Did you win the book lot?"

"That's your *first* question?"

"I'm trying to be pragmatic!"

That made me laugh, which then made me feel guilty. "Yes, I won the books, though I'm not totally sure how that's all going to work out, since the auction didn't actually finish. But they got my information to coordinate payment, so I'm assuming I still get the books. How much did the newspaper say about the death?" Imogen was levelheaded but not cruel, which made me wonder how vague the details had been if she was asking about the sale first.

"It just said someone died unexpectedly and the police were on-site. I assumed someone had a heart attack. Isn't it usually lots of older people at those? Eudora was always the one attending for the shop."

"Lots of middle-aged people, honestly. And I suppose you could call the death unexpected." I put the dishes into the kitchen and started a cycle on the dishwasher. When I returned, I dropped the real bombshell. "The woman running the auction was *murdered*."

Imogen spun around on her stool to face me, her expression stunned. "Excuse me? Someone was murdered at this auction? Are *you* okay?" She gave me a once-over to confirm I had not also been murdered. "What happened?"

It felt weird to be gossiping about this, but since I knew the news would arrive in Raven Creek sooner rather than later, it would be good to have Imogen on my side so she could set people right when they started sharing false versions of events. It was inevitable, when playing what was basically a game of telephone for adults, that some of the truth would get lost along the way.

As long as there wasn't a version of the story where people thought I was the killer.

"I found the body. Well, actually, Bob found the body."

"You took your cat to the auction?"

"In fairness, he kind of took himself."

Imogen suppressed a smirk, her gaze darting toward Bob where he was snoozing by the fire. Then she got back to business. "And did they catch whoever did it to her?"

"No, no one knows what happened. She was showing people around the property, she showed me all the books, and then an hour later she was dead. I *did* overhear her having an argument on the phone with someone, but I have no idea who. And her assistant left the event crying before the actual bidding got under way, which I thought was weird."

"Oh, she did it."

The bell chimed merrily, and Imogen turned around to greet someone walking through the door as I gave a soft smile to the customer. The new arrival made a beeline for the bookstore but stopped by the fireplace to give Bob a gentle scritch behind the ears, which automatically made me like her more. I just trusted people who liked my cat. Maybe it was a bad habit, but he hadn't steered me wrong so far. If Bob let you touch him, you were probably an okay person.

"I think it's a bit early to assume the assistant did it," I whispered, not wanting to spread the details with strangers. Mr. Loughery had been here the whole time, but as usual, by the lunchtime rush, he was snoozing, as was Bob. It made it a lot easier to talk about crimes when your only customer was fast asleep. This new customer, however, might not be so easygoing about the topic of murder.

Then again, who could tell? We got a lot of odd ducks in the shop.

"I mean, it's always the butler in those old black-and-white murder mystery movies, isn't it?"

"I feel like it's almost never the butler."

"But you know what that saying *means*, right? Not that it's the butler, but that it's the person no one thinks about, the person that was largely overlooked. Old-timey butlers and serving staff were basically invisible, hence why they'd be the last person you expect."

"Thank you for the lesson in whodunits. The assistant seemed pretty sad to me, one of those people who gets spooked by their own shadow. Plus she seemed so desperate to prove herself. Is that really someone who could commit a murder?"

"Well, I wasn't there, so I'll trust your gut if you think she was innocent, but anyone who is desperate about one thing in their life might be desperate enough to do whatever it takes to keep that thing." Imogen shrugged.

Franny didn't strike me as a killer, but who knew what people were capable of when they were pushed to their limit. I hated to say it, but Madeline Morrow seemed uniquely capable of pushing people to their limit. I remembered thinking I was glad she wasn't my boss.

I continued to tidy up the café and restock the glass display jars of tea, making a mental note of which ones were running low so I could make new stock tonight when I got home.

After my not-a-date with Rich, that is, and whatever kind of spectacle unfolded at the town council meeting.

The rest of the day went along relatively quickly, and by four o'clock things had slowed down at the shop enough that I felt more than comfortable leaving Imogen on her own. Amy had already confirmed that her oven was as good as new, but I made her promise to call me first thing in the morning if she ran into the same issue—that way I could come help well before she opened her doors.

I think we were both hoping that wouldn't be the case, but what were friends for if not to wake up at four in the morning to help bake bread?

I loaded Bob into his carrier and headed out on my bike, not straight home but rather in the direction of the grocery store. Lansing's, owned first by Leo's grandparents and then handed down the line generation to generation, was a decently sized outfit for such a small town. It looked like a bigger chain store and had tons of items in stock for those on unique diets, like gluten-free or keto, while also covering your more standard fare.

Unfortunately for me and my habit of overspending mindlessly when it came to food, I spotted something new and exciting whenever I went in. This afternoon I had enough time to kill before meeting Rich to run home and make fresh batches of loose tea, but I also wanted to grab some things to make iced tea samples tomorrow and see what worked.

With Bob strapped to my back—no one seemed to mind that I brought him in as long as he was in his carrier—I headed right for the produce department. I was on my bike, so whatever I got would need to be small enough to fit in my basket. I opted for a half dozen lemons and limes for a more classic iced tea flavor base, then a few early-season peaches and white nectarines, which were my favorite, as well as a clamshell container of strawberries. This would give me a good starting point to see what went well with berries, citrus, or stone fruit. I didn't want to get too carried away, but two iced tea specials that rotated out weekly seemed like a great idea for the summer months. Then I could prepare things in bulk and use them throughout the week rather than making small batches that might not last the whole day.

With my bounty of fruit collected, I made a quick stop in the pet food aisle to grab Bob's favorites: freeze-dried shrimp bites. While I personally didn't understand the appeal, I couldn't fault him for his tastes. After all, I liked putting pineapple on my pizza. He'd been so well-behaved all day and in the store, I figured he deserved a little treat, especially if I was planning on running out again for the evening.

Bob was, I had learned, something of a gentle, needy soul. He didn't always need to be in your lap or have you petting him, but he got a bit forlorn and pouty if I left him alone for too long. I thought it might have had something to do with the time he'd spent by himself after Eudora died, with only periodic visits from Leo and no regular company.

A few times I'd considered getting him a friend. Eudora's house was huge and could certainly manage two cats without us tripping over each other too much, but I wasn't sure I was at that stage just yet. I'd gone from being a no-pet person to being a cat owner to being a cat person who carried her baby around in a bag all the time.

Would two cats qualify me as a cat lady? Where was the line on that? A divorced woman with multiple cats was a creature to be pitied where I had come from, so I had to hold off on getting another cat until I decided how that fit my new lifestyle here.

I paid for my goodies and headed back out to my bike, making the rest of the trip home in about five minutes flat. The clock on the wall in my kitchen said it was only five o'clock, which meant I could use my free hour to make extra tea or get the fruit prepared for tomorrow.

Or I could go pay a visit to Honey.

Since I was meeting Rich at Peach's later, a quick trip over to Honey's new-age shop wouldn't take me far out of the way, since it was only two doors down from the diner. While Rich might be able to help me with finding phone numbers or addresses of people I could talk to about Madeline's murder, Honey could help me from an entirely different angle.

"Early dinner tonight, buddy." I cracked open a can of food and poured it into his freshly cleaned dish, then topped off his dry kibble and made sure he had fresh water. As a peace offering because I was leaving, I sprinkled a handful of the dry shrimp on top off his food, and he tucked into his evening meal with gusto.

I suspected he would forgive me.

I gave myself a once-over, assessing if my current outfit was cute enough to wear on a date without being too fancy for the meeting after, then found myself wondering if I could actually qualify this as a date when I had very insistently called it a professional meeting.

Nevertheless, it didn't hurt to look cute. I quickly changed out of my top and sweater—we didn't have a uniform at the Earl's Study, but my *personal* uniform was a T-shirt and cardigan plus jeans almost every day—and put on a black long-sleeved shirt with small white polka dots on it. The shirt tied in a bow at the back, so it made my typical dark jeans a little fancier than usual. I also swapped out my usual loafers for a cute (but not too cute) pair of heels. Something nice and low that wouldn't leave me with blisters and regrets later.

After applying some tinted lip balm and a tiny bit of blush and mascara, I gave a quick nod of approval to my mirror. I looked refreshed and almost presentable but not like I was trying too hard. If this *was* a date, I wouldn't feel overly casual, and if it wasn't, I wouldn't look like a fool. The perfect combo.

Now, to go see a witch about a murder.

Chapter Ten

I arrived at Honey's shop, New Moon, about fifteen minutes later. I'd briefly agonized over whether or not I should drive or take my bike but ultimately opted for the latter.

The weather was lovely and intoxicating, and while there was still the faintest evening chill and I might regret my decision later, I couldn't resist letting the wind blow through my hair.

Having come to Raven Creek from Seattle, I had found it a big lifestyle shift to be able to get everywhere I needed to go in a matter of minutes. There was nothing in Raven Creek I couldn't get to on my bike in under twenty minutes, and almost everywhere I went on a regular basis was less than a ten-minute ride away.

When I'd arrived seven months earlier, I hadn't been sure I was going to be able to adapt to small-town living. For one thing, everyone was constantly in your business and no one had the faintest awareness of what things like *privacy* and *decorum* were. Everyone I'd met in those first months automatically knew who I was and why I was there.

Thankfully, in the months that followed, I simply became Phoebe, owner of the Earl's Study and Bob's mom. People still mentioned Eudora, especially tourists who were in town only seasonally and stopped by the shop expecting to see my aunt. But now it didn't feel like I was living under her shadow. Instead, I was my own person and a part of the town itself.

I was still eager for the day when someone else moved to Raven Creek and I'd stop being considered the new girl, but as it was, I'd likely be the new kid on the block until I was forty.

Honey's shop didn't have a bike rack outside, so I just leaned the bike up against the side of her store. This wasn't the type of place I needed to worry too much about my things disappearing on me, but then I remembered that Honey had given me a spell for this. I didn't think anyone would steal my bike, but I wanted to give it a try. I figured the more regularly I used my magic, the more second nature it would become. Maybe if I got better at spells like these, I would stop worrying so much about locking my bike up on Main Street, which would be one less thing to manage when I got to work every morning.

I stood next to my bike and focused all my intention on it, visualizing it still being here when I got out later. "What's mine is mine and shall remain, till such a time as it's meant to be free. What meddling minds might try to steal, shall overlook this set of wheels."

One thing I'd learned, and that Honey continually tried to make me understand, was that the words you used were very rarely the most important part of a spell. Everything was about focus and intention. Aunt Eudora had been especially gifted with intention; it was her strongest skill. Just by focusing on something, she was able to amp up the power of the spell considerably more than what an average witch could do in the same scenario. Unfortunately, her magic worked only on others. That was why her magical teas packed such a punch, and why I was terrified to try duplicating them. I simply didn't have the same powers she did.

My skill with probability was a bit more mysterious. It was great if I needed to avoid getting hit by a bus but was unfortunately not something I could turn on and off at the drop of a hat.

A witch's gifts weren't limited to her strongest skill; that was just where she excelled most. I was still able to use the magical teas Eudora had already made and had achieved moderate success with some of the other spells I'd tried, but I worried that when I tried to make the teas myself, they would fall flat.

Watching *Bewitched* and *Sabrina the Teenage Witch* as a kid had certainly distorted my preconceived notions of what witchcraft looked like. There were two versions of it in my head: the fun, cutesy variety, like Samantha or Sabrina, and the *other* kind, like Bette Midler in *Hocus Pocus* or Anjelica Huston in *The Witches*—scary witches who used their power for evil.

I hadn't yet met any bad witches, but in fairness, I knew of only two other witches besides me: Eudora and Honey. And my aunt was gone.

Still, TV tried to tell me I could point at things and a little colorful blast of light and glitter would do my bidding. Or perhaps I could wiggle my nose and turn someone into a frog. Nope, not this lady. There were no pointed hats, no wands, and the only broom I owned was a Dyson cordless vacuum.

Needless to say, even months down the road, I still had a long way to go toward accepting or understanding what my powers meant. And because of that, I was always super hesitant to try using them on my own. I didn't want another incident like the Truth Be Told scones of the previous year.

I opened the door to Honey's shop, now satisfied my bike wouldn't go anywhere. The little overhead bell chimed merrily, and I was instantly hit with the blast of familiar scents. Honey's shop was laden with different kinds of oils and incenses for sale, not to mention a whole wall of clear jars that contained every herb or flower one might conceivably need to work a spell.

Whereas she and I were witches, with natural, *real* magical abilities, her shop still catered to others like Wiccans, or just spiritual types. There were also plenty of people with no magical powers who liked to burn incense and collect pretty crystals, so Honey's shop had no trouble staying busy. She was the only new-age shop for about fifty miles in each direction and also had a bustling online business.

She'd told me once that thousands of people watched her on weekly video streams while she live-packed orders of crystals. It was apparently a very popular thing on the internet now.

I brushed my fingers over some tall crystal points, each one at least as long as my forearm and twice as thick. Some were purple, others were white, but they all seemed to have rainbows trapped in them, depending on where you saw the light.

Sometimes I felt like a bad witch because my house wasn't covered top to bottom in different crystals—excluding those left behind by Eudora, most of which had been collected during her worldly travels—but Honey had laughed at me when I confessed my perceived shortcoming to her.

"Phoebe, you need to understand that these crystals are just talismans. They're just a way for us to feel like we have some control over our wants and desires. A person who wants love might buy a rose quartz and carry it with her, or someone who wants more money might slip some green aventurine in their pocket, but at the end of the day it's our own energy, our own desire to bring these things towards us, that does the job. Those who want success, fortune, and love can have it, as long as they're open to it. A crystal just helps us believe that we are."

That had certainly put a lot into perspective for me, and while I hadn't started clamoring for Honey's crystal inventory just yet, I did admire their beauty immensely. The thing was, I didn't *need* anything in my life that I wanted to manifest with spells or crystals. I had a job and a business I loved. I had a roof over my head and no mortgage to pay on the beautiful old house I now owned. I had new friends like Honey, Amy, Rich, Leo, and Imogen. And of course, I had Bob.

In seven months, I had come a long way from being the woman who first rolled into Raven Creek with everything she owned crammed in the back of her car and no idea what the future might hold. That woman was divorced, lonely, and lost. Not to mention more than a little broke.

Maybe manifestation had already brought me everything I wanted and needed right now, and that's why none of the crystals were compelling me to buy them.

Honey peeked her head through a beaded curtain at the back of the shop. As usual, her short-cut Afro was dyed platinum blonde, she wore impeccably applied makeup, including a mix of absinthe green and gold eyeshadow, and she sported her usual gigantic gold hoop earrings that were so big they almost brushed her shoulders.

"Phoebe!" She came fully into the room, beaming happily. "I wasn't expecting to see you today. What a lovely surprise."

Honey's age was still a mystery to me, and I had never bothered to ask. Her flawless brown skin made me think she was in her midtwenties, since there wasn't a single wrinkle to be seen, but she was also so much more poised and confident than I could have ever imagined being in my twenties, which made me suspect she might be a bit older than she appeared.

I was still from the old school of thinking where you didn't ask someone their age unless an opportunity presented itself naturally, and it hadn't yet. But if we got through a whole year of knowing each other and she didn't mention her birthday at some point, I was going to crack and make her tell me.

"Hey, Honey. I'm supposed to meet Rich for dinner at six, but thought I'd pop in, since we're going to Peach's."

She raised a quizzical, loaded brow at me and grinned. "You here to pick up a little rose quartz to slip in his jacket pocket, or what?"

I waved my hand at her. "It's not like that."

"Sure, and I'm blind and have never seen the way you two look at each other." Answering my own raised eyebrow, she sighed. "He looks at you like you're the last brownie on the tray and he's going to stick a fork in someone's hand if they try to take a bite."

This made me snort out a laugh. "Oh, please." But my red cheeks were impossible to hide. I could feel heat flush from my neck all the way to my ears. I knew there was chemistry between Rich and me, and heck, I had certainly dressed like this was a date, but he had spent so much time taking it slow, and then slower still, that I was starting to think we were going in reverse.

"We're just friends," I said finally.

"No, *we're* just friends. There's definitely something more going on with you two."

"*Definitely* not," I said, with a bit too much emphasis on the first word, completely giving away how frustrated I was.

"Oof. I'll stop teasing. Sorry."

I gave her a wan smile and shrugged. "Anyway, that's enough talk about Rich. How are you?"

Honey leaned on the glass counter that formed a U-shape around the back of the store and housed the more expensive items she carried, like custom jewelry and athames—ceremonial knives. I was sure she had plenty of spells and wards on the shop to keep people from walking out with things, which was why she was so trusting of all the smaller crystals in bins around the store, but the glass cases emphasized which items were of higher value and helped keep curious fingers from touching anything rare or delicate.

"I've got a date next week." Honey didn't sound too enthused about it, but this was the first time she had mentioned seeing someone new. I knew from our many previous evenings of wine and witchcraft that she hadn't been seeing anyone seriously, or even casually, since she broke up with her long-term girlfriend a year before I came to town.

My eyes widened at the revelation. "Excuse me, you can't play all casual like that. This is a big deal!" I tried to gauge her expression to determine if she was trying to *pretend* she wasn't excited or if she actually wasn't looking forward to it. "It's a big deal, isn't it?"

Honey smiled at me and gave a little shrug. "I'm trying not to get my hopes up too much, you know? It's been a long time since Emma, and I wasn't sure I was even ready, but every week like clockwork, Marco comes into the store with my orders. He's so sweet and lovely, and compliments me *so much*, that after a while I started thinking, *Maybe he's not just being nice*, and then after a while longer I started to think, *Maybe this guy actually likes me*, and then finally when I was starting to think I was a bit crazy and was *this close*"—she held her thumb and pointer finger a millimeter apart—"to doing a reading to see what he was thinking, he asked me out. So now we're going out."

I could tell, through all this, that her enthusiasm was growing and she was trying to play it cool. I'd been there. Heck, I'd be there again in about twenty minutes when I walked down the block to Peach's and tried to pretend it didn't make me crazy that Rich hadn't asked me out for real yet.

As Honey had implied, it took a long time after a serious relationship to be ready for something and someone else. There were trust issues built into big breakups—both in trusting others and trusting yourself. My ex-husband, Blaine, had cheated on me, which made me a bit more wary of trusting others.

Still, at a certain point you needed to open up again and let your-self be free to experience happiness, right?

I thought briefly of buying a little rose quartz to carry around with me, but it seemed like a terrible idea to use magic in any way when it came to getting Rich's attention. If he wasn't interested, he wasn't interested, and maybe it was time for me to accept that seven months was long enough to wait and start looking elsewhere.

Or I should just stop looking and hope that love found me again when the universe was good and ready for it to be my turn.

Instead of thinking of my own romantic life, or lack thereof, I decided to live vicariously through Honey. "Well, I'm super excited for you, and I expect a full rundown on every minute of the date as soon as it's over."

She laughed. "Can you wait until the next day? I promise a good bottle of wine and a complete minute-by-minute rehash. He's taking me out to this new West African place in Barneswood. I mentioned once, in passing, how much I missed my grandma's cooking, because she grew up in in Ghana and no one here makes food like that. And I guess he found out this place was opening and decided it was a sign we were supposed to go." Her smile was enormous now. "I don't mind telling you I'm possibly more excited for jollof rice than I am for the date. Is that terrible?"

I couldn't help but laugh. "Why do you think I made my not-date meeting with Rich at Peach's? If we're not going to smooch, at least I know I can get a decent burger out of the deal, right?"

Honey smiled. "Smart woman. Okay, now tell me why you're really here, because as much as I love seeing you, I know you're not just rolling in here unannounced, and on a limited timeline, because you wanted to say hello." She gave me a wink, letting me know she wasn't mad for seeing right through my plan.

What was lovely about my friendship with Honey was that she knew perfectly well she was my only friend in town—heck, in the world—who was also a witch. She never got annoyed with me when I needed her guidance with magic or had questions about my gift. I didn't want her to feel that was the only role she played in my life, though. She'd been one of the first people to welcome me into town with open arms and an offer of friendship, and our weekly get-togethers were more often hours of gabbing and sharing frozen appetizers than they were about learning any kind of magic.

Honey hadn't just been my first adult friend in Raven Creek; she'd been one of the first friends I'd made on my own since my divorce. I really had been starting from scratch when I moved here, and I was eternally grateful to those who had made me feel welcome so quickly.

There were a few folks in town who had seemed more interested in driving me right back to Seattle, but that was less about me and more about them being terrible people, I was learning.

I supposed every town needed to have a bad apple or two; otherwise, things might get a bit too idyllic.

"Okay, okay, busted." I clasped my hands together to mime begging. "But you're the best, smartest, most gifted, most wonderful witch in the world."

"Don't forget most charming, most beautiful, most powerful."

"Check, check, and double check."

"Consider me buttered up. What's up?"

I quickly gave her the rundown on what had happened at the auction the day before, from the murder to Bob's discovering the body to my concern that Detective Martin might think I was in some way involved.

"Did she *tell* you she thought you might be involved?" Honey asked.

"She wouldn't be a very good detective if she was like, *Hey, Phoebe, you're a suspect in my investigation*," I pointed out. Though I had certainly left our conversation feeling rattled and oddly guilty.

"No, but they can insinuate it in other ways, right? Like she might have said, *Don't leave town* or *I'll be in touch*—just something to make sure you knew she was keeping an eye on you."

"I mean, she did imply I shouldn't take any sudden vacations, but I'm telling myself that's normal when you're the one who finds a dead body." I tried to mentally replay Detective Martin's conversation with me, but nothing about what she'd said had been especially pointed. I had called her during my shift to ask if I could get fingerprinted in Raven Creek, but she had said she would prefer me coming to the station in Barneswood. But she also hadn't seemed in an enormous hurry, telling me it could wait until Friday if I needed more time, which had to be a good sign.

It was hard to say. She was a smart woman and a good cop, though, so I had a hard time believing she would show her hand if she thought I was up to no good. Keep your friends close and your murder suspects even closer, right?

"I don't know. I just can't imagine *not* being on the list of suspects. I did find the body, and I was one of the last people to see her alive. Probably."

"Probably?"

"I don't really know how many people she spoke to that day. She was making the rounds, really making sure everyone got to see whatever lots they were interested in. I have no way of knowing how many people she talked to before or after me. I was outside in my car with Bob for quite a bit."

"I can't believe you took your cat to an auction."

"I didn't do it on *purpose*," I protested.

"Still, it's pretty hilarious."

"It was terrible. When I saw him walk by those open doors, I thought for sure I was having a nightmare."

I paused.

The open doors.

As I remembered Bob passing through the big entry hall, the only reason I'd been able to see him at all was because someone had left the sliding doors partially ajar. And it was then I remembered the youngish couple at the back of the room and how one of them had ducked out in the middle of the auction. But my memory was muddled from there. I hadn't paid enough attention to them at the time to remember much about them except that they'd been in their thirties and that I'd found it weird that they were lurking at the back of the room rather than sitting down like the rest of us.

"Do you think you could help me sharpen my memory?" I asked.

"Like, revisit part of that day?" Honey tilted her head to the side and contemplated this request. "I mean, there's no saying it will be perfect, because our memory is imperfect. I can't actually take you back in time, but yeah, we could revisit a memory."

"Seriously?"

She beamed at me. "After all this time, Phoebe, isn't it obvious that there isn't much I *can't* do?"

Chapter Eleven

Honey pulled up two stools on the customer side of the counter and made her rounds through the shop, collecting various bits and bobs. While I was pretty sure she could have just closed her eyes and zapped me back into the memory, she seemed hyperfocused on performing a ritual along with it, so I wasn't going to interrupt her.

She muttered out loud as she worked. "Sage, to help with memory loss. Rosemary for concentration. Peppermint, to stimulate memory. Valerian root for memory and focus." Then she headed to the crystals, whispering, "Fluorite for clarity. Quartz to help amplify the other ingredients." She wasn't grabbing giant chunks of crystal but rather picking up a half dozen or so from the display of tumbled tiny pieces, ones that kids might gravitate toward and beg their parents for.

At last, she stopped in front of a rainbow-colored display of candles, hemming and hawing, her finger hovering between purple and yellow, then back, and back once more as she finally got a yellow one.

Bringing her haul over to the counter, she indicated I should take a seat on one of the stools as she put all her goodies on the glass countertop between us. She didn't sit down immediately but went to retrieve a small glass jar and a long candle lighter before hopping up on her own stool.

"Now, this isn't the kind of thing where I snap my fingers and suddenly you remember everything, okay? I'm sure Eudora could have brewed up a sensational, if slightly Thanksgiving-flavored, tea that would have worked wonders, but we're going to do things the old-fashioned way today. So you're not going to remember anything *now*, but tonight I want you to go home and put this under your pillow. By tomorrow, everything that wasn't clear should be a lot easier to remember. Got it?"

I nodded solemnly, though I was a little disappointed we weren't going to have a resolution immediately.

She took the stopper off the little jar, then methodically started to work through the herbs. She crushed everything up one dry ingredient at a time with her black mortar and pestle, then sprinkled the ingredients in perfect layers into the jar. Once she was done with the herbs, she added the tiny fragments of crystals, explaining what they were as she went. The fluorite was pretty purple-and-green chips that shimmered in the light, and the clear quartz, well, it looked like little shards of breakaway glass.

When everything was all neatly packed into the jar, she lit the yellow candle, holding it upright as the wick burned down and the wax slowly began to drip.

"Hold this with me," she instructed. "And as the wax drips, I want you to think of the moments you're trying to remember. Emphasize what has been lost and what you're hoping to regain. Then repeat after me: *What was lost, now is found. Memories gone again come round. Take these moments gone from mind, and make them once again be mine.*"

We recited the words together, over and over again, until the candle had completely melted down and the yellow wax had dripped down over the bottle's stopper, where it quickly hardened into place. When the candle was down to only a little nub, Honey held it out for me, and I blew out the flame.

She then handed me the adorable little jar, now sealed in wax, and said, "There you have it—a memory aid in a bottle. Under your pillow and have some sweet and fruitful dreams."

I took the bottle from her, surprised at how quickly the wax had cooled and hardened, then rifled through my purse for my wallet, but Honey was already waving her hand at me to stop.

"Put that away. This is a friend helping a friend. If you want to call it even after this, you can buy the next bottle of wine for girls' night, okay?"

"Are you sure?" I didn't want to take advantage of her kindness and expertise.

"If I didn't help you solve a murder, what kind of friend would I be?" She smirked at me. "Besides, the ingredients cost almost nothing. It's the intention that matters most, and that's all you."

"And you," I protested.

"Sure, but I'm not the one here who's on a suspect list, am I? I'd say you're more motivated to get this solved than I am."

My fitness tracker buzzed on my wrist, and for once I was glad it did, as the hourly reminder to hit my step goal was also a reminder that it was ten minutes before six and if I wanted to be on time to meet Rich, I needed to get going.

I gave Honey a fierce hug. "Thank you. Seriously. I'd be totally lost without you. And take notes on the date, because I want to hear absolutely everything about it next week, okay?"

"Deal. Now get out of here. And sleep well," she added with a knowing smile.

Chapter Twelve

Rich, ever punctual, was already standing outside Peach's when I left Honey's shop a few minutes later. He didn't look annoyed or impatient. If anything, his smile broadened when he saw me approaching.

I'd left my bike at Honey's, deciding this would be a good test for the durability of the protection spell and hoping it would be fine where it was. I probably didn't have much to worry about.

It didn't escape my notice that Rich did a complete head-to-toe look at me and my outfit, nor that the tops of his ears reddened as he did. Okay, so perhaps there was still some potential here after all, because he was definitely checking me out.

"I hope you weren't waiting long; I wanted to stop and chat with Honey for a little bit."

"No problem, I just got here." He ushered me in the direction of the diner's front door, one hand gently placed on the small of my back. It felt as if we were going into a much fancier restaurant, with my heels and him still wearing his nicely tailored trousers and suit jacket from whatever business he'd been attending to before this.

Come to think of it, he was *very* nicely dressed for someone who spent most of his time in a car staking out spouses who were potential cheaters.

"Sit wherever you want," came the usual cheerful voice of Lyla from behind the counter as she served up a big slice of pecan pie while simultaneously refilling someone's coffee. The woman had a gift.

Without asking, Rich led me over to the table where we'd first had dinner together, though I still wasn't sure if we were counting that as our first date or not. Probably not. At the time, I'd thought he might be a murderer, which was not the greatest way to kick off a budding romance, and it was also the evening I'd realized I might have special powers.

Overall, an insightful evening, but not exactly a *date*.

I settled into the booth, and he took off his suit jacket before sitting down across from me, folding it in half and putting it on the seat beside him. I watched him closely as he undid the buttons on his sleeves and rolled the cuffs up, exposing his toned forearms.

He smirked when he caught me watching him. "I'll never get used to the full suit-and-tie routine. I like having a little room to breathe, you know?"

"That's a shame, because you look good in a suit." I had not just said that out loud, had I? Oh, the horror.

Rich laughed. "Thank you. I should have told you earlier, but you look great tonight." He looked at me again, a long assessment, as if he wanted to make sure he wasn't lying, then smiled and nodded. "Really good."

I turned the same shade of red as the vinyl seats of the booth. I felt like I was fourteen again, trying to navigate flirting for the first time in my life and failing horribly.

Lyla, the diner's only full-time waitress, appeared at the table as if she'd popped out of midair. Her long hair was tied back in a sleek, black braid. "Evening. How are you guys doing tonight?" she asked with a genuine smile.

"Can't complain," Rich said, though he barely even glanced over at her, just kept his eyes on me the whole time. "You ready to order?"

I nodded, wondering if that was his way of telling me he wanted to speed this up so he could get out of here, or if he was just being polite.

"Yeah, I'm good. I'll have the smash burger, loaded, with a side of curly fries, and a strawberry shake."

Lyla looked at Rich. "Usual for you?"

"Yes, thanks." He handed her both of our menus.

Peach's was the kind of place where you went all in or you didn't go at all. While I was sure their salads were lovely, I could make a decent salad at home. Peach's was a greasy-butter-burgers, giant-order-of-fries, and milkshakes-mandatory kind of joint. You ate until you felt like dying and then ate a little more.

Part of me wondered sometimes if there was something super-natural in their food, because how else could it taste so good and *not* make you a good five pounds fatter?

I wasn't about to question it, though. It just meant that when I needed a guilty-pleasure meal, usually on a girls' night with Honey, I never felt bad about a Peach's burger platter.

With ordering out of the way, Rich leaned back in his seat, spreading his arms wide across the back of the booth, and then tilted his head to one side, trying to read me.

I didn't consider myself to be an inscrutable person. If anything, I was pretty sure my emotions were always painted directly onto my forehead like a tattoo that said *angry, annoyed, hungry,* or *happy,* depending on the day.

"Is this really a professional get-together, Phoebe?" he asked, a smirk lifting the corner of his mouth.

Did he want it to be something else? Was he trying to get me to admit to something? *Argh.* Why did it feel like he was trying to trick me into giving something away? He *knew* I liked him, and I was pretty sure he liked me, and we were in our midthirties, for crying out loud. We didn't need to be coy about this.

And yet I said, "What else would it be?"

Dummy.

He nodded and glanced out the window briefly. It was still bright outside, a true sign that summer was on its way. The trees were now all fully green, and a few of the storefronts had put planter boxes outside with cheery-looking flowers in them.

"Thought maybe you were just too shy to ask me out," he said finally.

"Maybe *you're* too shy to ask *me* out," I blurted, because evidently I was twelve years old and the best I could do was *No, you are.* Maybe I wasn't ready to date after all. At the moment I wasn't sure I was capable of being out in public with another adult. It was all I could do to keep from lowering my face into my hands and groaning out loud at how stupid I must have sounded.

But Rich laughed, a nice, warm, hearty sound that wrapped around me like the coziest of scarves on a chilly day.

"You're probably right about that."

"It *is* professional, though," I added. "I mean, you're not wrong— I suggested dinner because it sounded a lot more fun than just sitting in the bookstore together. Plus burgers, yum. But I do need your help. I think."

"You think?" He lowered his arms from the back of the booth and laced his fingertips together, putting his hands on his stomach. Now I had his interest, and there was nothing flirty about the way he was looking at me.

"I thought you might be able to help me find someone."

"Someone who?"

"Someone from the auction." I smiled innocently at him, hoping there would be no follow-up questions, but I already knew I wouldn't get that lucky. Rich evidently had already heard all about what had happened at the estate sale yesterday.

"Phoebe, I don't think that's a great idea. You should let Detective Martin handle the investigation. She's a good cop, smart. She'll figure out who did this."

"Except I think right now she might think *I* did this, and I'd really love for that to not be the case."

"Why would you assume she thinks you did it?"

"Well, she's a cop, and I can't help but think that when you find dead bodies in proximity to the same person on multiple occasions, you start to have some misgivings about that person. She also told me not to leave town anytime soon. She tried to tell me it was routine, but it still feels like she's keeping an eye on me."

"Hmm, you raise some very interesting points. *Did* you do it?" he asked, and for a second his tone was so serious that I stared at him in openmouthed shock. I guess it was only fair that he asked the question, since I had also once suspected *him* of murder.

"No, I didn't."

"Did Bob do it?" Now he was smirking broadly, telling me that his original question had been in jest. "You know what they say about the killer at the scene of the crime."

"That's not funny." I tossed a rolled-up bit of napkin at him, and it bounced harmlessly off his shoulder. "Bob will never forgive you for the implication."

"Bob loves me."

"Bob loves everyone. Don't think you're special."

"Ouch."

Lyla returned with our milkshakes, placing one in front of each of us along with a paper-wrapped straw, then disappearing as quickly as she'd arrived. Rich took a break from teasing me to sample his drink, and as I was doing the same, he asked, "Who from the auction are you trying to find?"

I took this as an opening and an indication that he might actually help me, so I quickly replied, "Franny? She was Madeline's assistant. I saw her leave crying right before the auction started."

He frowned at me. "Phoebs, that sounds like someone the police should be talking to."

"I know, I know. And I'll tell them everything, but I just want to ask her what happened. I would feel terrible if I pointed the detectives in her direction and she was just crying because she'd been fired."

"Which would be a *motive*," he reminded me.

"I don't know . . . she really didn't strike me as the killer type." Though what *was* a killer type? Rich was right, of course. If Madeline had fired Franny right before the auction started, she might have snapped. If tiny grandmas could lift up a whole car in a time of stress, who's to say Franny hadn't gone a little nuts when Madeline axed her?

"Not to mention if she *did* do it, she's not just going to incriminate herself to you. She'll lie."

I felt myself pouting a little, which was not the best look for a grown woman in most scenarios, but especially not one who's trying to convince their maybe sort-of romantic interest to help them out with a case. I straightened up in the booth as Lyla arrived with our food, and the overwhelming smell from the burger was all it took to center me back into reality and help me get my wits about me.

Peach's burgers weren't your run-of-the-mill burgers. I'm sure every diner on the planet has tried to claim they have the best burger, but Peach's had the edge. For starters, it was a classic smash burger, pressed thin while it grilled so the edges were nice and crispy while the center was perfectly cooked through and incredibly juicy. Not to mention the butter they grated into the ground beef mixture. Then they sneered at the idea of a standard bun with sesame seeds on top. No, no, that wasn't good enough for a Peach's burger. They had brioche buns, which were topped with onion bits prior to baking, so every single bite had a bit of an onion flare to it. Speaking of onion, they caramelized theirs in huge batches, topping every burger with a generous serving. The cheese was American cheddar, the bacon was perfectly crisped, the pickles were sliced lengthwise, not into little disks, and if you got a Peach's burger loaded, that meant all of the above *plus* a little signature chili, and the rest of the toppings were up to you. Every table had mustard, ketchup, relish, and barbecue sauce available, plus hot sauce if you needed it a bit spicy.

There was no way at all to eat a Peach's burger without getting messy. In hindsight, it was probably a terrible place to come if you were hoping to charm someone and look cute, but luckily for me, I was more hungry than I was concerned about my cuteness levels right then.

I bit into the burger—which required both hands to hold together, and even then, some of the chili would escape no matter how hard you tried to avoid it—and let the explosion of flavor wash over me.

This wasn't something you could eat every day, that's for sure. All of my arteries cringed in unison as I chewed, but my taste buds were holding a party in my honor, doing a happy dance as I went in for bite two. It was just *so good*. And thankfully, Rich was so focused on eating his own messy burger that he didn't have much chance to see how messy I was being.

After we'd both made a good dent in our burgers, I wiped my mouth and tried a different approach. "Do you think you could help me figure out who was *at* the event, at least? It was advertised in the paper, which was how I found it, but a lot of the people there looked, shall I say . . . fancy? I think maybe they were invited directly by the firm Madeline worked for. So there might be a guest list."

Rich dipped his fry in a combo of ketchup and mustard like an absolute maniac and finished eating it before he spoke again. "Why are you trying so hard to put yourself in the middle of this investigation, Phoebe?"

"Because I don't really feel like getting accused of murder?" I was still hungry, but my stomach churned at the memory of Detective Martin questioning me at the mansion.

"You didn't do anything, so you have nothing to worry about. Just let the police do their jobs."

I thought about the spell jar in my purse and how very much I intended to *not* keep my nose out of things. Rich was watching me carefully, and I decided that if he was really going to help protect me, like he'd promised Aunt Eudora he would, then he was going to have to do it my way this once.

"Look," I said. "I'm going back to Barneswood on Friday to go to the police station. I'm probably going to find Madeline's company and make a nuisance of myself. There's a really good chance I'm going to get into trouble, because I don't know the first thing about conducting a murder investigation. You, on the other hand, a former cop and current PI, are *very* good at this sort of thing. If you want me to stay out of trouble, don't tell me to leave it to the police. Tell me you're going to help me."

Rich blinked at me a few times, as if he couldn't believe I had just come out and said what I'd been thinking. Frankly, I was more than a little surprised myself. He thoughtfully chewed on another fry, trying to hide his smirk as he did so, but I could see it. I was pretty sure I'd won, but I decided to add a little icing to the cake.

"Pretty please?"

"Oh, you are absolutely incorrigible, do you know that?" He rolled his eyes. "This is *not* how I normally go about my business."

"That's probably a good thing. If everyone had to manipulate you into helping them, you would be pretty bad at your job."

"I will have you know I'm *very* good at my job."

"Prove it."

Chapter Thirteen

Rich and I walked from Peach's to town hall in companionable silence. It was still light out, as sunset kept getting later and later in the day. We now had sunlight until nine o'clock at night, though being surrounded by mountains did dampen the power of the sun somewhat.

A pretty evening glow painted the mountains pink and gave it a hazy, buttery filter that was magical. The streets were golden yellow, and the sinking sun glinted off the tall windows of town hall.

There weren't a lot of tall buildings in Raven Creek. Every shop on Main Street was only two floors, and while some of the Victorian-style homes around town—like Lane End House—were three stories, there was nothing else that really blocked out the views of the surrounding landscape.

Only two buildings in town were taller than everything else around them. The second tallest was the movie theater, which was so old it had an upper balcony and cute little mini balconies on each side of the stage. I knew there was a word for them, but no matter how many times I went to the theater, I forgot to Google it after.

That building was four stories tall, though the upper balconies were all closed and converted into storage—mostly for the seasonal decor the town used to liven up the streets at each holiday—and newer, comfier seating had been installed on the main floor for moviegoers. We still didn't get new releases until about a month after they came out in other theaters, but that didn't seem to make the venue any less popular.

The tallest building was town hall. With its large bell tower, it was about equal to five or six stories tall, though counting windows told me there were only four actual floors of usable space, plus the basement, which I'd been told housed even more decorations. Raven Creek was wild for holidays, and I frequently wondered how many of those stored items had been paid for from Eudora's funding.

Not that it bothered me. If my aunt loved anything, it was over-doing it on decor, so she would absolutely want me to keep using the money from her properties to keep Raven Creek's supply of giant red bows and comically large candy canes well stocked.

People were filing into the old red-brick building in groups of two and three. The population of Raven Creek was about two thousand, give or take, and while most people did not attend the meetings, enough did to make them feel like an event. Small-business owners were generally present, which meant most of my friends would be here, so perhaps that was why it seemed like everyone I knew was going to be in attendance.

When we got into the building, we headed into the auditorium, where permanent seating—rescued from the upper balconies of the movie theater—had been installed some years earlier to avoid needing to set up folding chairs every time there was a meeting.

Rich and I scanned the crowd inside, and from near the front I saw Amy get up and wave enthusiastically at us, then gesture to the empty seats beside her. We made our way down the aisle, and just in the nick of time too, because Tamsin Heartly, who owned the knitting shop, was edging closer to the spots Amy had saved.

"It's first come, first served," Tamsin said haughtily. She was in her seventies and had a posh-sounding British accent. I knew she'd lived here for almost forty years, but she'd never quite lost the sound of her home country.

Tamsin had a beige tote bag slung over one shoulder with knitting needles protruding from it. I admired that she had come here prepared to completely ignore everything that was happening. It made me wish I'd brought a book.

Amy rolled her eyes at Tamsin. "It's not a queue for concert tickets, Tam. Just find another seat."

Imogen, who was sitting in the row ahead of us, glanced over her shoulder like she was ready to intervene if things started to get heated, but Tamsin didn't argue any further and scuttled off to sit a few rows behind us. Imogen was sitting with Leo, Honey, and Charlie Bravebird from the pet store, and when I scanned the room, I saw other familiar faces in the crowd.

While I had been living here more than half a year, I still hadn't gotten to know so many of the people in town. I'd learned the names and faces of those whose businesses were in the spaces I owned, but there were a lot of people I still needed to meet. Perhaps there was a better way to get to know everyone outside of coming to these meetings, which could be great fun to observe but were rarely good for mingling.

I made a mental note to ask Amy and Honey what they thought about the idea of a cocktail hour or barbecue for local business owners to get together and get to know each other. Who knew, maybe we could help find ways for local businesses to support each other, the way Amy and I did by sharing our goods with each other.

A microphone whined from the front stage, followed by a loud *thump-thump-thump* of someone tapping on the mic. The bright-red hair of Dierdre Miller was visible around the whole room, making her a beacon you couldn't look away from. Like a petite, rude car accident.

"Ahem," she declared, and I had to suppress a giggle, because she didn't clear her throat, she actually *said* "ahem."

"Did anyone bring popcorn?" Honey whispered.

"I have a box of Junior Mints that has been in my purse for three months," I offered.

She looked over her shoulder. "Opened or unopened?"

I wrestled through my bag, which was so full it would make Mary Poppins proud, and handed her the unopened box. "Go to town."

"Thank you for joining us for our monthly council meeting for May," Dierdre announced. "We will first revisit lingering business from our last meeting and share any decisions we've made on those projects, then any new business can be brought up at the end. Please refrain from interrupting the discussion process, as you will have plenty of time for questions at the end."

It was cute that she issued this reminder, because in about five minutes people would be talking over each other no matter what she said.

Dierdre, who was seated at a long wooden table with the other council members, dramatically straightened some papers that were sitting in front of her. You didn't need to know her to be able to tell how much she enjoyed the power this position gave her. She wasn't in charge of the town council—the eight members all had equal votes—but it seemed everyone else was so scared of getting on her bad side that she probably got her way more often than not.

I couldn't blame them. I'd been on her bad side once before, and now, even months later, I'd been there so long I was considering buying property.

Dierdre held grudges as if it were an Olympic sport and she were Michael Phelps.

"First order of business," said the mayor. "The rejuvenation of the covered bridges."

A loud groan echoed through the crowd, and in front of me Imogen booed. This had been ongoing for four months.

"As I have previously made abundantly clear," Dierdre began, "the bridges are historical, and I don't believe we should be doing anything that might hinder their historic value to the town." A few more groans followed this. "That's quite enough from the crowd, please."

"I think what Councilwoman Miller is forgetting is that historical buildings are, by definition, old. And old things will fall apart if we don't care for them." The mayor wasn't usually too outspoken in these meetings, but this was a real passion project for him, and we'd all learned how badly he wanted to paint these bridges over the past few months.

"Just let him paint them," someone in the crowd yelled.

"That isn't how this system *works*," Dierdre complained. "This is a *democracy*."

"Who here votes we let the mayor paint the bridges so we never have to hear about this again?" someone else shouted.

Every hand in the room went up, including mine.

The bridges were lovely, and sure, the rustic paint gave them a nice aged vibe, but the mayor was right: unless they were cared for, the constant rain would eventually destroy them. A little paint wasn't going to make them any less historic.

Dierdre stared out at the raised hands, and her face twisted as if she had swallowed something sour. Then she looked at the other seven council members at the table, who also all had their hands up, and let out a long, dramatic sigh.

"Very well. Motion to paint the bridges passes."

A whooping cheer spread through the crowd. Honey munched happily on the Junior Mints, chuckling to herself.

Old business from the previous meeting was reviewed, then the floor opened for new business. A few people got up to approach the microphone in the middle of the main aisle, and I squeezed past Rich and the others to join them. Mr. Young complained that the new LED streetlights were too bright, saying he wanted to return to the older, yellow style. The mayor pointed out that the LEDs were more energy efficient and that the old type was still being used in the lamps on Main, but Mr. Young was specifically annoyed about the lights on his street.

Notes were made, and the council said they would take the matter under advisement and get back to him. There were then some complaints about the types of annuals that had been selected for the flower displays. Dierdre reminded everyone they were more than welcome to join the town beautification committee if they wanted more input on those choices.

Mrs. Pomeroy wanted to know if we could do anything about the mess made every spring by Canadian geese, to which the answer—I presumed the answer given this time every year—was no.

Then it was my turn to speak at last.

"Oh, Ms. Winchester. Hello again," Dierdre said coolly.

"Good evening, council," I replied, trying to keep my tone upbeat and friendly. "I'm actually just hoping I might be able to get some insight as to why it's taking so long for me to get approval to open my shelter?"

"You mean your little cat café?" she snarked back.

I had to restrain myself from saying anything I might regret or that would give her any ammunition to say no. It was okay if Dierdre didn't like me, but I wasn't going to let her use that to turn down my proposal.

"It's not a cat café. The animals wouldn't be free roaming; they would have dedicated space. I've outlined all this very clearly in my proposal. I know this plan has been under consideration for quite some time, but I was hoping I could impress a little urgency on you. We're going into spring and summer, which is the busiest time of year for shelters, and as most of you are aware, there is no local shelter, humane society, or even vet office in Raven Creek. The kitten population booms this time of year, and I happen to know that the Barneswood shelter is already at capacity. Without a little help, they won't be able to accept new intakes, which means dozens of new kittens born feral over the coming months will have nowhere to go. If my shelter is allowed to open, we can help ease this burden by taking longer-tenured residents from Barneswood and giving the shelter more room to help kittens, while also offering a local option to those right here in town or nearby who are looking for pets." I took a deep breath. I hadn't expected to say so much, but once I'd started talking, I hadn't been able to stop myself. "I'm just really hoping that we can settle this matter; otherwise, a lot of innocent animals are going to be the ones who suffer as a result."

The members of the council, or at least seven of them, were nodding quietly in agreement, but before anyone else was able to say anything, Dierdre cut in. "Yes, well, as sad as that is, we must abide by zoning regulations. So I'm sure you understand when I say you'll just need to wait your turn." She said this last part as if each word were its own sentence. *You'll. Just. Need. To. Wait. Your. Turn.* She might as well have exclaimed *period* at the end, because she'd made her point very clear.

The discussion was closed.

"Thanks," I grumbled, making my way back to my seat.

When I sat down again, Amy leaned forward across Rich and said, "Don't you worry, hon, you had them in the palm of your hand. You're going to get that shelter, just you wait."

But that was the problem, because if Dierdre was involved, I knew I could be waiting a very, very long time.

Chapter Fourteen

I was surprised to find how quickly I fell asleep that night, despite my unfortunate interaction with the town council.

After putting the little jar Honey had given me under my pillow, I put my head down and pictured the day of the auction and the way I remembered the room. The tricky thing about memory is just how slippery it can be. It doesn't matter how good you think you are at recognizing faces or if you believe your mind is an impenetrable vault; there are little things that drift away and change in the hours and days following an event.

I believed I had given the police my best possible recollections about the day of the murder, but if there was a way to make those memories more clear and more accurate, I wanted to do it.

I drifted off with that one goal in mind: to remember.

As soon as sleep settled over me, I understood that this would not be a normal dream. This wasn't a fantasy or an imagined space; instead, I found myself drifting through the rooms of the Weatherly mansion like a ghost. I slid past Bob as he brushed through the front door and found myself hovering in the ballroom where the auction had taken place.

To make things even more unsettling, I could see *myself* sitting in the room, almost as if instead of being inside my own memory, I had been transported back to the day of the auction and given more time to pay attention, only this time from another angle.

As with all magic, I had no idea how long this spell would last or what the limitations might be, but the problem was I was also *asleep*, making it a bit harder to control myself like I might in my waking hours.

I observed myself for a moment, but then watching my own anxious face and bouncing knee made me feel uncomfortable, and I had to focus my attention elsewhere. First, I noticed the girl who had been sitting in the same row as me.

When I'd seen her during the auction, my first impression of her had been that she was mousy and nervous. Now that I was watching her again, I saw something different. She was still hunched into herself, trying to take up as little room as possible, but rather than it being a gesture of nerves or a lack of confidence, it felt somehow *intentional*. She was trying not to be seen, like she didn't want anyone else in the room to look at her.

Interesting.

My attention shifted to the back of the room, where the polished-looking couple in their midthirties were standing. While the woman's expression looked passive, even bored, the man's seemed almost pained. His mouth had formed a thin line, and his countenance was somewhere between having indigestion and feeling genuine rage toward something.

Or maybe he was just gassy.

He leaned over to the blonde woman at his side and whispered something into her ear, then slipped out the door at the back of the ballroom. I tried to follow after him, but the limits of my memory wouldn't allow me to leave the room. I supposed the only reason I'd been able to "see" Bob sneaking into the house earlier was that I *knew* it had happened, because he had to have entered somehow. Since I didn't have the faintest clue where this man was going, I couldn't follow along.

Crestfallen, I turned my gaze back toward the room. Everything was quiet, as if the scene had been muted. The auctioneer's lips were moving, but no sound came out.

I watched the young woman seated in my row a moment longer as she pulled out her phone, typed out a quick message, then put it away. Sadly, I couldn't see the message or the name of the person she was contacting.

Off to the side of the room, a waiter shuffled uncomfortably with a tray of champagne flutes precariously balanced on one hand. He checked his watch with the other, one of those clunky-looking high-tech numbers that had probably cost him a full month's salary.

I had been a waitress in college, and watching him hold the tray made me think either he was new to the job or he didn't care too much about whether or not all the flutes tumbled to the ground.

I was about to move toward the front row when something tugged at me, like a hand grabbing me by the back of the shirt and yanking backward.

I glanced over my spectral shoulder only to see myself—the self of my memory—ducking out of the room in an awful hurry. I must have spotted Bob.

As I was dragged out of the room to follow the path of my actual memory, I noticed one final thing. The girl who had been sitting in the row beside me wasn't watching the auctioneer, and she wasn't looking at the other guests.

Instead, she was staring right at the waiter, watching his tray wobble, and she wore a smirk that suggested the greatest joy in her world would be watching him drop all those glasses right onto the floor.

I woke up before I could see if he did.

I felt as if I had more questions than answers about the people who had been in the room with me, none of which could easily be resolved by a mere spell. But I also felt as if I had a more solid recollection of the faces and behaviors of the people at the auction.

One of whom might have been a killer.

Chapter Fifteen

Since I needed to go to Barneswood on Friday, I called Daphne to ask her to come in and split the evening shift with Imogen. This was the third time in a week I'd called her in for an extra shift, and I was surprised it took her as long as it did to speak up for herself.

"Um, Phoebe?" she said, after we'd confirmed she could come in on Friday. "You know I don't mind picking up extra shifts. And of course I love working on the weekends." I knew this was true, because weekends were a bit slower and gave her time to work on her university assignments. "But I was hoping, um, you know, that . . ." Her voice started to drift off, and I wanted to give her a little shake to motivate her, but we were talking over the phone.

"Daphne, just ask. It's okay."

"Well. It would help me out a lot if maybe I could get an extra shift or two a week? Not even long ones, but, you know, maybe helping Imogen in the evenings. Or I can come in over lunch on Tuesdays and Thursdays. I know you're really bad at remembering to take your breaks."

That made me chuckle. She was spot-on, too, because unless I had something I needed to do away from the shop—which more often than not involved going to the grocery store to pick something up *for* the shop—I usually worked my shift all the way through. It might have been a different story if I had been working for someone else or I didn't like my job, but being at the shop every day filled me with so much joy and enthusiasm that it barely felt like work.

Sure, it could be exhausting, and it was retail, which meant we sometimes had customers who could be demanding, but ninety-nine percent of the time it was just making tea and selling books to people I really liked. Not to mention I was able to have a creative outlet in designing the book displays, and I was also able to express my culinary creativity with the minimal baking I did in the petite kitchen.

Every day was a new opportunity to have some fun, and that wasn't true of everyone's job. Plus I lived alone—or with Bob, I supposed—but I liked spending time with people. Being at the Earl's Study rarely felt like a chore.

I was pleased with Daphne for coming come right out and asking me for more shifts. She could often be shy and reserved, and I was proud of her for taking a mild stab at being commanding for a change.

"You do really good work, Daphne, and I know our customers love you. I just want to be sure that you're ready for the extra responsibility. You're sure it's not going to be too much to handle with your school schedule?"

"Oh, no." Her voice was immediately enthusiastic, as if she could sense that I was about to give in. "Actually, school is done for the summer next week. I'm just finishing my exams, so I'm going to have a much lighter load. I'm only taking two summer classes."

I knew she would do her homework in the store, and it didn't bother me. I'd be a pretty giant hypocrite if I called her out for it, since Imogen spent half of every shift with her nose in a book, and I myself had been known to enjoy some downtime in the fireplace sitting area when it was quiet. The shop was always tidy and things were put away; who was I to argue with what my employees did, as long as customers weren't neglected and the daily checklist was completed?

I think that was honestly a huge part of the appeal of working at the Earl's Study. That and the proximity to the Sugarplum Fairy, which certainly didn't hurt.

Well, it might be hurting my waistline, but that was all the more reason to use my bike more often.

"As luck would have it, I do have a pretty big project I'd like to start soon." I explained my goals for the website and how the new batch of books from the estate sale would be a great place to start.

"Please," she said, her eagerness apparent. "I *love* cataloging things. And I even have a little Etsy shop where I sell some of my knitting, I could totally help you in setting up an e-commerce site. Oh, Phoebe, this is going to be so fun. Thank you."

We agreed that I'd give her full-time hours for as long as it took to catalog the new books, and then we would play it by ear from that point. I made it very clear that I couldn't afford to have three full-time employees long-term, but I did need more assistance with all those new books coming in, and I wanted to be able to help Daphne out.

When she hung up, I got the sense I'd just made her day, but I was also starting to feel a renewed sense of excitement over my ideas for the shop and what might be possible. If the online sales did take off, I'd be able to keep Daphne at full-time hours, too, which would be great.

I was jotting down some ideas for the website—perhaps we could sell things like the reusable drink cups, and maybe porcelain mugs?—when the door chimed. I glanced up to say hello but did a double take when I saw who my two new customers were.

It was the young couple who had been standing at the back of the auction. A little lump formed in the back of my throat, and I wasn't sure if it was nervousness or excitement. The two so often felt the same.

"Hello," I said again, trying to maintain my cool. I didn't want to spook them, but when else was I going to have an opportunity like this dropped into my lap? It felt so surreal to see them again in person after I'd just seen them in my dreams last night. I wondered if maybe I'd gone a little overboard on the manifestation and that had brought them to my doorstep, perhaps without them even realizing why.

"Hello," the woman said, her tone polite but disinterested. She didn't even glance at me, which also meant she likely didn't recognize me from the auction. As she wandered into the bookstore, the man lingered by the door, taking in the entire space.

"Nice shop," he said casually. "This is a lot of space. Is rent pricey?"

"I own the building," I replied.

"Oh. Well, that's a rare treat."

Technically, I owned most of the block, but we didn't need to get into that. "Yeah, it's pretty nice getting to be your own boss and your own landlord," I said with a small smile.

"Was this originally two buildings?" he asked, eyeing the dividing arch between the tea shop and the bookstore.

"Yes, a very long time ago. It had already been connected when my aunt bought the property, but she had two distinct shops in mind, and it just worked out that we were able to join them." He probably wasn't that interested, and I wasn't sure why I kept chatting, but if he was being open and friendly, maybe I could find out what they'd been up to at the auction, since I hadn't seen them bid on anything.

"Cool." He glanced into the bookstore, his gaze trailing the woman as she slowly moved down the aisles. She had the look of someone who did a fair bit of book shopping. Her head was tilted sideways as she meandered, and she already had two books tucked under her arm. I couldn't see the titles; otherwise I might have directed her to something similar.

The sorting of our shelves was imperfect. We tried to divide everything by genre and again by author last name, but books got moved and rearranged by customers so frequently that it wasn't always a sure bet that you'd find Agatha Christie in *Mystery, C.* She might pop up in *Romance, A* because someone had decided at the last minute they were in the mood for a rom-com instead of *The Murder at the Vicarage*.

We tried to do a nightly pass over the shelves to see if anything was obviously misplaced, and we even had a table at the end of one of the rows with a sign that said *Changed your mind? Let us reshelve it for you!* to try to resolve the issue, but not everyone looked at the signs.

The man must have concluded his partner would be occupied for a while, as he drifted into the tearoom; his gaze immediately fixated on the glass cabinet where I kept the treats. Since it was fairly early in the morning still, it was pretty much entirely full. No bread yet—that was in the process of baking and would be used for lunch.

"Wow, quite the array you've got there. Do you make everything yourself?" he asked.

"Some of them. The scones and our signature Earl Grey shortbread are house specialties. The rest come from the bakery next door, the Sugarplum Fairy. Amy has loads of stuff there, so if you're in the market for some cake or perhaps some treats to take home with you, I recommend stopping in."

The man seemed briefly confused, something that happened on occasion when people realized there wasn't any rivalry between

Amy's shop and my own. "You send people to another business?" he asked.

"Sure. She stocks my tea; I stock her treats. It's mutually beneficial. I'm just saying she has a wonderful selection of things we don't carry here. But the stuff I *do* have is excellent."

He gave a little shrug and said, "Well, we'll have to stop there next, then. But in the meantime, I'll take a half dozen of the shortbread, if they're your specialty."

"They go really well with our Strawberry Fields Earl Grey, which is only available in spring and summer," I suggested, filling a little carboard box with the cookies.

"You twisted my arm. I'll take some of that as well."

"Bag or tin?" The bags held fifty grams, while tins neatly held a hundred. I had just switched over to branded tins, and they were the same mint green as the cups. I loved them.

"Tin sounds lovely."

I filled it up with the loose-leaf tea, holding the bigger canister out to him so he could get a good whiff of the freeze-dried strawberries we mixed into it. Sometimes I would use this tea in the daily shortbread, which gave it a completely different flavor than the plain Earl Grey did. It always amazed me how changing or adding just one ingredient could create a unique experience with the tea.

One of the main ingredients in Earl Grey tea is bergamot, and while most people are familiar with the distinctive smell of bergamot—enjoying its notes in candles and even perfume—not many know it's actually an inedible citrus fruit, coveted for its oil. The citrusy notes of bergamot played really well with the strawberry, making it a perfect summer tea.

I took the man's items to the cash register and let him continue to browse, his gaze drifting over the names of my teas the same way his partner's were looking over the books. Watching him read gave me an opportunity to get a good look at him for the first time since he'd entered. He was probably in his early to midthirties, and was starting to develop fine lines around his eyes. He wore a pair of thin, gold-framed glasses, and his haircut looked fresh and expensive.

He was wearing a plain button-down underneath a nice navy-blue sweater that looked pricey and soft. Cashmere, probably. His pants were neatly pressed, and he wore polished brown leather loafers. A man like that wouldn't have been out of place at a country club, or a yacht club, or anything else that ended in *club*. The only clubs we had around here were the Knit and Sip crew, who came in on Fridays, and Becky Scranton's monthly book club, which typically ended in the middle-aged mothers of Raven Creek not speaking to each other for about a week, then making up and selecting the next book they were going to read and fight about.

I loved the book club because they all insisted on owning the books they read and would place bulk orders with me for the monthly titles, which guaranteed ten books for the members and a handful more for others who just liked to be in the know about what had caused this month's fight.

I had learned, retroactively, that things had almost come to blows the month they read *The Help*, and that since then merlot was no longer allowed, and Jenny Marcotte had been disinvited for three months.

Living in a small town was the best.

"Are you up here on a little getaway?" The area around Raven Creek and Barneswood was festooned with cute B and Bs and charming little hotels that even had their own spas. It was a great way to promote year-round tourism and was usually the reason couples were wandering around Raven Creek in the middle of the week. Our mishmash of European-inspired architecture and proximity to hiking trails kept us busy all year, and during the holidays people made the trip just to see how the shops and homes were decorated. Raven Creek took holiday decorations very seriously.

I didn't think he was here to hike, though.

"Oh." He glanced quickly at the woman, who wasn't paying any attention to us, and then back to me. "Kind of, but not really. Visiting family. My family." He offered me a hand. "My name is Riley Weatherly."

It took a moment before the familiarity of his name registered, and once it did, I had to keep my mouth from literally falling open. I pretended to have no idea that I recognized the name and introduced myself back, shaking his hand firmly. "Phoebe Winchester."

"Like the rifles? And that crazy house in San Jose?"

I preferred references to the Winchester Mystery House over the *other* most common reference I got. "And the fictional demon-hunting brothers, yes."

"Ah, you get that a lot, I bet."

"You have no idea."

"Well, I have to admit it's sort of nice to not have someone react to my name for once. Where I'm from, the Weatherly name is . . . well, it's pretty well-known."

I bit my tongue, not wanting to mention that I'd literally just bought thousands of dollars' worth of books from his family—or who I assumed was his family—only days earlier.

"Famous or infamous?" I asked, trying to keep my tone light.

"Maybe a bit of both. You know how it can be with old-money families."

I gestured around my shop and then at my dirty apron as if to ask, *Do I?*, and that made him laugh. "Sorry, maybe not."

The woman had finished browsing and had a decent stack of books in her arms when she got to the counter. She smiled at me, but the gesture didn't reach her steely blue eyes.

"I see you've been busy," she said, looking at the items Riley had on the counter. He'd added a branded mug while we'd been chatting.

"You too," he replied. "Phoebe, this is my wife, Yasmine."

"Charmed, I'm sure." Then she pointed toward her pile of books. "Cable doesn't work. No Wi-Fi." She sighed as if she were explaining years spent in a gulag rather than time at some nice B and B or family home. "I swear, the second you leave a big city, *nothing* works. I don't know how you people live like this." She smiled again, and I tried not to take it personally.

Besides, my Wi-Fi worked just fine.

"These should help distract you for a little while," I replied cheerfully. She'd picked a solid assortment of classic beach-read fiction. Some romance, some mystery, and a few that bore the distinct sticker of a famous actress's book club. I always front-faced those when we got used copies; they sold instantly. "Great choices," I added.

"Thank you. I do love to read." She had an accent, or was trying to have one, anyway. That specific wealthy Transatlantic accent made famous by Katharine Hepburn. Only hers didn't sound entirely natural, and I suspected she was using it to make herself sound a bit fancier than maybe she actually was.

I rang up their order, my heart pounding. When was I going to get another chance to grill them about the auction? I'd be a fool not to say something now while I had the chance.

"Wait, did you say your last name was Weatherly?" I asked, making sure to process Riley's credit card and bag up their goods before I accidentally offended them or drove them from my shop.

"Yes," he said, a newly wary tone in his voice.

"I thought you two looked familiar." I snapped my fingers as if the memory had just come back to me. "The estate sale. The auction at Weatherly Manor earlier this week. I saw you two at the back of the room, didn't I?"

Yasmine went pale almost immediately, all the color draining from her face and her expression twisting into something ugly and defensive. Her gaze darted to Riley, whose own face was now considerably whiter. They both took a step back from the counter.

"Oh, you were there?" he asked. "What a small world."

I could tell they were about three seconds away from running out the front door, which in and of itself was a curious reaction, but I had to ask just one final question before they did.

"What's funny is, I remember the auction hostess telling me there was no immediate family left, and that's why the estate was being auctioned."

Riley's expression went from worried to angry in an instant, and it was so sudden and so scary I took a step back from the counter, wondering if I'd made a big mistake.

"She didn't know what she was talking about," he spat. "That stupid woman got what she deserved."

Chapter Sixteen

I stared at Riley in openmouthed shock. I couldn't believe he'd actually said what he had out loud, and evidently neither could Yasmine, or Riley himself, for that matter.

He began to stammer almost immediately, while Yasmine let out a long, exhausted-sounding, "Riley, no."

She must have sensed that damage control was necessary, because she looked at me, plastering on her best politician's wife smile, and said, "You have to understand that there's quite a bit of drama going on behind the scenes with the Weatherly estate. We were, of course, shocked about what happened at the mansion earlier this week, and Riley didn't mean what he said just now, did you, darling?"

Riley, who was sputtering like a fish out of water, fixed me with a worried stare. "No, of course not. It's the stress talking. Absolute tragedy what happened to Marianne."

"Madeline," I corrected him, stunned he could forget the name of a woman who had died when we were all at the house. Though perhaps he hadn't met her.

"Yes, Madeline." He nodded a few times and tried his best to smile, but it was definitely fake and made him look like he was stepping on a sharp tack while he did it. "Like my wife said, there's a lot going on we can't really get into, for legal reasons, but we were at the sale that day hoping to put a stop to it."

"Riley," Yasmine warned, the meaning of her tone evident even to me.

If he'd wanted to stop the sale, killing Madeline certainly would have been a quick way to do it. It was obvious Riley had a lot of animosity toward the sale, and Madeline in particular, but while that might have given him motive, I couldn't immediately say it made him a killer.

Nevertheless, I wasn't too thrilled to be alone in my shop with two people who might have had a hand in Madeline's slaying.

The Weatherlys and I stared at each other uncertainly, and just as Riley moved to take a step toward me, the sound of the back door opening and closing drew our attention. I hazarded a quick glance over my shoulder to see Imogen entering.

Her braids were hanging loose today rather than in her usual high bun, and the little metallic clasps woven into them clicked together musically as she entered.

"Morning," she said brightly, obviously missing the thick wall of tension hanging between me and the couple at the door. "Ohhh, looks like y'all did some damage." She smiled at them and headed into the café to pour herself a cup of tea.

The Weatherlys took this as the perfect opportunity to duck out the front door without saying another word, and while I was sorry I hadn't had a chance to grill them more, I was happy to have been given the reprieve and the added layer of safety brought on by a witness.

I let out a breath I'd been holding for heaven knows how long and sank onto my stool once the door clicked shut. The scent of Cinnamon French Toast tea wafted into the air and was an immediate balm to my nerves. I wrestled with the idea of telling Imogen what she'd just walked in on, but she was in such a happy mood I didn't want to upset her.

It was less likely Imogen would be upset and more likely that she'd immediately go into question mode like a high-octane Nancy Drew. I wasn't sure I had the energy for that right now. I definitely planned to tell Rich about this later, and most likely would tell the detectives when I went to Barneswood tomorrow.

It wasn't as if they could get mad at me for meddling if two potential suspects had wandered into my shop, could they? All I'd done was mention seeing them at the estate sale. I hadn't gone knocking at their door.

Which was precisely what I planned to do with Franny tomorrow when I wrapped things up at the police station. Rich had grudgingly agreed to give me her address, but with the major caveat that he was going to come with me. I appreciated—and maybe even enjoyed—the protective approach he was taking, but I also had to wonder if showing up with a big man towering behind me, especially one whose entire aura said *cop*, might make it harder to get any information out of Franny.

We would play that one by ear.

Before I could say much else to Imogen, Mr. Loughery walked in, the overhead bell chiming, and waved his most recent Sue Grafton at us. It was a bit late in the morning for him to arrive, but I hadn't started to worry just yet. There were days here and there he didn't come in, so I would start to fret only if we missed seeing him two or three days in a row.

"The usual, Mr. Loughery?" Imogen asked, setting her own steaming mug on the counter.

"You know it, my dears. Is Bob expecting me?"

It warmed my heart a thousand times over to know that not only were the regulars okay with me bringing my cat in, but they'd started treating him like part of the experience. It made me believe we had a good shot at having a successful rescue operation out of the store. The more people saw and loved Bob, the more they might imagine themselves having a feline reading buddy of their own to hang out with. That was the goal, anyway.

First, I had to get Dierdre Miller to finally agree to let me have the animals on-site. It wasn't like I was having a full-blown cat café. They would be in nicely outfitted cages. And I planned on having only two or three at a time. I think she just enjoyed making my life difficult, and if we was being honest, I hadn't given her much reason to warm to me since my arrival.

Sighing out loud, I resolved to try to mend fences with the redheaded menace and make my life easier in the process.

Mr. Loughery took my sigh the wrong way, asking, "Bob's okay, isn't he?"

"Oh!" I started to blush immediately. "Yes, oh my goodness. I'm sorry. He's waiting in his usual place, of course. My mind was somewhere else entirely."

He gave me a compassionate nod, as if having a head in the clouds was something he was accustomed to himself, and shuffled slowly into the bookstore. Soon I heard the familiar creak of old leather and Bob greeting him with a soft "Brrow?" which told me that the cat had been asleep and Mr. Loughery had given him a little greeting pat.

I loved the familiarity of their routine, and it helped take some of the edge off what had just happened with the Weatherlys. What a weird encounter that had been, and one that certainly put Riley at the very top of my suspect list.

Using the little notebook I kept at the front counter to track special-order requests, I quickly jotted down everything they had said to me about the estate sale, and specifically Riley's most telling words: "That silly woman got what she deserved."

How on earth could someone believe murder was deserved, for any reason? Even if Riley and Yasmine believed they had a claim to the estate, that would have been something to take up with their lawyers, not to blame on poor Madeline. And it most certainly wasn't a reasonable excuse to kill her.

There was no good reason to kill someone. All the potential motives I was finding while looking into this case were just such empty, thoughtless reasons to end a life. Losing a job? Not inheriting the family wealth?

Madeline might have come across as cold and a little uncaring, and I certainly didn't know her well, but I felt terrible that no one seemed to care she was dead.

Even my own reasons for wanting to locate her killer weren't entirely altruistic. I just didn't want anyone thinking I'd been the one to do it.

After making notes about the encounter with the Weatherlys, I sent Rich a quick text. *Two people from the auction were just in here. I think one of them might be a good suspect.*

Three little dots jumped up and down in the text window, letting me know he was typing his reply.

They just HAPPENED to come in on their own?

Scout's honor.

You were never a Scout, Phoebe. I'll come by your place later to chat about tomorrow. Did you get their names?

I gave him the pertinent details and tried to ignore the fluttering excitement in my chest at the idea of him stopping by my place. I quickly remembered what a disaster it was and swore inwardly, knowing I'd need to do a clean of the living room and kitchen before he showed up or he was going to think I was an absolute slob.

The truth was, the kitchen was upside down because I'd started experimenting with some new seasonal blends for fall and winter—yes, far too early, but I wanted a chance to try things out before the holidays arrived—and the living room was a mess because I'd been steadily going through all of Eudora's old photo albums over the past several months. Part of the reason was to see if she'd hidden anything else inside them—that was where she'd tucked millions of dollars' worth of real estate deeds, after all—but I was also enjoying visiting all the moments of her life she'd felt were worth saving.

I kept finding great photos of her that I wanted to make copies of, so that every room in the house would have one or two pictures of Eudora. I might live there now, but it was always going to be her house in my mind, and even as I started to decorate and change things slightly, I didn't ever want to lose her from the place.

Putting my phone down and tucking the notes into my cardigan pocket, I took the tea Imogen had just finished making and brought it into the bookstore. We'd started giving Mr. Loughery the big mug instead of our usual small teacups so we didn't need to offer him refills quite as much and risk interrupting either his reading or his naps.

He was settled comfortably into his chair, one foot resting on his knee and the Grafton novel open in his lap. He was wearing his familiar tortoiseshell reading glasses almost on the tip of his nose, and absently scratched at his short white beard.

While he was an older man, there was something wonderfully vital about him, a mischievous twinkle in the eye and a redness in the cheek that kept me from worrying about him. Plus, I thought, the routine of getting out of the house every day to interact with other people was good for him.

"Mr. Loughery, do you ever think about hanging out a bit later on Fridays? There are some lovely ladies that come in for Knit and Sip, you know? I sometimes hear them talking about you." I gave him a little wink.

From my understanding, it had been over a decade since his wife had passed, which I assumed had been the thing that started this daily routine to begin with. I hoped he wouldn't take any offense to my teasing.

"Oh." He gave a soft chuckle. "No, no. I couldn't possibly. That's an event for the ladies. I'd just get in the way."

"I don't think it's an exclusive club. I bet they could teach you to knit too. I'm terrible at it, but I've started to pick up some of the basics just from watching them." Not that you'd ever know it to look at the truly pathetic attempt at a scarf I'd begun over the winter, with holes in the middle, uneven rows, and tension all over the place.

He flushed and took the cup from my hand, setting in on the little circular table beside him.

"Something to think about, I suppose, but maybe us bachelors need to stick together, right, Bob?"

Bob opened one eye slightly upon hearing his name, but he offered only the smallest trill of acknowledgment before going right back to sleep.

Maybe finding him a girlfriend wasn't the right move.

Maybe finding Mr. Loughery the perfect cat of his own should be my new mission.

Chapter Seventeen

After doing a speed round of housecleaning when I arrived back at Lane End House, I thought the place looked decent enough for me to let company in. I didn't think Rich would have a negative opinion of me if my house was a little messy, but it wasn't the image I wanted to project to someone coming over. I also knew Eudora would roll over in her grave if she saw me playing host with dirty dishes in the sink.

Bob trailed after me from room to room, and I found myself chatting with him as I went.

I carried some clean laundry up the stairs to my bedroom, where I neatly folded everything and put it in its designated drawers. Even though it was fresh from the dryer, there was cat hair on it somehow.

It had taken me several months to feel totally comfortable unpacking my things into the dressers and closets, and subsequently I had spent an awful lot of time living out of my suitcases and moving boxes before finally getting fed up with the whole thing and giving myself permission to actually *live* in my new house.

In fairness, the first month of me moving to town had been a very eventful one, during which I'd almost been killed. So I thought it was okay to be gentle with myself for being a bit lax with the housework.

Ever since then, it had been a matter of the giant house being so much more than I could maintain on my own while also working at the store full-time. I was beginning to think I might need to hire a part-time cleaner. Someone who could handle coming in once a week, just to make sure the house didn't fall into total disrepair and that my free time wasn't entirely consumed by keeping up three floors and ten bedrooms as one person.

Still, hiring a cleaner was one of those things rich people did, and while I might technically be rich, I certainly wasn't in terms of my personal bank account. But I probably could afford someone if I reworked my budget a little bit. And heaven knew how good it would be for my mental well-being to not feel like I was constantly falling behind on things like vacuuming and dusting.

I made a mental note—not for the first time—to ask around and see if there was anyone local who might be a good fit. Leo would probably be a good person to ask; a lot of people posted flyers for their various side hustles on the big cork board at the front of Lansing's, and if someone was going to be offering their part-time cleaning services in town, that would be where they would share it.

It was decided, then. I'd leave it to fate, and if there was an ad up for a housecleaner at Lansing's when I went in for my weekly groceries tomorrow, I would call them.

While I tidied, I thought about the murders, unable to avoid dwelling on the mystery. "You were with me at the Weatherly mansion, and you found the body. What did you think of Riley and Yasmine?" I asked Bob, who was still at my heels.

Bob had watched me go through this whole mental process, which was largely done by me hauling things around the house and then loudly announcing "Okay!" to myself as I nodded and moved on to the next thing. He didn't answer my questions about the Weatherlys, but I supposed I hadn't really expected him to.

He also hadn't reacted to them when they'd been in the store. I thought if Riley had been the killer, Bob would have hissed or given some indication of it. I tried to recall if he'd been sleeping the whole time, or if he'd noticed the married couple at all, but I wasn't sure. He'd been dozing when Mr. Loughery arrived, so there was a chance he had slept through the whole thing, which might explain his lack of response.

I sort of wished I could bring him along to Barneswood with me tomorrow, just to see what kind of response he might have to Franny, but I wasn't about to get pigeonholed as a crazy cat lady who brought her pet with her when conducting non-interrogation interrogations. It was just going to be a friendly chat.

I had just given the house one last look to assess its present-ability when a knock sounded at the door. When I'd first moved to town, there had been a big uptick in neighborhood kids running up, pounding on the door, and running away. It had scared the heck out of me at the time, but by now I had sort of gotten used to it. However, it did mean I was always a little dubious whenever someone knocked.

As I braced myself for an empty porch, I opened the door and found that I had real company instead.

"I half expected no one to be there," I admitted to Rich.

"Are those kids still playing pranks?" He glanced over his shoulder down the hill toward town as if he were going to see a kid running away, even though he had been the one who knocked.

"Not as much now. I think offering full-sized candy bars at Halloween helped endear me to them at least a little bit. Though they definitely all still think I'm a witch."

"You are a witch," he reminded me.

"I know, I know. But they think I'm like an *Oh no, Auntie Em, I squished this green lady* witch and not an *If I get spooked, I stop time* witch." Rich didn't fully understand my gift, as it wasn't something I could demonstrate at the drop of a hat, but it was nice to have someone other than Honey around who I could actually say the word *witch* to.

Both Rich and Leo knew what I was, and others, like Amy and Imogen, had a version of the truth that they understood. Everyone else in town had just decided I was a weird lady whose tea was special, like my aunt's had been, and continued to trust me the way they'd trusted her. They also tended to believe many of the items purchased from my shop had some delightful bonus side effects, which the magical teas stored in the kitchen most certainly did. The term *witch* didn't get used too liberally outside of a small circle of trust.

In the case of Rich and Leo, Eudora had been something of a surrogate mother to them even when I hadn't been here, and that trust had extended to her asking them to look out for me when I moved back to town. They'd both interpreted this instruction in different ways. Leo was a keen observer, keeping an eye and ear out at all times but never putting himself too directly in my way. I suspected that Leo knew more about what people were saying about me on any given day than I ever would.

Most people thought men, especially burly, bearded ones, had no interest in town gossip, and as a result they were willing to speak much more freely in front of him, assuming he was rarely paying any attention to them.

Since he spent all day at a grocery store, this made him privy to pretty much everything that went on in Raven Creek, whether he opted to share or not.

Rich took a very different approach to looking out for me than Leo did. He'd previously tried to keep some polite distance, but now he would pop up whenever I least expected it just to let me know I was safe. He was more hands-on, certainly, and a bit more ever present. Living in the apartment right over the shop made it very easy for him to keep track of my comings and goings. Ever since the big kerfuffle last fall, which I suspected he blamed himself for, ever so slightly, he'd had no problem whatsoever letting me know he was watching.

Between the two of them, I definitely felt looked after. Eudora would be proud of them, I thought. But I also suspected she would be sneaking polished rose quartz into their jacket pockets whenever they weren't paying attention.

She'd never liked my ex-husband, Blaine, and thought the absolute world of the two men I knew best in town. It didn't take a genius to see that part of her was hoping that by putting them in my orbit, she might find me a new husband.

That almost made me chuckle, except for the fact that I was looking directly at one of those men right now.

"You let me know if they keep being a nuisance, okay?"

"What are you going to do, stake out the porch and run some poor preteens off into the night? They're not hurting anyone. I bet a hundred dollars you were dared to knock on that door once."

"And look where it got me," he said with a knowing wink. "I'd be doing those kids a favor, running them off. Otherwise, they'll end up just like me, indentured to the house for a lifetime."

I rolled my eyes at Rich and guided him toward my dining room. It was a space I never actually used, and because of that it still looked exactly the way Eudora had left it. I ate in front of the TV more nights than I cared to admit, and when I didn't, I sat in the kitchen at the cute two-person table there so I could chat with Bob while he ate his fancy wet food.

Chat might be a bit too kind a word for it, but he listened politely well I thought aloud and worked through my plans for the evening or the following day. Sometimes I'd ask his opinion on whether he'd prefer the car or the bike, but he was usually very open to my suggestions.

The dining room was a much more formal space than most of the other rooms in the house. Here, Eudora's maximalist decorating style was a bit more subdued, and instead of every inch of wall space being adorned with art and knickknacks, there were only framed photos of my family, dating all the way back to my great-great-great-grandfather Black, the first of the family to move to Raven Creek when it had originally been founded. He had built Lane End House.

All the photos were in black and white, with black frames and large white mats, giving them an almost gallerylike quality. You could trail the entire lineage of the Black clan from one end of the room to the other, ending with my brother Sam and me at the far side of the room. My wedding photo had hung there once, but I noticed Eudora had replaced it with a different snapshot, one she must have gotten from my parents, where I beamed brightly while standing on a beach all by myself.

Blaine had *been* there when that photo was taken, but the message was clear: she'd erased him from the family by removing any evidence of him from the walls. That was kind of a relief, honestly.

The red damask wallpaper gave the room a cozy, inviting warmth, but the newspaper clippings spread out across the big oak table made it look like the lair of a madwoman. I'd fallen into the rabbit hole of looking for any information I could find on Madeline's murder the last couple of days, wondering if comments from friends and loved ones would give me any indication of what had happened to her.

So far, however, no clues stood out. No one had commented about feeling bad because they'd fought with her on the phone just before she passed. No one had outright said, *Gee, I feel terrible for killing her*. I wasn't an expert on reading between the lines of written statements either, which put me at a major disadvantage in terms of deciding if any of the quotes gave something away.

What I did gather, though, was that she didn't have any immediate family, and most of the people reporters had spoken to about her mentioned only her career mindedness and how passionate she'd been about her job. It was a bit sad, really, that no one seemed to be friends with her, that no one had known who she was outside the world of estate sales.

I hoped that when I died, people would have much more varied stories to tell about the life I'd lived and who I'd been.

"This is quite the reading material you've amassed here," Rich observed, picking up one of my clippings, then putting it down again. "Phoebe, what are you doing? This looks nuts."

I pretended not to be offended but failed to keep the indignant huff out of my voice. "I'm just trying to figure out what happened to her, that's all."

"That's Detective Martin's job. You don't have to solve this case."

"You know, you keep saying that, but this time around you're not a person of interest, and I don't know if you remember much about what that feels like, but it's not really enjoyable."

"I'd like to point out that I wasn't really a person of interest last time to anyone but you." He winked to let me know that all was forgiven on that front. I thought he understood why I'd been so suspicious of him at the time, even if I felt guilty now for being willing to think he was a killer. Not cool.

He sat down at the table, clearly not too put off by my DIY investigation, and pulled out his laptop, setting it on top of the newspaper clippings.

Bob entered the room and jumped up into one of the other empty dining room chairs, sitting down and looking from Rich to me as if to ask, *When are we getting started?*

Well, if they boys were poised and ready, who was I to hold them back? I sat down at the head of the table, which put me right beside both Bob and Rich but at an angle. Rich automatically turned the laptop screen so I could see it, and a frustrated Bob, who could not get a good look, jumped up onto the table and lay down right in the middle of all the other newspaper clippings, his striped tail flicking hard against the table's wooden surface and yellow-green eyes narrowing into contented slits. It didn't take long before he was purring loudly, the newspapers underneath him all crumpled and creased beyond repair.

"I did some research on the supposed Weatherly heir who came into your shop today."

"Riley," I added.

"Yes. So, as it turns out, he wasn't lying when he said he had a connection to the estate. His grandfather *was* Patrick Weatherly, and he is one of six grandchildren that were left behind when the elder Weatherly died."

"*Six*?" I couldn't help but be shocked. The way Madeline had explained things to me, it had seemed like Mr. Weatherly had no living relatives at all, or at least none who had laid claim to his luxurious worldly goods. "That doesn't make any sense."

"He has three children, or I should say *had*. He had two daughters and a son, and I gather that the son was very much his favorite, something he didn't bother hiding from the girls. This led to quite a bit of resentment, and when his daughters married, he said he didn't approve of either of their husbands and would no longer support them. He cut the girls and their future families out of his will."

I couldn't hide the gasp that emerged from my lips. While I'd been busy admiring all of Mr. Weatherly's beautiful things, there had been a substantial storm brewing under the surface, one that had torn a whole family apart. I felt awful for Weatherly's daughters, who had spent their lives feeling unloved and unwanted, only to find love and be punished for it by the very man who had denied them his own warmth. How awful.

"What about the son?" I asked. "The favorite child."

Rich gave me a grim half smile, as if he wanted to apologize for what he was about to show me, then opened a new tab on his laptop. On the screen was a newspaper article from fifteen years earlier.

Weatherly Wood Heir Declared Dead One Year After Boat Accident.

I didn't get a chance to continue reading, as Rich was already giving me the shortened version. "Warren Weatherly, Patrick's only male heir, was a seasoned sailor, and not unfamiliar with how to operate a sailboat, but he decided he wanted to take one of the family's boats from Fiji all the way to Hawaii. About two days into the trip, they lost contact with him. Two days after that, the boat was found, capsized, but with no obvious signs of damage. Warren's body was never found. The Weatherlys continued to look for him for a year, but it became obvious that he was never coming back."

I was stunned. The family had suffered such an unimaginable loss. After hearing what Weatherly had done to his daughters, I didn't have much sympathy for him, but no one deserved to endure what he had. To lose a child, and in such a terrible way, must have broken everyone's heart.

"That poor family."

Rich shrugged. Almost to himself, he continued, as if he didn't feel comfortable dwelling on the story of Warren's death. "They were multimillionaires several times over. They are partially responsible for the founding of Barneswood, and the Weatherly Wood company continues to employ hundreds of people in Washington and Oregon."

"If he disowned his daughters and his son is dead, then who inherited the company?" I had been so focused on the estate that it had never occurred to me that there was something bigger at stake.

"The company is run by a board, of which Weatherly was only a minority shareholder at the time of his death. The board will maintain their ownership over the company, and Weatherly had willed his shares to other members, as well as ten percent to his assistant, Keely Morgenstern." The way he emphasized the name *Keely* made me think there was more to that story than just a very deserving secretary getting her due.

"What's the story there?" I asked.

"Well, for one thing? Keely is twenty-two and exceptionally pretty. And she's now a millionaire who owns enough of the company to get to vote on board matters."

"And what's the other thing? You can't just say *for one thing* without there being more."

Rich's eyes glinted.

"She's the one who arranged to sell off the Weatherly estate, without giving Weatherly's daughters or grandchildren any opportunity to take a single thing."

"*What?*"

"She's the one who hired Madeline Morrow."

Chapter Eighteen

I could barely sleep that night as Rich's information danced around in my head, doing the exact opposite of what counting sheep might. Now, instead of adding up fluffy farm animals, I was thinking of potential suspects who might have had a hand in Madeline's murder.

First, there was Franny, who I still planned to grill the following day when we got to Barneswood. Then there was Riley, who definitely had a motive, now that I knew what had happened to his family. I bet his mother had filled his head with all sorts of toxic notions about her father and what they were owed. His sense of entitlement had been apparent when he'd had his outburst in my shop.

Yet, it had also been obvious that money wasn't exactly tight for Riley Weatherly. He and his wife had both been outfitted to the nines in very expensive casual wear, and he hadn't flinched for a second about continually adding accessories and books to his purchase pile at the store. They'd spent several hundred dollars between them.

But being rich didn't negate someone's sense of entitlement; in fact, in my own experience, it tended to make that entitlement worse. I certainly never expected things to be handed to me, and that hadn't changed a lick since I'd inherited, well, half the commercial buildings on Main Street.

Riley was still high up on my suspect list, especially since I'd seen how he could have bursts of rage in person. It had been pretty alarming, and Yasmine hadn't seemed all that surprised by it, suggesting it wasn't uncommon for him to lose his cool.

With Rich's big reveal to me today, though, I had another suspect to add to the list, one whose motives were still unclear. Suddenly I wanted very badly to speak to Keely Morgenstern.

Why had she decided to sell off the estate rather than keeping it for herself, or letting Patrick Weatherly's family have access to it? The things in that house had been a part of a long family history, and in spite of the rift formed between Weatherly and his daughters, it felt especially cruel of Keely to simply sell off the items that had once been theirs.

Could that kind of cruelty indicate someone who was a killer?

Maybe Keely had caught wind that Riley, and perhaps other Weatherly grandchildren, were in attendance at the auction and had lashed out at Madeline as a result, but that felt like a flimsy excuse for murder. I didn't fully understand why Keely might kill Madeline, but I also didn't trust a woman who was so willing to sell a family's possessions and childhood home out from under them just because they had been left to her. That felt nasty.

After I'd rolled around in bed long enough to see the sky begin to pinken through my window, I decided not to bother pretending I was going to get any real shut-eye. I left Bob curled up in his place at the end of the bed, snuggled up in a throw blanket that was now officially his, and changed from my pajamas into my running gear. I needed to clear my head and hoped a run could accomplish that.

I had declined Rich's offer to drive us to Barneswood and said I'd meet him at the store for eight. Imogen was already taking the morning shift, but I wanted to stop at Amy's to grab myself a customary chocolate hazelnut latte and maybe one of her savory hand pies for the road. I also wanted to leave Bob at the shop for the day so he wouldn't feel lonely all cooped up in the house, though this time I'd be extra careful I didn't end up with a ginger stowaway.

I also suspected Mr. Loughery would be let down if Bob wasn't around. The ladies of the Knit and Sip wouldn't mind his presence either, if it took me that long to get back tonight. The store was in good hands with Imogen and Daphne; I didn't need to worry. Being at the store bright and early had become part of my routine, and since Rich lived right above the Earl's Study, I didn't think it would hurt anything to check in before we left.

But first, my morning run.

The air was crisp and had a lingering, chilly dampness to it that seemed to stick around in Washington for much of the year. By noon the sun would be bright enough overhead to burn off most of the wet chill, but it was still early enough that the air was moist and almost drinkably thick. I took a deep breath, and it was like having a big glass of cold water.

Unfortunately, the moment I took a step onto my front porch, my foot went through the wood. I let out a little whoop of surprise as I staggered and went calf-deep into the porch, but before I could fall farther, I found that I had actually frozen in place. Bits of dandelion fluff being carried by the breeze hung suspended in the air, while a flurry of apple blossom petals from a nearby tree were captured like frozen snow falling to the ground. The trees themselves had stopped swaying, and a squirrel who had been chittering angrily at me a moment earlier was stuck midsqueak on the porch railing, his little teeth exposed in an expression of the total indignation that small animals are uniquely capable of feeling.

This was my special little magic gift, showing up when I least expected it, pausing time and keeping me from falling all the way through the rotten wood. There was a good chance I would have sunk up to my hip, considering how high up the porch was. I carefully extracted myself but overcorrected on my balance and fell directly onto my butt next to the now enormous hole in my deck.

A bird who had been caught midflight in my little magic show began to fly again, proving that I really *had* stopped time and didn't imagine it.

I counted my lucky stars that I'd been wearing sneakers instead of heels and that I'd fallen in such a way that my leg bent naturally, so nothing was broken. All in all, it could have been much worse. That didn't mean it was *good*, though.

I looked myself over for damage. A few scrapes that would look pretty icky after a day of healing, and definitely a bruise or two, but nothing was bleeding or broken. The porch, however, now had a nice Phoebe-sized leg hole in it, and I wasn't sure what was safe to step on at this point.

"*Ugh*," I managed.

I'd been bemoaning the condition of my porch for weeks, knowing this moment would come, but I hadn't done anything about it, and now I was paying the price for my laziness. Stupid porch. Stupid hole. Stupid adult life that meant I was the one responsible for maintaining my own house. This was not at all how I'd wanted to spend my morning. And with plans to head to Barneswood looming, I also knew I couldn't immediately take the time to do anything about this.

It was just after six o'clock, but I knew Leo would be up. He took the morning shift at the grocery store, which let him ensure all the shelves were nicely stocked and tidy before the place opened at seven. Funny how many friends I now had who could be considered *morning people* when I'd never thought of myself as one.

I hobbled back into the house, my pride hurting worse than anything else but my lower leg not far behind. Bob was sitting on the bottom step of the staircase, doing that slow morning blink, and he gave me an uncertain, "Meow?" as if to ask I why I was back so soon.

"I broke the porch," I mumbled sadly, gesturing behind me to the open door where the hole was visible.

He came closer and wound himself around my shins as I closed the front door, purring loudly. What a guy.

I pulled out my cell phone and headed for the back door, dialing Leo's number from the contact list.

"Mornin'," his voice answered after only three rings. "Early for you."

Leo was typically not a man of many words, so his greeting was unsurprising.

"How are you with a hammer?" I asked him.

This was evidently enough to give the man pause, because a lengthy silence filled the air, then he cleared his throat and said, "I manage."

"Well, *I* have managed to put a giant hole in the front porch using only the power of my legs."

He let out a soft chuckle, and I suspected he was picturing it. Then he stopped laughing and asked, "You all right?"

"I am, and I'm mostly just happy no one was around to witness it." I was back outside now, going down the steps outside the kitchen that led to a little shed in the backyard. "I'm wondering if you might be willing to help me out this weekend with a little emergency surgery on the old girl?"

"I hope you mean the porch and not you," he said.

This time it was my turn to laugh. "Yes."

"Yeah, be happy to." He didn't even hesitate, which made me want to hug him. "You're gonna need some wood, though. Don't have any."

"That's not a problem. Rich and I are going to Barneswood today, and I'll stop by the lumberyard there on the way back to get some."

Leo scoffed. "In your car?"

"My only other option is my bike."

I could practically hear him shaking his head. "Tell you what, you go do what you gotta do in town. I'll come measure up the porch at lunch and call 'em to tell 'em what you need. Then you go pay on your way home and I'll stop in later tonight to put it in the truck."

Leo had a huge cube truck for the grocery store, since he sometimes needed to go all the way into Seattle to pick up items that weren't available in the weekly delivery.

"Leo, I can't ask you to do that. It's too much."

"Nah, you didn't ask, I offered. And I gotta go get some brackets for a few storage shelves I'm installing. Now I can't put it off. You're really helping me."

"Then make sure you get them to add the brackets to my order, okay? You're doing me a huge favor." We argued about it for another five minutes before he finally gave in and agreed to let me pay for his parts, as well as for the gas he would use going to and from Barneswood.

"You really don't need to do that," he argued again.

"I do, and I'm doing it. End of story." I didn't mention to him that I would also be ordering pizza and have a case of cold beer ready when he came by to help. I knew he wouldn't let me pay him for his time, so I had to make sure I could repay his kindness in other ways. I'd probably stop at Amy's to get some treats for him as well, since I wouldn't have time to bake anything between now and tomorrow. "I'll twist Rich's arm a bit and get him to help with manpower."

Leo chuckled. "Good luck with that."

When I hung up, I ducked into the shed and rifled through the unlit space. This little side mission might make me a bit late getting to the store to meet Rich, but I couldn't just leave a hole in the porch. I sent him a quick text to let him know I was running behind thanks to a carpentry-themed disaster.

He sent back a puzzled-face emoji and a thumbs-up.

The shed looked like a hurricane had blown through it. Organizing it had also been a long-standing item on my to-do list, and much like with the porch, I was now kicking myself for having avoided it so long. The area was crammed to the rafters, quite literally, with more yard decorations beyond those in the basement, and a ton of gardening equipment, like tomato cages and big rolls of ground cloth. There were empty planters stacked inside each other, reminding me that this would be my first spring being responsible for the garden of Lane End House. Yet another project I was going to need to do research on. I didn't know the first thing about creating a decent garden. I could barely keep a succulent alive. Though in fairness to me, the lovely croton gifted to me by the Tanakas was still alive and well in my store window. Maybe I wasn't a total lost cause.

But Aunt Eudora had always had such a gorgeous yard, with planters overflowing with brightly colored flowers and hanging baskets all around the porch rafters. Not to mention a huge amount of the herbs for the tea she sold came right from her own herb garden.

I would need to ask Imogen to order me a few books like *Gardening for Dummies* when I stopped in at the store later. Eudora had plenty of books for her own reference, but I was worried my black thumb needed something much more basic than her higher-level gardening books.

What I was hunting for now, however, was something I'd seen when I first explored the little shed in October after moving in. I hadn't thought much about it since then, but after I put my foot through the porch, it was the first thing that had come to mind once I got myself free. There, tucked in at the back of the shed behind all the other clutter and supplies, were two large sheets of plywood.

I spent a good ten minutes wrestling one of the sheets out and another ten dragging it around the house and up the front steps. The darned thing must have weighed about thirty pounds, so by the time I got it situated between the steps and the front door, I had worked up more of a sweat than I would have on my run.

It wasn't a perfect solution, but it would help distribute the weight of anyone who came by while I wasn't home, so I wouldn't accidentally trap the mailman or find myself with a lawsuit if a poor Girl Scout came by trying to sell cookies and fell right through my porch.

I gave a little test hop on the plywood and was relieved that it held my weight just fine and managed to keep the wood on the porch from breaking any more. It would do the trick until Leo and Rich could help me properly fix the real problem tomorrow.

Once I'd done my hasty construction job, I barely had time for a quick shower. I put my damp hair into a messy bun at the top of my head, trying to make it look like an intentional choice rather than one of necessity. Then I put on a long plaid skirt with a cute caramel-brown belt and a dark-green turtleneck tucked in. With my slouchy knee-high brown boots—ones I didn't dare wear to work anymore because they hurt to wear all day—I thought the look was a nice cross between hot librarian and *attending a British polo match*. It was cute but also professional enough that I didn't think anyone would deny me admittance to their homes if I came knocking.

I hung the necklace Eudora had left me around my neck, rubbing the dark stone for luck. I'd shown it to Honey, and she had told me it was meant to protect me. A lot of what Eudora had done for me when I moved here involved protection, which made me wonder if there was something sinister she was trying to protect me *from*, but in my seven months in town I had felt safe almost the entire time.

Maybe that was just the necklace and my new guardians doing their jobs. Or perhaps it was because there was nothing for me to really worry about in a small town like Raven Creek.

I hoped it was the latter.

I loaded Bob into his backpack, since I currently didn't trust him to be loose in the back seat, grabbed my bag, and got us both into the car with about fifteen minutes to spare before I was supposed to meet Rich. Five minutes later I was parked in front of the store, freeing Bob to spend the day on his favorite chair. Imogen poked her head out of the kitchen when she heard the bell jingle.

"You're not supposed to be here today," she scolded.

"I'm just leaving my furry son in your care until I get back," I joked. "Hope you don't mind." The smell of baking cookies wafted into the air. I had prepped everything the night before so Imogen wouldn't have to struggle getting things ready in the morning. The shortbread had been left in logs in the fridge, so she only needed to cut and bake. The sourdough loaves were already in their Dutch oven homes with Post-it instructions on precisely how long to bake them, when to start, and when to remove the lids. I'd also premade some bacon-tomato jam and left fresh ricotta in the fridge with instructions on my intended assembly: smear toast with ricotta, spoon on jam, drizzle with spiced honey, then top with a sprinkle of fresh thyme leaves.

She would be fine. I just overprepared sometimes.

Imogen laughed. "Bob basically owns the store. Sometimes I think I work for him and not you."

"We *all* work for Bob, realistically. He thinks he owns both this shop and our house. And me, for that matter."

I left her with the request to order me a few books on beginner gardening, a chore she seemed excited to tackle, and headed next door with a farewell wave to Bob, who was already in his favorite spot by the fire.

Next, I had just enough time to run to see Amy, who was surprised to find me coming through her front door. "Aren't you off today? Imogen was already in this morning."

"I'm here strictly in a customer capacity today," I assured her. "One chocolate hazelnut latte, and a black coffee to go. And what do you have for savory hand pies this morning?"

"Bacon, egg, and cheddar, which is probably our best seller. And then I did a crab, chive, and goat cheese as the daily special. You're too early for the lunch ones, which is too bad for you. Butter chicken today."

I was practically drooling. "I'll take one of each of the others, but let me know when you make those butter chicken ones again, because yum."

"Super yum. I make this sweet-and-spicy cilantro dipping sauce to go with them." She set to work making my latte, and I checked her levels of loose-leaf tea on the counter. She had hers displayed in cute apothecary jars above all the baked goods.

"You need more Peppermint Bliss already. Wow."

"There's something about baked goods that makes people want peppermint tea, I've never been able to figure out what the connection is, but it's by far my best seller."

"I'll bring you some extra tomorrow."

"You're the best." She handed me the cup with my finished latte and poured the big cup of black coffee for Rich, before putting a small cardboard takeout box together with our two flaky, wonderful-smelling hand pies. I didn't know how adventurous Rich was with his food; after all, we had eaten together only at the diner, and that was delicious but not adventurous. So the bacon-and-egg pie would be for him, while the idea of the crab one made my stomach growl.

When I got outside, Rich was crouched down in front of the window to my shop, moving his finger back and forth across the glass. I was about to ask if he was checking to see how clean my windows were when I saw little orange paws going *bap, bap, bap* along the inside, Bob chasing Rich's finger.

Well, if that wasn't the darned cutest thing I'd ever seen in my life.

"Got you a coffee." I handed him the big cup. "I took a shot in the dark that you were a black-coffee kind of guy."

"Maybe you should be a PI too." He took a sip and smiled. "Amy's coffee is so good. I'm not sure what she does to it, but it's just so much better than making it at home."

"I think the whole *not having to make it yourself* thing is one of the biggest nods in its favor," I pointed out.

"What's in the box?" He raised both eyebrows, waggling them at me in a way that made me let out a very unbecoming giggle. Why was I suddenly thirteen years old again whenever I was around this man? And trust me, at thirteen I had been one of the most uncool people on the planet.

"A treat for the drive."

"Mmm. Remind me to go for drives with you more often."

I flushed, because I *wanted* that. I would love more one-on-one time with Rich, but even when he said things like that, it was hard to know what he really meant. Right now, though, I had other things I needed to focus on. I'd settle for the inconsistent flirting a little longer.

As we drove, I told him about my ordeal with the deck that morning, and before I could even ask for his help, he told me he'd come around in the morning and help Leo and me with the labor.

Whether or not Rich and I ever became a *thing*, it was nice to know I could count on him as a friend.

Considering how few friends I'd felt I had in my corner when I left Seattle—precisely zero—it warmed my heart to know how many people in Raven Creek cared about me now, after such a short time living here.

The drive took forty minutes, and while I would have loved to detour to Franny's first thing, Rich was a big ole stick-in-the-mud and insisted on going directly to the police station. I might have been the one driving, but he wasn't going to let me go off course.

I pulled into the parking lot, and we headed inside together. The woman sitting behind the desk at reception beamed when she saw us, and I suspected her look of obvious adoration was not aimed at me. "Rich! Oh gosh, it feels weird to just call you Rich. Is that weird for you?" She was smiling ear to ear, flashing every single one of her pearly white teeth at him.

I tried and failed to ignore the little ping of jealousy in my stomach. She was pretty, and maybe twenty-five, which made me feel every inch of my thirty-six years.

"It's good to see you, Chelsea. How's your dad? Retirement driving him crazy?"

She laughed brightly. "Oh, you know the captain. He was insufferable all winter, tried to take up woodworking but only built one really ugly birdhouse. Now that he can golf again, though, I think we might actually have a bit of a reprieve from his sparkling personality."

"You tell him I said hey and to let me know if he ever needs a golf buddy, okay?"

"Will do." Her gaze cut to me for the first time, and I gave an awkward smile, like I'd somehow become the third wheel on a date I didn't know was happening.

"I'm here to get fingerprinted for comparison prints?" I phrased it like a question. "From the murder at the Weatherly mansion?" *Way to sound confident and poised, Phoebe.*

"Oh, sure, one sec. Detective Martin isn't here today, but Detective Kim is. Let me call him up." She did just that, continuing to smile at Rich the whole time, until Detective Martin's partner came into the lobby to greet us.

"Kwan!" Rich said enthusiastically.

"Rich, my goodness. I feel like it's been eons. How are you doing, man?" The pair exchanged a hug rife with hearty back pats.

"I'm great. PI life is a bit of a drag sometimes, but I love it. You know Phoebe Winchester, right?" He gestured toward me.

This was too surreal. We were at a police station, and I was here to get fingerprinted, but everyone was treating it like a high school reunion. It was only occurring to me now that *this* might have been the police department Rich worked for. I had assumed all this time it was the Raven Creek Police Department, but his close bond with all these people was leading me to question that assumption. I had already learned that detectives worked between several small-town departments, so it made sense that Rich would have moved around.

"Ms. Winchester. Nice to see you again. We really appreciate you coming all this way. I know it's a bit of nuisance, but since the investigation is centralized here, it's a lot easier for us to collect all the evidence at a central headquarters. I'm sure you understand."

"Of course. I don't mind making the trip, and Rich kept me company. Is it okay if he stays with me?" It was exactly like having a lawyer—something I hadn't even considered until this moment—but I anticipated Rich would keep me from accidentally implicating myself in the murder.

"Not at all. We're not questioning you today. This is just a formality, really."

Did that mean I was off the radar in terms of being considered a suspect, or was Detective Kim just trying to make me feel comfortable so I might let something slip? Both options seemed equally plausible. I had to admit, though, I wasn't exactly getting *we think you're a suspect* vibes from him the same way I had with Detective Martin.

Detective Kim led us into the back area of the station, past several other officers both in and out of uniform working at desks, to an area that looked a lot like a copy room, where the printer and stationery for the station were kept.

"Some people find this a little unpleasant, but I promise it's painless." His brown eyes glinted warmly, and while I wasn't thrilled about the idea of being fingerprinted, he was working overtime to make me feel comfortable.

He took a blank card that had designated boxes for each of my fingers and filled out the top, asking for some basic details, like my date of birth and other personal information. He then pressed each of my fingers into an ink pad and, one at a time, pushed them to the thick card.

He was very gentle with the process, but he still had to use considerable pressure rotating my finger back and forth to get a good impression. By the time we were done with both hands, my fingers looked like I'd been rifling around inside a fireplace.

Detective Kim offered me a packet of makeup remover cloths, and I set about cleaning off my fingertips, trying not to look at him, my cheeks ablaze with an unexpected wash of embarrassment.

Rich saved me here, making small talk with the detective, until I was as clean as I could get without a proper soap-and-water wash. At least I didn't *look* like I'd just been fingerprinted, so that was something.

"Phoebe, you should tell Detective Kim about what happened in your shop on Wednesday," Rich urged, which of course gave me no choice in the matter. I felt a bit like I'd be thrown under the bus. I'd been planning to tell them, but since Rich had brought it up, it made it seem like I might not have been intending to. I gave him a quick glare.

"Riley Weatherly and his wife came into my shop."

"Well that *is* interesting. How did you know who he was?" Kim asked.

"I recognized him from the auction but didn't know right away he had a connection to the Weatherly family. The two of them had been standing behind me at the auction. When I realized they'd been there, I brought it up, and that sort of . . . excited things a little." I explained the outburst from Riley and everything he'd said to me as best I could remember it.

Detective Kim took notes and asked a few questions about Riley's behavior—if I'd thought he might be violent, if I'd ever met him before. When he seemed satisfied with my responses, he said, "And you're sure you'd never met him or spoken to him or his wife before?"

"Definitely not. We didn't speak at the auction either. I suppose there's a chance they might have been nearby when I told Madeline where my shop was, but they seemed genuinely surprised I recognized them from the auction. I don't think they knew who I was."

Kim nodded a few times and made a couple other notes on his little notepad. Were those something made specifically for police officers? Was there a line of tiny little notebooks made exclusively for cops? I'd always wondered how they all seemed to use the exact same kind.

"You'll let us know if they come by again, right?" he asked.

"Absolutely."

It didn't escape my notice that Rich hadn't divulged any of the other information we'd gathered during our little research session—specifically, the Keely Morgenstern connection. Though if Rich had that information, it was pretty likely the police had it as well.

I liked the feeling of it being a little secret between us, even if it wasn't a secret at all.

As we were leaving the police station, Rich stopped to chat with a few more people he knew, further confirming my suspicion that this was his old stomping ground. I headed outside to enjoy the spring sunshine, feeling like a third wheel. My fingers were still throbbing from the hard scrubbing I'd done to get all the ink off, so much so that I almost didn't hear the rising voice.

It took me a moment to realize someone was shouting, someone nearby, though I couldn't see them.

"No, this is ridiculous. Why do I have to go talk to anyone? That woman dying isn't my fault." It was a woman's voice, and she sounded young. I glanced back over my shoulder into the police station but didn't see any sign of Rich coming out to find me, so I moved in the direction of the voice, which sounded like it was coming from near the adjacent parking lot.

Normally, I wasn't one to stick my nose in other people's business, but the tone of her voice and the way she said *that woman* raised several alarm bells, and had me thinking there might be a connection to the Madeline Morrow case. After all, how many homicides were being solved between Raven Creek and Barneswood on a regular basis?

I got to the edge of the police station and peered around the corner, scanning the lot for the mysterious—and vocal—young woman.

There, perched on the hood of her Mercedes, was a well-dressed blonde in a gorgeous plaid coat, wearing knee-high black leather boots and a tailored red dress with a pencil skirt, showing every inch of her figure to its best light underneath the coat. She wore a large pair of sunglasses, but even with most of her face covered by the big, black frames, it was easy to tell how annoyed she was.

"No, listen to me. This is the *third time* I've been asked to come here. Do you know how that looks from an optics perspective? *Not good*. It makes me look guilty of something." She glanced down at her polished red nails as she listened to the person on the other end of the phone. There were a few huffs and sighs in the mix as her conversation partner spoke at great length.

"I don't think it's fair, and it's really starting to make me wonder if the money was worth all this trouble." Again, she paused and listened, then put one hand on her hip, as if the person on the line might be able to see the gesture. "Well, you're not the one being questioned in a *murder*, are you? No, I didn't think so. What did she even say to you on the phone that day? She was absolutely livid with me before the auction started, threatening to call the whole thing off."

I found myself leaning in closer, wondering if the volume on the phone might be up high enough that I could hear. Then a branch on the little cedar hedge by my feet snapped, and the woman looked over just as I ducked back behind the building.

I didn't think she'd spotted me, but I heard her saying, "I'm here now, I have to go," as I hustled back to the front steps of the station. Rich was just emerging, and I did my best not to look guilty of anything, though I wasn't sure what I was guilty of, honestly. A moment later the woman came around the corner, giving the two of us an unimpressed once-over as she passed.

Before entering the building, she pushed her glasses up on her forehead, and I let out a little gasp despite myself.

The woman I'd just been spying on was the same woman who had been sitting next to me at the auction. The difference in their appearance was almost night and day. The girl who'd sat near me had been mousy, reserved, not at all flashy. Everything about this woman screamed to be noticed.

Something had changed in the last three days, taking her from quiet and fearful to bold and overstated.

"Do you know who that is?" Rich asked, monitoring my response.

"She was at the auction. She was sitting next to me before I went to find Bob. I don't know who she is, though."

"Phoebe." Rich settled a stern look on me, distracting me from watching her walk in. "That was Keely Morgenstern."

Chapter Nineteen

The news of the blonde's true identity hit me like a ton of bricks. Very expensive bricks, based on how she now looked.

Since I had used Honey's dream spell just recently, the girl's face was fresh in my mind, as if I'd just been chatting with her, and I had no doubt at all it had been Keely who was in my row.

I supposed there was an element of logic to her attending the auction. She was selling off the property, and perhaps wanted to know what price she would be receiving for the items in the Weatherly estate she wasn't interested in. Maybe she'd just wanted to make sure that Madeline's company was running things well.

But why the massive change in appearance, and which version of Keely was the real one? Was she the mousy girl you wouldn't look at twice, or was she the blonde bombshell who had just passed us on the steps?

This also raised numerous questions about her phone conversation, some of which were even more sinister now that I knew who she was. Perhaps I was jumping to conclusions, but some of the things I'd heard from her end of the conversation suddenly had me wondering if whoever she was talking to might have been involved with

Madeline's murder. Could whoever Keely was talking to have been the same person I overheard Madeline arguing with?

I wasn't sure if the timeline would work, because Keely had mentioned that this mystery phone call had caused an argument between her and Madeline. If that was the case, Keely could have quite possibly been the last person to see Madeline alive. Or the argument could have happened much earlier and I was trying to squish together puzzle pieces that weren't meant to fit.

If Keely *had* been the last one to see Madeline alive, however, it meant she might know who else had been around, or who could have had motive, like the person on the phone.

It could also mean that Keely was the one who had killed Madeline.

That last notion swirled around in my mind. The police had spoken to her . . . how many times did she say? Three times. That was a lot of conversation for someone who was just being asked casual questions. But she was also here alone, without a lawyer—unless she was meeting one inside—which seemed to indicate she wasn't threatened by the questioning, merely annoyed.

That didn't mean she was innocent, of course, but it did suggest she didn't feel like she had any reason to worry.

Part of me wished I could care that little about what the police thought about me and that things like questions and fingerprints didn't bother me in the slightest. But they did.

Instead of saying any of this to Rich, I said, "I guess this means the police already knew the stuff you told me last night."

"Of course they did. They know where to look, to follow the crumbs left behind. Talking to Keely would only be a logical step, since setting up the sale and hiring Madeline had all been her idea."

As I processed this, I wondered something aloud. "You know, it would have made a lot more sense for Keely to be the victim than Madeline, if greed and anger about the estate were at the heart of all this." I glanced back at the door before I started to follow Rich toward the parking lot. "I guess I just don't understand the motive behind killing Madeline. She was just doing her job."

"I think you're trying to apply logic to murder, and while that might be a lovely concept in the books you sell, you have to remember, murder doesn't always have a logical explanation in the real world. Sometimes people get mad, sometimes people lash out, sometimes . . . sometimes we just can't explain it, and that's what makes real murder a lot scarier."

I wrinkled my nose at him, not loving the dismissive way he'd implied that my love of reading was making me take this less seriously. I'd been the one who'd found her body, after all. I'd had to wash her blood off Bob's feet. It didn't get much more real than that.

Seeing my expression, he paused at the car door. "I'm sorry. I didn't mean it like that. I just know you're looking at this like a puzzle to solve, but the reality is we might never get all the pieces, and we can only hope that we find enough of them to put together a picture of the killer and bring them to justice."

"You say *we* like you're still a cop."

He glanced over at the building. "Old habits."

"You used to work here, didn't you?"

"You are a little sleuth at heart, aren't you? Was it that obvious?"

"They practically threw a *welcome back* party when you walked through the door. It's pretty obvious they missed you. Why did you leave?"

Rich slid into the passenger seat, literally ducking my question, and I got in on the driver's side, refusing to start the car until he looked at me.

"It's a long story, okay? But the shorthand version is that I didn't feel like I could do my best work and still work for the department. So I left, and I became a PI, and now I help nosy bookstore owners harass former auction employees."

It wasn't the answer I'd wanted, by any means, and it hurt me that he was hiding things from me, especially about something so important, but I didn't push. Instead, I focused on the last part of what he'd said. "I am not going to *harass* her; I just want to ask some questions, that's all."

"Sure, sure, Sherlock Winchester."

Ever the fully grown woman, I stuck my tongue out at him, which made him laugh, a rich, hearty sound that filled my heart to bursting. I glanced over my shoulder, partially to see if there was anyone behind me, but also to confirm there wasn't a stowaway cat along with us, then we hit the road on our way to Franny's house.

Having spent much of my adult life living in Seattle and experiencing Seattle real estate, I was frequently gobsmacked by the property that people could afford on relatively middling salaries.

The same was true for Franny Houseman, who lived in an adorable little bungalow in Barneswood, only a ten-minute drive from the police station. Her street, literally called Charm Crescent, was lined with old oak trees that bowed over the road and were just starting to turn green as the spring buds properly unfurled. The Oregon white oak was the only oak species native to the area, and it was rare to see them, so it was a treat to find so many on one block looking so strong.

In the Pacific Northwest, there was always an undercurrent of green. Even in the winter it never went away entirely, with hardy plants sneaking out through the dusting of fresh snow and the incredibly array of conifers staying verdant all winter. I knew there were plenty of places where winter was just white on white on white—I'd lived in Chicago for several years, after all—but now I couldn't imagine going a whole season without green.

The spring buds were lush and full, morning light dappling through the green to give the impression of a stained-glass window over our heads. Franny was obviously an eager gardener as well, with pots of fresh pink and red flowers lining the sidewalk up to her sweet little yellow house. There were planter boxes under each window, and an actual white picket fence.

I couldn't get over how cute the place was.

Rich trailed behind me, staying on the walkway as I jogged up the stairs and rang the doorbell. There was a red car parked outside, one I thought I'd remembered seeing at the estate, so I suspected she was home.

A moment later my assumption was proved correct as the white door swung open to reveal Franny Houseman.

Her personal appearance didn't match the charm and polish of her house's exterior. Her red hair was frizzy and worn in a messy bun atop her head that didn't look like it had been brushed in at least a day. She wore no makeup whatsoever, which showed the heavy, dark bags under her eyes, and the skin on her cheeks was blotchy from crying.

In fact, there was a tissue clutched in one hand and her eyes were glistening, as if she'd just finished a good crying session, or was about to start one. She sniffled loudly and dabbed her eyes.

"Hello?" Her gaze swept between the two of us, and I wasn't offended when it lingered on Rich longer than it did on me. I would probably soak in the view, too, if a handsome guy showed up on my front lawn. "Can I help you?"

Rich glanced at me and made a gesture, letting me know this was my rodeo and he was just here for the show.

"Franny, my name is Phoebe Winchester. I was at the estate sale earlier this week. I'm . . . well, I'm actually the one who found

Madeline's body? Or I should say my cat was. Bob. That's my cat's name?" Now I felt like an absolute fool for prattling on about my cat, but the entire babbling discourse appeared to have softened her, and she opened the front door wider so we could come inside.

"What kind of cat is he?" she asked, sniffing loudly as she did so.

"A big orange tabby."

This brightened her mood, and as we entered the house, I could immediately see familiar cat owner earmarks. There were crinkly pom-poms on the ground and a well-loved cat tree in the front window. *Hmm, maybe I should get a cat tree for Bob*, I thought.

"Have you ever heard the joke about ginger cats?" she asked, guiding us toward two overstuffed love seats with floral-print upholstery.

"I don't think so."

"That all ginger cats have one brain cell. And they share it." She beamed, chuckling softly at her own joke, which was admittedly funny enough to garner a genuine snort laugh from me and Rich alike.

"That's perfect. I love it."

A flash of gray passed from the living room into the kitchen, and I had to assume that was her own cat getting away from unwelcome intrusion. Franny sat on one love seat, sinking into a well-loved crevice in the middle, and Rich and I were forced to sit side by side on the facing love seat, our thighs pressed together. I was not going to be distracted, however.

"Franny, I hope you don't mind, but I just had a couple of questions for you about the day of the auction?"

The suspicious, uncertain version of Franny returned in a flash, and her entire posture changed. She stiffened and crossed her arms awkwardly in front of her. "I don't know if that's a good idea. Are you with the police?"

I glanced at Rich, trying to gauge which approach to take, but he sat quietly, letting me know that this had all been my idea and he wasn't about to interrupt now.

"No, not exactly. Rich is a private investigator." I then realized I hadn't bothered to introduce Rich yet. "This is Rich Lofting. He's a private investigator, and, uh, a good friend of mine. We're just doing some independent inquiries about Madeline's murder."

"Why?"

The question was too obvious, too simple, and I didn't have an answer prepared for her. Why? Why *was* I doing all this?

"Because I was the one who found her, and I want to make sure that whoever did that to her is located. It's not that I don't think the police are capable—the two detectives working on this are very smart and good people—but I thought it couldn't hurt just to poke around."

It was close enough to the truth without being the whole truth. She didn't need to know that my primary motivation was finding out who did this so the police didn't wind up deciding I was the most likely suspect. I *did* want to find Madeline's killer; that much was also true. So I left it with the partial truth, which I hoped would be good enough for her.

When Franny sat quietly without kicking us out, I continued, "You left before the auction started. I bumped into you as you were leaving the house, and you were crying."

She seemed surprised by this, then looked me over one more time, trying to place my face with the people she had met that day. "Oh. Sure. I probably should have recognized you sooner. I'm sorry."

I suspected she hadn't because she'd been too busy looking at Rich, but that was okay. I was used to blending in in most crowds. You got used to being part of the scenery after a while.

"It's okay. But Franny, why were you crying?"

She let out a sigh that was so dramatic, so burdened with feeling, it would almost have been funny if not for the new sparkle of tears wetting her lower lashes.

"My mother used to tell me I was an overcrier. I cry about everything." She gestured toward her face, just in case we needed evidence of the fact. "I cry at commercials. I cry over love songs on the radio even when I'm single. I cry when I eat a really good meal. I'm just a bit . . . emotional."

That wasn't exactly an answer. "What made you cry that day? I got the impression from Madeline that perhaps she wasn't happy with your work, and that she might have let you go?"

The tears that had been clinging to Franny's lower lashes began to stream down her red cheeks, and her bottom lip quivered. "She said that? To you?"

Now I felt like the world's biggest jerk for telling her what Madeline had told me. "I'm sorry. She didn't say she was planning to fire you, but she'd made comments about your work that weren't very flattering."

Franny swiped at her eyes and picked up a nearby floral throw pillow, hugging it tightly. "I guess I shouldn't be all that surprised. I knew Madeline didn't like me; she spent most of her time criticizing me, telling me what I was doing wrong, how I needed to improve, that I needed to grow a spine. She thought our industry was too cutthroat for someone like me. When I bumped into you that day, I wasn't crying because she had fired me; I was crying because she'd yelled at me in front of a couple that had been wanting to buy some of the one-off jewelry pieces after I hadn't given them the correct information about their historical significance or whatever." She rolled her eyes, the first time she'd shown any kind of noncrying feeling regarding Madeline. "She said I was useless and I'd never go anywhere in this job. I wasn't actually *leaving*; I just needed to go get my head right."

"But she didn't fire you?"

Franny shook her head. "She couldn't fire me."

"Why not?" Rich asked, suddenly leaning forward with keen interest.

Franny gave a warm smile. "My dad owns the company."

Chapter Twenty

Whatever I'd been expecting to come out of my chat with Franny, the revelation that Madeline actually worked for Franny's father was *not* it. This completely threw my theory about Franny, and her potential motive to kill Madeline, right out the window.

Yet it didn't absolve her entirely. If, as she claimed, she had only gone out to *get her head right*, she could have easily come back into the estate when the rest of us were at the auction. She could have snuck upstairs and taken out her frustrations on Madeline. While she hadn't been fired, she *had* been humiliated in front of others at the auction, something that was sure to have a sting to it.

But looking around Franny's butter-yellow living room, with its antique teapots filling a china cabinet on one wall and framed pictures of her cats adorning her packed bookshelves, it was very hard to picture her as a homicidal maniac.

Sure, the opportunity was there, and she still had motive with or without losing her job, but I tried to picture Franny killing someone and it just didn't click. She looked like the kind of person who caught spiders under a cup and ferried them outside rather than squishing them on sight.

Honestly, she looked like someone who would cry if you squished a spider in front of her.

"Can I get you guys some tea?" she asked, setting her cushion aside and smoothing down the front of her very wrinkly sweatshirt.

"I'd love some tea," I said, wanting a moment alone with Rich to confer over what we'd just learned.

"Do you have a preference?"

"That's a very big question to ask Phoebe," Rich said with a laugh. "I'll take whatever you have."

Franny looked at my quizzically. "It's a big question?"

"I own a shop in Raven Creek called the Earl's Study. We're sort of famous for our tea blends."

Franny's hand went to her chest, and an excited look flashed over her face. "Eudora Black's shop. I used to go there a lot; I didn't realize it had opened up again after she died. Oh, that's so exciting." Then her face fell. "I didn't mean exciting that she died." She seemed horrified by the prospect of being misunderstood, and I was worried she might start crying again.

"Yes, Eudora was my aunt. We reopened last fall when I moved to town and took it over. All the recipes are the same; I promise it's all as good as you remember. You should come by sometime."

"I will. Oh, how wonderful. I have some of her Cinnamon Hearts tea in the cupboard. Would you like that?"

Cinnamon Hearts tea was more for winter evenings, in my opinion, but knowing that the batch she had in her home would have been hand-blended by my aunt made me feel a sudden pang of nostalgia and miss Eudora fiercely. "Yes, that would be lovely."

As she vanished into the kitchen to make up our mugs, I turned toward Rich, which was exceptionally difficult to do, given how tightly wedged together we were on the love seat. "What do you think?" I whispered.

"Are we really going to talk about this here? *Now?*" he asked me.

"Well, yeah."

He shook his head. "Don't let people's kindness, or seeming innocence, throw you off. Yeah, she comes across as a nice lady, but she was still there. She was mad at the victim, and she could have easily gotten alone with her without raising eyebrows. Means. Motive. Opportunity. You said yourself that for the Weatherlys, it would make more sense to kill Keely. And for Keely, why would she kill someone that was helping her make money?"

I sat back in the squishy love seat and let his words sink in. Was I just letting the illusion of Franny throw me off? She was so lovely, and seemed so completely incapable of doing harm to anyone, but maybe that was all an act and I was eating it up without question. I liked to consider myself a pretty good judge of people's character. After all, I'd disliked Dierdre Miller immediately, and I'd trusted Imogen and Honey without question right out of the gate. None of those decisions had yet to be the wrong ones. But I was sure Eudora would have gleefully pointed out that I'd married my ex-husband, and that had obviously not gone even remotely the way I had planned.

I supposed we couldn't eliminate Franny as a suspect, even if she seemed to be someone who wouldn't hurt a fly.

One of her cats trailed cautiously into the room, bright-green eyes flashing at us. It was a little gray tabby, her perfectly round face giving her the appearance of a kitten in spite of the fact that she was obviously an adult cat. She was too uncertain of us to approach, but she did jump up onto the cat tree so she could watch us from a better vantage point.

"Oh, I see you've met Vivi," Franny announced as she brought a loaded tray into the room. She set it down between us. Three mismatched bone-china teacups, each with their own disposable tea bag set to steep, were sitting in the middle, along with a little plate of cookies.

Come on, this woman couldn't possibly be a killer, could she?

Killers didn't serve adorable little fruit crème cookies like the ones my grandmother used to have on hand at all times. Franny was younger than me, probably still in her twenties, but everything about her home and the way she behaved made me think she was secretly eighty years old.

What an odd duck.

I removed my tea bag from the cup after five minutes had passed and set it on my saucer so it wouldn't damage her serving tray. The others followed suit. As we sat in companionable silence, I decided to test the waters of her openness now that we were all on friendly terms.

"Franny, was that the first time Madeline had yelled at you during an event? In front of clients?"

Franny shook her head. "Oh goodness, no. She was always doing that. You know, I hate to say it, but I think she believed it made her look more authoritative to prospective buyers? A lot of times people coming to those events, especially for the bigger lots, are very wealthy. Madeline was a real snob sometimes, and I think she got it into her head that being mean to subordinates was something that rich people would approve of seeing." She gave a little shrug of both shoulders and sipped her hot tea. "I don't say this to sound braggy or anything, but I grew up fairly wealthy. Not Weatherly wealthy, but my parents own quite a few businesses around the area that have done well. As kids, we never wanted for anything; we always had a job waiting for us after we graduated. I just mean to say I've been in the presence of wealth, and I don't think Madeline had any idea what would make rich people respect her. As much as she wanted them to."

I thought about how Madeline had dressed, so polished and poised, looking like she'd stumbled right out of a fashion magazine article about being haute couture at the office. Everything had been tucked and pinned and glossed. I wouldn't have been shocked to learn she ironed her skirt while wearing it, she had been that crisp.

The insight from Franny into Madeline's mind-set gave me food for thought about some of the wealthy people in that room that she might have tried to impress in the wrong way. Had she said something to the Weatherlys to set them off? Had she made a mistake somewhere along the line that made her a very powerful enemy?

"Franny, did she know your dad owned the company?"

Franny shook her head. "No, we have different last names—I was married really briefly right after high school—and I told him I wanted to see how I could do for myself without the entire office knowing who I was. Madeline immediately disliked me, and that's okay; I'm not everyone's cup of tea." She looked down at her cup and giggled softly at the unintentional pun. "But I think it was also a way for Daddy to see how I could do working with the rest of the staff, to see if I was cut out for taking over the business one day. And I guess the answer is, probably not. I don't think I have the heart to be a manager. I never want to think I can treat someone the way Madeline treated me."

"That's not how managers should treat their staff," I told her. "I would *never* yell at my employees, let alone do it in front of customers." I was having a really hard time staying objective when all I really wanted to do was give Franny a hug.

"I know. I think I knew deep down she was just kind of a mean person. But I look at Daddy, and he's tough; he can deliver feedback, even when it's bad, and he doesn't cry. I think If I had to give *nice* feedback, I'd start crying. Anyway, he has me doing the accounting now. That's a lot more my speed."

Rich spoke up. "Why were you crying when we came in?"

Franny set down her teacup and picked up a tissue, bracing herself for another round of tears at the mere mention of her recent outburst.

"I got the email about Madeline's funeral tomorrow, and I just got so sad thinking about what happened to her." Tears flowed down her cheeks.

Funeral, eh? I leaned across the table and offered her a fresh tissue. "Did the email mention where that was going to be?"

Chapter
Twenty-One

"**A**bsolutely not," Rich insisted.

We were wandering the aisles of the local hardware store as I looked for anything else I might need for the porch renovation tomorrow. So far, my cart was loaded with new gardening supplies that I hadn't planned on buying when I'd come here, a gigantic bag of birdseed, new bird feeders, and a *very* heavy plaster birdbath.

At first, I thought Rich was telling me no to the red glass hummingbird feeder, but then I realized he was still thinking about my last question to Franny, regarding Madeline's funeral.

"Why not? It's open to the public, I'm sure. And don't you want to see who shows up? Isn't that a thing cops do, look at the guests to determine if one of them might be the killer?"

"*Yes*, Phoebe, that's precisely why you shouldn't be going. The detectives are going easy on you right now, but if you show up at that funeral, I'm pretty sure they're going to put you at the top of the suspect list. You already know Franny is going, and as far as I'm concerned, she's probably the strongest suspect."

I snorted as I added a heavy bag of white sugar into my cart to make syrup for the hummingbirds. "Sure."

"I know you liked her, and you got swept up in that whole act she was putting on, but she is still the most logical fit. No one else had as much emotional baggage with the victim; no one else had as much unfettered access."

"I'm sorry, but after talking to her, I really don't think she did it."

"Liking cats and tea doesn't make someone a good person by default."

I narrowed my eyes at him. "I *know* that, Rich; I'm not stupid. But nothing about that conversation made me think she had *killer* written in her biography. I'm trusting my gut on this one."

He threw his hands up in the air. "I'm not sure why you asked for my help if you're just going to ignore everything I say."

I held up two boxes of nails in front of him, and despite his clearly being annoyed with me, he tapped the box on the left, which I threw into my cart.

"See, I don't ignore *everything* you say."

He laughed then, unexpectedly, and knocked into me with his shoulder. "You might be the most frustrating woman I've ever met, and that includes the one I'm divorcing."

"Is this your version of sweet talk? Because if it is, it could probably use a little workshopping."

"Just my natural charm, I'm afraid."

"Yikes. I'm really sorry."

We headed for the checkout, where I quickly felt a rush of guilt over how much I'd spent on bird accessories and the lumber Leo had called in an order for. The cashier also informed me Leo had suggested a certain brand of deck stain, which I agreed to add to my total, along with the shelf brackets I'd promised to buy for Leo.

We agreed that the wood and brackets would remain at the store for Leo to collect later, but the cashier told me that the store now did weekly deliveries to Raven Creek, so if I ever needed anything in the future, I just had to call my order in before Friday at noon to make it for the Saturday delivery truck. Good to know, because there were definitely a lot of future projects on my list for Lane End House.

It was midafternoon by the time we'd finished all our errands in Barneswood, but I was hoping Rich might humor me with one more non-murder-investigation stop.

I pulled into the parking lot in the front of the Barneswood Humane Society and looked over at Rich with my best *pretty please* smile. "We'll just go in for a couple minutes, okay? I'm on a mission."

"I thought Dierdre put the kibosh on your cat rescue plans."

I held up a finger. "First, no, she merely *paused* my plans. I will still be victorious once the other town council members see the plan. Second, not having the rescue in place doesn't mean I can't *look* at cats that need a home, especially when I have a great one in mind. And third, there is never a bad time to look at cats."

Rich shook his head, but he was smiling. "You know, when you moved here, you claimed you weren't a cat person."

"I wasn't. That's the thing; sometimes you don't know you're a cat person until the universe gives you a cat. You should consider it."

"Absolutely not."

"You'd love having a cat."

"I love not being covered in hair all the time."

"Buy a lint roller."

"This better not be a convoluted plan to get me to adopt a cat, Phoebe, because it's not happening."

"Never say never, pal. But we're not here for you. I've noticed how much Mr. Loughery brightens up when he spends the day with Bob, and I think it might do him some good to have a cat of his own to go home to."

"You're not going to get him one today without asking him first, are you?"

I rolled my eyes. "I wasn't born yesterday, Rich. No, but I'm going to see if there are any good senior cats who have been here a while that I think might be a good fit for him."

We walked into the shelter together and were greeted warmly by a young woman sitting behind a desk. "Have a look around, and if there's anyone you'd like some one-on-one time with, let us know. Dog kennels are all in the center, puppies are down the hall to the right, and all our cats are down the hall to the left. If you're looking for rodents or birds, they're next to the gift shop to my left over here." She pointed to a wall of smaller cages, where I could hear the distinct chattering of birds.

We followed her directions to Kitty Cat Corridor, where there were several Plexiglas-fronted community rooms in which multiple cats could spend time playing together, and there were other smaller versions of those rooms for cats who had special health requirements or needed to be isolated. On the back of the wall was a tower of cat "condos," each containing one resident awaiting visitors or a new home.

There were cats everywhere you looked. Black cats, tuxedo cats, tabbies, torties, and calicoes. There were lovely, rich-looking Ragdolls and even one sweet, cross-eyed Siamese. Each one had a name tag pinned to their door and a little write-up about their demeanor and what kind of home the staff thought they would be suitable for.

Cheddar would do well in a home with no children.

Luna was a snuggler and would spend all her time on your lap.

Tractor would probably spend most of his time hiding, but he was a sweet boy when he finally came out.

Their ages were also listed on the sheets, and in an effort to garner some sympathy from prospective adopters, several of the cages had neon-pink starburst signs on the corner to indicate "long-term residents." It was working, because I wanted to scoop every one of them into my arms and take them home.

There were plenty of cute, fresh-faced kittens, but that wasn't what I had in mind for Mr. Loughery. For one thing, he was already in his eighties, and cats could live up to twenty years or more sometimes. Not that I was expecting anything to happen to him soon— he was still in good health for his age. But he wasn't going to live forever.

Plus, younger cats had a lot more energy and could be prone to getting into trouble. Even Bob, who was hardly a spring chicken, liked to dig up the dirt in my indoor houseplants and got a major case of the zoomies at three in the morning.

Mr. Loughery needed someone like him. An old guy who liked comfort and wanted to spend his afternoons napping.

Rich, who had tried to pretend I was dragging him in here against his will, was transfixed by the cage belonging to a lovely calico cat named Dolly, asking her who was a pretty girl. She was indeed, and seemed instantly smitten with Rich. Was it possible to be jealous of a cat?

Actually, yeah, pretty much all the time. Cats had the best lives.

I was more focused on the cages with the pink signs. There was a grouchy-looking tabby named Emilio, who hissed at me when I got close. Not great at first impressions, poor guy. Every cat deserved a home and someone to love them, but Emilio might be a bit more of a project cat than an eighty-something-year-old man could take on.

I kept looking, finding things to like about every single long-term stay, but none of them seemed like the right fit. Several of them did, however, strike me as good potential cats to bring to the store when we were finally able to function as a satellite adoption center. I was sure some of the shyer cats would thrive when there weren't so many other things around them.

Finally, when I was almost out of options, I came across the cage for a cat named Frodo. Frodo was a black-and-white tuxedo cat with black covering one side of his face and white over the other, with two black ears and plenty of black spots over his body. He even had black and white spots on some of his toes, making it look like he'd dipped his paws in a container of ink, then shaken it off.

He blinked his giant green eyes at me as I approached and let out a lazy yawn. He was a bit on the chubby side, and the write-up said he was very much a lounge cat who only got up to move with the sun. The pink sticky on the corner of his cage said he'd been at the shelter for five years, and he was only eight years old, meaning he'd been here most of his life.

Frodo squinted at me, and I could hear him purring inside the cage even though he hadn't bothered to get up to beg for pets. Apparently just having someone look at him was enough to make him happy.

My heart absolutely broke. If my car hadn't been full, and if I hadn't been unsure if Mr. Loughery would even like him, I would have snatched Frodo up on the spot and taken him home with me.

Heck, my lack of impulse control might bring me right back here tomorrow to collect him regardless of what Mr. Loughery said about it. Bob would probably hate it, but that was a fight I was willing to have.

I snapped a photo of Frodo on my phone and another one of his write-up. I had to go now, before I decided to be reckless and get myself another cat. I'd come here with the good intention of helping an old man, but I had only so much willpower.

Rich was still talking to Dolly, who had stuck her paw through the bars of her cage and was holding on to his finger, licking it. He looked utterly smitten with her.

"I thought you said you didn't want a cat," I teased him.

"I didn't." Then he quickly corrected himself. "Don't. I don't."

"Mm-hmm, sure. She seems to think otherwise." Dolly's eyes were an almost teal-blue color, not something I'd ever seen in a cat before. She was more arresting than cute, a truly beautiful little cat.

"We could make room for her in the car," I said, nudging him in the ribs with my elbow. "Charlie Bravebird over at the pet shop would get you set up with everything you need."

"I'm not getting a cat." He was laughing when he said it but tried to sound firm. He gave Dolly's paw a farewell shake. "A pleasure to meet you, pretty girl."

If Dolly was still around when I was able to open the adoption center, I was definitely going to request her. A few visits would break Rich of his *no cats* philosophy. I happened to have it on good authority his landlord didn't have a problem with pets.

The entire drive back to Raven Creek, I thought about Frodo and wondered whether I was crazy to think he might be the exact right thing for Mr. Loughery. More importantly, our little side mission had caused Rich to entirely forget about my plan to attend Madeline's funeral the next day.

Chapter
Twenty-Two

I awoke at seven thirty to the sound of pounding coming from the general vicinity of my front door. As I blearily wiped sleep from my eyes, checking the digital alarm clock on my bedside table, I wondered if it would be poor form to ask Honey to teach me how to curse my own friends.

When I'd told Leo to come over in the morning, I'd envisioned us kicking things off around nine, giving me enough time to wake up, get myself somewhat presentable, and make a nice breakfast for him and Rich. Of course, I hadn't indicated a time to Leo, and had mostly forgotten what an early riser he was.

My mistake. Evidently the sun being up was reason enough for him to come over. Why waste a minute, right?

I grabbed my phone and noticed a few missed messages from him, and rather than leaving him hanging on the porch knocking endlessly, I sent a quick message back. *Slept in, give me five.* At least he would know I was awake and wouldn't leave while I was getting ready.

Since I didn't have enough time to look *good*, I had to settle for not looking like I'd been hit by the bad-sleep truck. I pulled on a pair of old jeans with holes in the knees that I wouldn't mind ruining and a threadbare AC/DC T-shirt that I'd had since high school. Bless the trend of oversized Ts that had been so popular in my formative years, which meant a lot of my most beloved shirts still fit me twenty years later.

I ran a brush through my long, dark hair and pulled it up into a messy bun, then brushed my teeth, because if I was going to take an extra two minutes to do at least one thing, it would be brushing my teeth. You're welcome, Leo. A speedy slick of lip gloss was the only makeup I had time for, but overall the effect was passable. I didn't look like a zombie, which was all I could hope for.

Jogging down the stairs, Bob trailed behind me, his tail held high in the air, and while I made a beeline for the front door, Bob directed himself to the kitchen. When he realized I wasn't going that way, he sat in the kitchen entrance and meowed loudly at me, as if I'd betrayed our most sacred trust.

"Just a minute," I pleaded, both to him and to the door, where I could see the shape of Leo through the opaque glass panel on the side. I unlocked the front door, and there he was, an absolute mountain of a man, with a toolbox in one hand and a cardboard tray of coffee in the other. I immediately recognized Amy's cups.

"I'm supposed to be bribing *you*," I reminded him.

He blushed immediately, red going all the way up to his ears. "Was nothin'."

Amy's wasn't really on the way to my house at all, meaning Leo had gone out of his way early in the morning just to get coffee, something he absolutely hadn't needed to do. But I wasn't going to look a gift latte in the mouth.

I relieved him of the tray and ushered him inside. "Just give me a minute to feed Bob before he starts plotting my death."

Leo chuckled, closing the door behind him and setting down his toolbox. "I liked your makeshift solution out there."

Bob went over to the big man and rubbed back and forth against his shins, telling him the sob story of his momentarily delayed breakfast. Leo leaned over and gave the cat a hearty rub on his side, then thumped him a few times, as if he were a dog. This momentarily distracted Bob, who wasn't accustomed to being roughhoused with, but he seemed to enjoy it.

I went into the kitchen and topped up his dry food, and the second the can lid opened on his wet food, he was next to me, as if he had appeared out of thin air. Maybe my cat was a little magical too. Nah, he was just sneaky. With his dish filled, he set about devouring his breakfast.

"Did you eat?" I yelled into the foyer, since Leo was lingering near the door.

"Yeah, earlier."

"Can I make you anything?"

"Nah, all good. But you go ahead."

I wasn't going to sit down and make myself a feast, but if we were going to be doing hard labor, I should probably put something in my stomach to fuel me. But I didn't want to waste more time either. I gave the fridge a quick scour and decided a fried-egg sandwich would be the easiest way to fill me up *and* use some of the leftover sourdough I'd brought home from the store earlier in the week. Leftovers were rare, but sometimes I could sneak home a few slices, and this had been a lucky week for that.

I set the bread into the toaster, then dropped a pat of butter onto my frying pan and got two eggs out of the fridge, as well as two orange cheese slices wrapped in plastic. I could pretend to be fancy, and I often bought Brie and extra-old cheddar from the grocery store, but sometimes you just needed the super-gooey melty deliciousness of a cheese slice that had been perfected by food science.

The eggs cooked quickly, and once I'd flipped them, I topped each with a slice of cheese. The toast—which I generally preferred to be just on the brown side of blond—popped up, and I did a quick smear of mayo on each piece. The whole process took less than ten minutes, and I soon had two slices of toast, each adorned with a cheesy egg and a drizzle of hot sauce.

I made a mental note that this would make an addition to our lunch menu one day. Our regulars really seemed to enjoy egg-themed options, and this one couldn't have been easier.

Mulling over what type of toast would work best—perhaps a roasted-red-pepper sourdough?—I met Leo back in the foyer with my plate in one hand and the coffee tray in the other. There were three drinks, meaning he'd kept Rich in mind.

"I'm ready if you are," I announced.

"Nah, you sit and eat. I'll get started."

I shook my head adamantly. "I'm not letting you go out there and work on *my* porch without help. Nuh-uh. No way."

Leo smirked and held the door open for me. "Then you can eat out there and I'll get started. Fair?"

I couldn't really argue with that. I couldn't exactly eat a sandwich *and* wield a hammer, so no matter what, I'd need to sit down and finish breakfast. I followed him outside, grateful to see that the makeshift plywood solution had done its job overnight.

"This is cute. Sure you don't want to keep it?" He playfully toed the big plywood board.

"I'm not looking to start any fun new home decor trends, thanks. Proper wood is perfectly fine by me."

"Suit yourself."

I sat in the big porch swing on the right side of the door and set the tray of coffee in the wood slats in front of me, taking one for myself and leaving the others for the boys. The swing groaned ever so slightly, but only damaged my ego in doing so. Aside from needing a fresh coat of paint, it was still in good shape, and could very likely survive another few years without needing to be fortified.

But if the front porch was teaching me anything, it was that I shouldn't put things off just because I thought they might last a little longer. I was going to need to do a better job keeping stock of Lane End House to make sure the old Victorian mansion didn't fall apart around me while I wasn't paying attention. Like Bob, it needed constant care and vigilance, though also like Bob, it spent most of its day dormant.

As I munched through my breakfast, I watched guiltily while Leo unloaded all the wood from the back of his truck. Twice I tried to get up and offer my assistance, but both times he shook his head and insisted I sit down and eat. He even apologized to *me*, saying if he'd realized I slept in so late, he would have unloaded first before knocking.

Because sleeping until seven thirty was *late* according to Leo Lansing.

He finished unloading at the same time I finished eating, which coincided perfectly with Rich walking up the path to greet us. There was no sign of his car, so I assumed he'd made the walk from the store. The morning was nice, though the sky was overcast, leading me to believe that the warmth would give way to rain before all was said and done.

While the rain wasn't ideal for our work, the porch itself was covered, and for the funeral later, rain just felt appropriate. Sunny-skied funerals felt like an oxymoron.

I doled out the coffees Leo had brought, and the three of us set to work fixing my porch.

We fell into a comfortable rhythm, Rich ripping up the old boards, me hauling the debris off to a tarp on the lawn, and Leo cutting the new boards down to size. Both Leo and Rich confirmed that the actual supports underneath the porch were in fine shape, being of much thicker, sturdier wood, and that it was just time and the elements that had worn down the most heavily used boards.

It took the three of us about four hours to finish the project, from tearing off the old wood to applying a nice, even coat of stain to the new boards.

"Ideally, we'd've stained 'em before installing them," Leo lamented. "But they're pretreated lumber, so shouldn't cause you any extra headaches. I just like getting into all the nooks and crannies, and that's harder when they're hammered down."

It was one of the longest sentences I'd ever heard from him, and he'd said it all with a loving gaze directed toward the wood. Ah, if only I could find a man to look at me the way Leo Lansing looked at fresh-cut two-by-fours.

The porch looked incredible.

It was obvious where the new wood was, mostly because the stain was still fresh. It would need a second coat tomorrow, but Leo had done a great job of selecting a stain that matched the existing boards, so when everything was dried down, it would be a lot harder to notice the difference.

The two men did a walk around the entire wraparound porch, and I'm pretty sure they stomped on every single board the whole way. Rich and Leo mumbled, their heads bowed together, much the way they used to when we were kids and they had something to discuss that they didn't need a *girl* hearing. Except now I was an adult, and they were mumbling about my house.

"Um, hello?"

I quickly realized they weren't whispering to keep things from me. They had simply forgotten I was here. They both swiveled their heads back toward me, surprised expressions twinning on their faces.

"I think you're all good here," Leo said. "Some of the other boards are showing some signs of wear, but you've got at least another year, I think, before anything is at any real risk. We can do another round of replacements after winter, when we see what the snow and ice amount to. They're the real kickers for this old wood."

Rich nodded his agreement. "Shouldn't be too worried about stepping through these." He jumped up and down on the porch, the wood bowing slightly—enough to make me cringe. But the boards didn't give, making him a man of his word.

Since I had them there, and since I didn't want to give the impression I was hustling them off so I could get changed for the funeral, I asked, "Do you think you guys could help me get the birdbath out of my car?" The staff at the hardware shop had helped me load it in, and it had turned out to be too heavy for me to move on my own when I'd gotten home last night.

"I've actually got to head out to a job. You got this?" Rich asked, directing his question to Leo.

"Yeah, no problem." They gave each other a quick hug, patting backs roughly, then Rich stopped and gave me a hug as well. This was a lot less bro hug and a lot more lingering hand on the small of my back, the faint scent of sawdust clinging to his hair.

When he left, I was a bit dizzy.

Leo followed me to my car and helped me unload the concrete birdbath. We took the base out first, placing it in the middle of one of Eudora's big flower beds, where perennials were starting to peek their green heads up. I was hoping we weren't smushing something that might be a late bloomer, but it was a risk I'd have to take.

He then helped me carry the large circular water dish and balance it on top, so the whole structure wouldn't fall over if a squirrel or larger animal tried to climb in. Leo, being Leo, even filled up a watering can next to the outdoor hose, then transferred the water into the bath itself.

"There. Done." He nodded at the birdbath, seemingly more pleased with having finished this small task than the laborious work of getting the porch back up to code. Or maybe he was just happy to be done helping with my to-do list. I couldn't blame him.

"You are the absolute best; do you know that?" I wrapped my arms around him as much as I could, and he lifted me right off the ground. I didn't think he could have hugged me *without* lifting me, he was just so much bigger than I was.

"Aw, it's nothing." He set me back down, and when I stepped back, I could see his cheeks flaming red above his beard. "Eudora always knew she could count on me and Rich. You can too. Anything."

My heart felt full to bursting for the kindness Leo and others in town showed me. Sometimes I felt like I didn't deserve it, but other times I was grateful to the universe, or maybe to Eudora, for putting me in a situation where I had found everything I needed.

Leo loaded his supplies back into his truck, thanked me for buying his brackets, and headed on his merry way a little before one in the afternoon. The funeral, at least according to the Barneswood newspaper I'd scoured online, was set to begin around three o'clock, with the burial slated to happen around four.

Since I'd stick out more at the funeral home, I opted to skip the service and head to the cemetery directly, hoping to avoid curious eyes and just get a look to see if any familiar faces popped up in the crowd.

But first, I was covered in sweat and sawdust, a combo that wouldn't fly in any public setting, let alone a funeral. I showered, dried my hair and tied it back into a low chignon, then rifled through my closet for my most somber, most funeral-appropriate ensemble.

I found a jersey cotton black dress that was impervious to wrinkles jammed in the back of my closet and slipped that on over some black tights and a nice sensible pair of black pumps. Something I could wear on grass without looking like a giraffe with a broken leg.

Covering the entire outfit with an emerald-green trench coat, I assessed the look and deemed it appropriate for lingering in the back of a stranger's funeral. I hadn't known Madeline, but she was so chic that I thought she would have appreciated the touch of green from the trench. It was the single most expensive piece of clothing I'd ever purchased, an impulse buy during a trip to London where I'd foolishly decided to step into Harrods "just to look."

I avoided Bob on my way down the stairs, hoping I might make it all the way to my car without him rubbing orange hairs all over my dress. He seemed to recognize the effort and sat in the middle of the staircase, grooming himself, pretending he didn't care about me.

That was fine, as long as he didn't try to come along with me to the funeral.

I had a feeling I'd stop blending in entirely if I carried a big orange cat with me instead of a handbag.

Chapter
Twenty-Three

The drive between Raven Creek and Barneswood was getting so familiar to me at this point that I was pretty sure it was actually becoming a faster trip. I'd entered the directions to the Barneswood cemetery on my GPS and found that it was nestled just outside of the town proper, about ten minutes away from the Weatherly mansion.

It seemed so odd to be back near the mansion's front door. It had been only a few days ago that I'd been inside, but it felt as if years had passed since I'd stumbled on Madeline's body. Now I was on my way to her funeral and hoping that her killer might have a similar plan in mind.

I arrived at the cemetery before the rest of the assembly, but it was obvious which plot was hers. A tent was set up to protect the grave site from the impending rain, which had held off so far but seemed likely to begin in earnest at any moment.

I waited in my car a little way away from the burial plot and scanned the area around me. I hadn't been able to attend Aunt Eudora's funeral, nor had I been to visit her grave site since coming home. Raven Creek had a small local cemetery where she was buried, and it wouldn't have taken much time or effort on my part to go bring her flowers. Yet it never felt like the right move.

A lot of me still felt she was alive in so many ways. Not that I believed she'd faked her death, but rather that her home, her shop, her town all still radiated her presence back to me. When I walked through the halls of Lane End House, it always felt as if I was entering rooms just after she left them. I'd catch little bits of her favorite perfume lingering in the air.

At the shop, I'd sometimes find a favorite book of hers left out by the fire, as if she'd just set it down and wandered off. Or a particular tea would call to me in the morning, and the smell of it would take me right back to summers spent in her kitchen, telling her my trivial thirteen-year-old problems, which she listened to as if they were her own.

Maybe it made me a bad niece to not visit her grave, but it didn't feel like she was there. She was everywhere else in town. She was also always there, the little voice in the back of my head, telling me what I should and shouldn't do. Sometimes I thought she might be my new guardian angel.

Other times I thought she might be a literal ghost.

The most likely truth was somewhere in between, that she was just a memory I would carry with me forever, and that was okay. Plus Honey had assured me that ghosts weren't something I needed to worry about.

I just liked knowing Eudora was still there in some small way.

The rain had begun to fall, just as I'd anticipated. Fat, heavy drops splattered onto my windshield as the funeral procession pulled into the cemetery's winding drive. The hearse stopped first, right next to the low hill where the tent was set up, and a long line of cars began to park behind it.

As difficult as Madeline had apparently been in life, it seemed like plenty of people were sad to see her gone, if the number of cars was any indication.

Black umbrellas appeared as if by magic—a rare sight for native Washingtonians. I had one in the back seat as well, ready for when I got out to join the crowd. It seemed like a more austere choice than my vibrant yellow Van Gogh *Sunflowers* umbrella that I'd purchased as a very pricey whim while visiting the Neue Pinakothek art museum in Germany.

I loved that umbrella a lot, but it wasn't the right choice for a funeral.

People clustered together beneath the large black umbrellas and shuffled their way over to the tent. There wasn't enough room under the protected area for everyone to sit, so the immediate family—I assumed—took the dry seats, and everyone else grouped together nearby with their umbrellas overlapping to create a makeshift secondary shelter.

I waited until it was obvious that everyone was done getting out of their cars before silently getting out of my own, my umbrella in hand. I had no intention of mingling directly with the group. I wanted only to watch from a distance.

As I ducked under a nearby tree that was still a good dozen or more yards away from the funeral, my gaze raked over the attendees, trying to match any of them to my dream, or to my memories from the day at the estate.

I half expected to see Riley Weatherly and his wife, but there was no sign of either of them in the crowd. Franny was there, under the tent, her arm looped around the elbow of a very large older man with a silver mustache. She'd mentioned her father being the owner of the company Madeline worked for, so I assumed the older man was probably Franny's dad. It would make sense for him to be here to give his final farewells to an employee who had died on the job.

He didn't look very moved by the ceremony. His expression was stern, his eyes looking straight forward at the casket.

Franny, for her part, looked inconsolable. She wept openly, tears streaming down her cheeks, which she blotted regularly with a hankie.

"She did say she was a crier," a voice announced behind me.

I let out a little yelp of surprise, which was thankfully not loud enough to draw any attention away from the droning voice of the pastor. Spinning around, I found Rich standing behind me, wearing a very smart black suit and black tie and carrying an umbrella of his own.

He sidled up next to me, so our umbrellas were overlapped, and gave me an unreadable expression. Was he amused? Annoyed? It was really hard to tell right now.

"Yes," I agreed finally. "Definitely a crier."

"I thought I told you coming here was a bad idea," he said, and again I was utterly unable to gauge his feelings from his words or his tone. Inscrutable. Just put his picture next to the word in the dictionary, because that's what he was to a T.

"You might have mentioned something along those lines, come to think of it."

"And yet."

"And yet." I couldn't help but smirk to myself, because even if he was annoyed, he wasn't yelling at me, which meant he had known I'd intended to do this the entire time.

"I'm impressed you weren't hustling Leo and I out the door earlier. You played that really cool. Well done."

"Couldn't lay all my cards on the table. And what about you, Mr. I Need to Leave Because I Have a Job to Do?"

He gestured at the assembled crowd. "Who says this isn't the job?"

"You doing a little murder investigation on the side?"

"That would make two of us, and what are the odds?" This time he did smile, a real one that made my heart flutter a little, and also told me he probably wasn't going to lecture me about this too much later on. Thank goodness. "No, I was heading this way to drop off some paperwork for a client and decided to see if my gut was right and that you would be here sticking your nose in other people's business."

"Hey now, my nose is at a very safe distance from being in their business. Look how far away I am," I protested.

"Mm-hmm. A regular Miss Marple, you are. So, have you noticed anything interesting?"

"A very annoying private investigator who follows me wherever I go," I teased.

"Is he handsome? I feel like that's relevant to whether his presence is actually annoying or secretly kind of enjoyable."

"I'm sure he *thinks* he's handsome."

"Ouch."

"And no, nothing standing out. The Weatherlys aren't here, at least the ones I've met."

Rich scanned the crowd, then leaned closer to me, pointing to the other side of the tent, a good distance away on the opposite side of the plot. "Did you spot Detectives Kim and Martin, by any chance?"

I had not. Even though he'd told me they would likely be doing the same thing I was, it was still alarming to see how well they'd hidden in plain sight. I hadn't even noticed them until he pointed them out.

Like us, they were dressed all in black and huddled together under umbrellas. They spotted us, and while there was a good amount of distance between us and them, it was clear they weren't thrilled to see me standing there. Rich's presence might ease their minds slightly, but I was sure I wasn't doing myself any favors in terms of getting off their potential suspect list.

My cheeks felt warm, and it was only in that moment that I realized what a silly idea this had been. Rich had warned me over and over again not to come, yet I'd pretended to know better. So stupid.

Just as I was chastising myself for acting without thinking, I noticed one figure drifting away from the main crowd of mourners. She wore a dark-burgundy dress and heels that were not made for walking on grass, but she took long, intentional strides and never wavered, in spite of her precarious shoe choice.

I couldn't make out a face under the umbrella she carried, but she was moving in the direction of a white gazebo perched up on a hill about a hundred yards away. As she got closer, I realized a man dressed all in black was already sitting in the gazebo, waiting for her.

From this distance I couldn't make out any of his facial features, but his general build and coloring suggested he wasn't too old, probably no older than forty, though I wouldn't have bet money on my estimation. He might have been twenty-five, might have been fifty with good genes.

The woman closed her umbrella as she mounted the steps and took one quick look over her shoulder before sitting down next to the man.

I gasped.

"What is it?" Rich asked.

"Isn't that Keely Morgenstern?"

Chapter
Twenty-Four

I wanted to make a dash around the cemetery's main drive in hopes of seeing the man Keely was meeting with, but Rich was dead set against me going anywhere.

For one thing, leaving a funeral wasn't immediate grounds for suspicion, though it was odd that Keely was here to begin with, and even stranger that she'd be meeting with a stranger while Madeline was being laid to rest mere feet away.

If it was Keely Morgenstern, that is.

She and the man were far away, and it was raining, but I recognized the blonde hair and the regal way she was holding herself, just like at the police station yesterday. Every bone in my body was screaming at me, telling me that was Keely, and that whoever she was speaking to in that gazebo was important to this case.

Rich got out his phone and sent a quick text message, and a moment later Detectives Kim and Martin left their perch and moved toward their nearby car. They weren't going with a lot of haste, but I supposed they didn't want to draw too much attention to themselves.

Unfortunately, as they reached their car, the funeral came to an end, and people began moving back toward their own vehicles. With everyone in a post-funeral haze of melancholy and umbrellas obscuring their vision, the drive was soon cluttered with people ambling around looking for their cars, or helping more senior mourners get into their vehicles.

I let out a little moan of frustration.

"Rich," I said. "*Rich*."

He saw what I was seeing and knew perfectly well that if we didn't get a move on, Keely and her mystery man were likely to disappear on us before we were able to get a good look at who he was.

I couldn't help but think of the argument I'd overheard in the police station parking lot, which had heavily implied that she was speaking to the exact same person Madeline had fought with on her phone right before she died. Something in my gut told me there was a very good chance this mystery man was connected to, and quite possibly the same person involved in, both arguments. I was desperate to get a look at his face in case I remembered him being at the auction.

Thanks to my dream spell, I had a pretty good memory of every face I'd seen that day, so I felt certain I'd be able to recognize him if he'd been there.

Rich grabbed me by my elbow and hustled me over to my car, which was parked right near the tree. I climbed in wordlessly, barely getting our umbrellas closed and into the back seat, and I started the engine as he got in on the passenger side. I pulled out, narrowly missing a Town Car that was whizzing past.

My heart was in my throat, but I was running on pure adrenaline at this point. I needed to get over to that gazebo. Triple-checking that I wasn't about to cause a collision, I pulled out and drove the loop that would get me to the other side of the cemetery where the gazebo was situated.

It had taken us a few short minutes to get around, but the white structure now appeared empty, and I spotted Keely's burgundy dress traipsing back across the lawn under her umbrella.

I didn't want to believe we'd missed them both, not when we were so close. I jumped out of the car, not bothering with my umbrella in spite of the sheets of gray rain pelting down, and jogged across the driveway over to the gazebo.

Just as I'd expected, it was totally unoccupied, and even from the higher vantage point inside, the only person nearby I could see was Keely, who was already almost all the way back at Madeline's burial site.

I hadn't *imagined* a man. Rich had seen him too, but there was absolutely no sign of him now that I was here.

"What on earth?" I muttered out loud, sitting down on the wrap-around bench inside the gazebo. Each bench seat was marked with the name of a benefactor, and I noticed the name *Weatherly* prominently featured on a plaque on one of the big white pillars.

Interesting.

It could have been a coincidence. This was, after all, the only dry place to meet someone where you could hide from prying eyes. Though it was strange to me that Keely would make plans to meet someone at the funeral of a woman she had barely known.

That the gazebo was dedicated to the Weatherlys was likely nothing of note. They had lived in Barneswood, they were buried here, and they'd been exceptionally rich. I was willing to bet I'd find things all over this town with the Weatherly name on them.

Still, it bothered me a little, for reasons I couldn't entirely put my finger on.

Rich joined me a moment after I sat down, scanning the surrounding area himself but seeing exactly what I had: nothing.

A mere two minutes later, the two detectives parked behind my car and followed us into the gazebo. "Did you get an ID?" Detective Kim asked.

"No, they were both gone by the time we got here. It was definitely Keely Morgenstern, though," Rich answered.

"Yeah, we spotted her among the guests when she arrived," Detective Martin said. "We're a bit surprised to see her." She then pivoted toward me, brown eyes practically boring a hole in my head. "Surprised to see you as well, Ms. Winchester."

I gave a weak, apologetic smile. "I was seeing if I recognized anyone from the auction."

"Funny, because so are we, and we noticed one. You."

"Oh." I wasn't sure what I could say that wouldn't look worse for me, so for once in my life I zipped my lip, not sure the truth would make me look any better.

Detective Martin sat on the bench across from me, her hands clasped together. She looked more put together than usual, wearing a black blazer with a silk blouse underneath and black slacks. The blouse was dotted with water stains now and would need to be dry-cleaned if she had any hope at all of saving it.

"Phoebe, I know you're trying to be helpful, and I can't tell you what an enormous assistance you've been just based on your original witness statement. We appreciate that very much."

There was a big loaded *but* hanging in the air, and I knew it was going to drop on me like the proverbial sword of Damocles. I practically winced waiting for her to say it.

"But." There it was. "You need to let us do our job. I promise you Madeline's murder is getting every bit of our attention right now, and we are putting in the time and effort to solve this case. We're very close."

"How close can you be if you're at her funeral hoping to catch the murderer, the same as me?"

I instantly regretted the words, because Detective Martin recoiled as if I'd slapped her.

"Just leave this to the professionals, Phoebe, before you wind up getting hurt." She placed emphasis on these last words, reminding me without actually adding *like last time*.

"Fine," I replied, hating the sullen tone of my voice, which made me sound more like a teenager than a grown woman. "I'll leave it alone."

Detective Martin gave a satisfied nod, but I didn't think either of us believed a word I was saying.

Chapter Twenty-Five

The police lecture had been enough to deter Rich from giving me his own *I told you so* speech, which I appreciated. I already felt like I'd been pulled into the principal's office and given a stern talking-to; I didn't need the guy I had feelings for getting in on the same party.

I dropped him back at his car, now the only other vehicle parked in the drive, and waited for him to get in and drive away. The cemetery crew were hard at work, one man folding the chairs under the tent and putting them in a wagon while the other two shoveled dirt onto Madeline's grave.

The rain was relentless now, coming down so heavily I could barely see the men working. I couldn't even make out the gazebo anymore. It had become nothing more than a white smudge on the horizon.

I felt silly, and whenever I felt this way, I had the completely irrational urge to cry. Tears welled up in my eyes, threatening to fall, and my hair was already so wet that it was dripping down my face, so no one would be able to tell the difference.

But I refused.

I might feel humiliated, but I was trying to do something good. I wanted to find the person who had killed Madeline, because someone willing to hurt a person in such a public way, with so many potential witnesses, was someone who could do it again.

I briefly considered going to see Keely and grilling her about her part in the murder. I knew she knew more than she was letting on. However, If I were to confront her in private, I might just be setting myself up for more trouble.

I decided that instead, I would go home and poke around on the internet to see if there was anything I might be able to dig up in a more low-risk setting.

As I started the car, my stomach gave a rumble of protest, telling me I would be a nightmarishly hangry monster by the time I got home and I wouldn't have the patience to cook anything.

Pizza it was.

The Busy Bee Bistro was empty when I arrived, and the teenage boy behind the counter looked excited about the prospect of having *anything* to do. I was guessing they had a pretty strict no-phones policy, because he looked bored out of his mind.

I placed my order, then sat in one of the empty yellow booths to wait for my pizza and salad to be prepared. While I idled, my phone buzzed in my pocket, and I pulled it out. There was a text from an unknown number, which I almost deleted, assuming it was spam, but curiosity tickled the back of my neck and I couldn't resist.

Stay out of it.

I stared at the message, trying to understand what it meant. Clearly *it* referred to the case, but was it Detective Martin reminding me to keep my nose out of their business? It definitely wasn't Rich, I had his number saved in my phone, and he wouldn't send something quite so ominous sounding. He knew better than to freak me out like that. Come to think of it, I also had Detective Martin's number in my phone, so it wasn't her either.

I continued to look at those four words, dumbfounded, until the clang of a bell almost made me jump out of my skin.

"Order up," the teen boy hollered. "Meat lovers' pizza, Caesar salad, side anchovies."

Snapped out of my musing, I went to the counter and collected my food, slipping a five-dollar bill into the tip jar as an extra thank-you for the salty fish goodness for Bob. My car was parked right outside, so I was able to dash from the door to the passenger side easily and slip my pizza onto the seat before rounding the other side to get in.

All the while, I couldn't stop thinking about the words.

Stay out of it.

Was it a warning?

A threat?

I didn't know what to make of it or who would send me such a thing, but the message itself was clear, and did a better job sending a chill down my spine than the rain did.

I briefly considered stopping at the police station to show the text to the detectives, but thought better of it. For one, driving home was going to be a nightmare if it got any darker, and I wouldn't be able to see any of the wildlife that liked to dart out into the middle of the road. Who knew how long the officers might keep me.

I'd sleep on it before telling anyone about the message, though it had certainly succeeded in making me want to back off from the case than any of the other warnings I'd been given from Rich and the detectives up to this point. Was someone watching me, keeping track of all the people I'd spoken to and questions I'd been asking?

Someone who might have been at the funeral today and seen me taking the whole thing in?

With the number blocked, I couldn't reply or look it up to gain any kind of clarity, so I had no option but to stew on it. I should probably be scared, but if anything, I was perplexed. Had I been getting close to figuring out the truth?

If so, that meant the killer had been right under my nose and I just had to look at the details I already knew in order to figure it out.

I was back on the highway, the sky dark and ominous overhead as evening settled in. While the drive back to Raven Creek wasn't a long one, I wasn't going to rush it. I stayed below the speed limit and kept my wipers going on their highest setting.

Driving in the rain wasn't exactly new to a native Washingtonian, but I'd also seen plenty of accidents on the side of the road from people who got a bit too confident in their ability to best the weather. The last thing I needed was a deer or coyote running across the road looking for shelter and finding the hood of my car instead.

I also liked to use an umbrella on rainy days, so maybe I wasn't a true Washingtonian. People in Seattle loved to look at you like you were a tourist if you're not just suffering in the wet.

It was incredible just how dark it had gotten since I'd left the pizza place. With no lights on the road and no other traffic to speak of, it was just me and my headlights, and even the light from my car was barely cutting through the rain. I slowed further, tempted to pull over to the side of the road and wait out the storm, but I knew it could last all night.

The drive was just a straight shot from Barneswood to Raven Creek, and while I did have forty minutes ahead of me, I should be able to do it if I was cautious and kept my eyes glued to the road.

I turned down the radio, and soon all I could hear was the routine *swish-swish* of the wiper blades and the hum of my tires on the slick blacktop. My pulse hammered heavily, and every few minutes my gaze drifted to the side of the road just to make sure I wasn't missing anything in the ditch.

That must have been how I missed the lights creeping up behind me, because one minute I was alone on the highway, and the next there was a car coming up from my rear.

Initially, I was relieved to see someone else driving. It meant that the road might not be as risky as I'd imagined, that there was another brave soul out here with me. It also meant if I happened to end up in the ditch in the next few minutes, at least someone would see it and maybe call for help.

But my initial relief faded quickly when I saw the way the car was gaining on me. At first, I thought maybe they were intending to drive around me and just wanted to get close before pulling into the other lane. But soon my heart was in my throat, because the car was *right* behind me, so close I could no longer make out more than the glow of their headlights, and *much* too close considering I was going almost sixty even at my reduced speed. If I had to slam on my breaks for any reason, they wouldn't be able to stop and would drive right into the back of my car.

I gently tapped my brake twice, hoping to give them the hint, but they continued to ride my back bumper.

Their closeness was distracting me from the road ahead, and every time my gaze drifted back to the side of the highway, my mind played tricks on me, with shadows that pretended to be deer or raccoons.

"Just go around," I breathed out through gritted teeth. I certainly wasn't going to speed up. Speed limits were made for *ideal* weather conditions, and it was hardly what I would call ideal out there. I wasn't sure what this guy's deal was, but if he was in such a hurry to go faster, he could pass me.

I let me speed drop ever so slightly, hoping it would give the other driver the hint and they would decide it was time to pass. I even edged a bit closer to the shoulder, giving them ample room to see that there was no oncoming traffic and the coast was clear.

They slowed to match my pace, continuing to ride mere inches from my bumper.

"What the heck?" I'd been sure that would be the thing to push them over the edge of annoyance and was braced for them to blitz by me with a middle finger in the air. I hated driving confrontations like that, but it would have been a welcome reprieve at this point.

At last, the car pulled into the opposite lane and started to pull past me.

"*Finally*," I said, speaking to myself to calm my ragged nerves.

The car, a dark-colored SUV with tinted windows, began to slow its pace again as it pulled alongside me. I hazarded a quick glance over, trying to see if I could get a good look at the driver, but the dark windows and darker night made it all but impossible.

Then the car swerved, sideswiping me, and sent my car into a tailspin on the wet asphalt.

As my car spun, I stopped fighting the wheel and thought, *I'm going to die.*

Chapter
Twenty-Six

Time stopped.

One minute the car was spinning out of control and my headlights were illuminating the ditch, the nearby pine trees, all the things I might drive right into now that I had no way to stop myself.

The next minute everything was still. The rain outside had stopped falling, the car had stopped spinning, and the taillights of the car that had just hit me were frozen in place, two hovering red orbs partially obscured by the rain.

It took me a few seconds to recognize what was going on, because it had been quite a while since something this frightening had happened to me and the adrenaline coursing through my body was blocking out logical thought.

I'd done this.

My powers had allowed me to stop time, and as a result I was able to clearly see my surroundings, and my brain had a chance to reason it out.

The SUV had hit me, and it had done so intentionally; of that I had no doubt. The way it followed me, the slow way it had crawled up beside me, and the absence of any kind of animal on the side of the road that it might have been swerving to avoid told me all I needed to know.

I was profoundly tempted to get out of the car, jog through the frozen night, and look into the window of the person who had done it to me, but my abilities were still a bit suspect, and I didn't know how long I'd be able to control the time stoppage. Sometimes when I did it, the effects lasted only a few seconds—like when I'd fallen through my porch—other times it could be a minute or two. There seemed to be a direct connection between how much danger I was in and how long the effects lasted, but I wasn't a scientist, and more importantly, this wasn't science. It was magic.

If I got out of my car and the spell wore off, I'd be standing in the middle of the highway while my unmanned car spun, heading heaven only knew what direction, and all the while I would be out in the open next to the car of someone who had just tried to kill me.

I thought of the text message I'd received not even an hour ago. *Stay out of it.* I had been hesitant at the time to report the message to the police, but now? What if this was the person who had sent it trying to hammer home their point? Had this been the unspoken *or else* lingering at the end of the message?

I felt a lot more certain now that it *had* been a threat.

No, I didn't have time or the guarantee of safety to go after the car, and thanks to the rain and the distance between us, I couldn't quite make out the license plate number, though I could read a B and a 9. And "dark SUV" was just vague enough to be almost no use at all. Not enough to help the police find whoever had done this to me, but better than nothing, I supposed.

I took a deep breath, assessing my situation. The car was pointed at the ditch, and if I didn't do anything, I would drive right through the ditch at full speed, and probably hit a nearby tree.

I slammed my foot down on the brake and roughly turned my car's wheel as far back toward the highway as I could. The pause, giving me just enough time to see where I was pointed and what was happening, might be enough to save me. The only other option would be to climb out and let the car go into the ditch without me, but what would stop the SUV from turning around and finishing the job?

With my teeth gritted, I waited for things to start moving again. I had only activated this power a handful of times, but from those experiences I knew that once I was out of immediate danger, everything would begin moving again. I usually had less than a minute to take action if I was going to use the time stop to my advantage. I had done all I could for myself, so I braced for the world to start moving again.

After a moment the blurry scenery around me shuddered. I slammed my hand down on the pizza beside me, as if it were a passenger I was trying to protect from the force of the spin, and hoped with every ounce of my being that I'd done all I could do to save myself.

The tires screeched so loudly it sounded like they were screaming, and even through the night I could see smoke drift up off the asphalt where I'd burned a streak of black rubber onto the highway. Gravel popped and snapped under the tires as I drifted onto the shoulder, but with my car pointed toward the highway, I didn't shoot into the ditch.

I released the brake and hit the gas, just lightly, and the car skidded back onto the blacktop proper. I braked again and put the car into park, hitting the four-way blinkers on autopilot.

I was stopped right in the middle of the proper lane. Behind me were black lines illuminated red in my taillights and huge tire-shaped divots in the gravel. My heart was beating so loudly I couldn't hear anything else. I took one ragged breath after the other until I felt my pulse coming back down to something that wasn't on the cusp of a heart attack.

The SUV was long gone, its red lights so far ahead of me I could barely see them as they took a turn in the road and vanished.

My purse, phone, salad, and Bob's container of anchovies had all slid off the seat thanks to my violent braking, and the interior of the car smelled of salad dressing and fish.

The pizza box was still on the seat, my hand pressed down firmly on top of it, and when I lifted the lid, I saw the pizza had slid forward, crushing against the side of the box, and certainly wasn't pretty to look at, but it was still relatively in one piece.

I started laughing.

I pressed my forehead to the car's steering wheel and laughed until my chest hurt, because the only other option right now was to cry. And if I cried, I might realize that someone had just tried to kill me, and I wasn't sure I'd ever be able to drive another mile if I had to carry that thought with me the whole way home.

So I laughed, and then I wiped the tears of laughter from my eyes, popped a piece of pepperoni into my mouth, and turned off the four-way blinkers.

I still had a half-hour drive ahead of me.

Then I could call the police.

Chapter Twenty-Seven

Rich sat next to me on my couch, tucking a big fluffy gray blanket around me and handing me a fresh cup of tea. He hadn't steeped it long enough and it was weaker than I would have preferred, but the thought was there and that was all that mattered to me right now.

Bob was curled up in my lap, kneading the blanket like it was a loaf of bread and he was trying to win Star Baker on *The Great British Bake Off*. His loud purrs were so intense I could feel the vibration against my chest.

Detective Kim sat in one of Eudora's big armchairs, a notepad out and a serious expression on his face as he jotted down details. Detective Martin was walking the perimeter of the house, checking to ensure that there wasn't anything here we needed to worry about.

I'd felt safe the moment I got out of my car and walked through the front door, carrying my battered pizza and my salad-stained purse. It hadn't occurred to me that my own home might be somewhere that this person would target me. I was glad Detective Martin was looking out for me, but I sort of wished she hadn't told me what she was doing.

I was never going to sleep tonight at this rate.

Bob finished his biscuit-making efforts and curled up in my lap, resting his head on my knee. I held the warm mug of tea in both hands, and between the tea, the blanket, and my furry personal space heater, the chill of the storm was finally dissipating.

"Can you just walk me through the details of what happened one more time?" Detective Kim asked. I could see something about the story bothered him—that made two of us—but I wasn't sure what I could do to help make it all make sense to him when none of it made sense to me.

I walked him through everything again, letting him see my phone so he could read the text message for himself and forward a copy to his own phone. I wasn't sure what kind of digital forensics a small-town police department might be able to use on a blocked-number text, but if they could use it somehow, all the power to them.

When I got to the part where I stopped the car, he shook his head, his expression incredulous.

"It's a miracle you're alive. I looked at the damage to the side of your door, and this person wasn't messing around. I don't know how you kept it together enough to stay on the road, but I might need to take a lesson or two in defensive driving from you once this is all over."

I sputtered into my tea, because of course I'd left out the part about using my magic powers to stop time. Can't really easily explain something like that to the police. I was just glad to be relaying these details to Kim instead of Detective Martin, since she had once been impressed with my ability to seemingly dodge a literal bullet.

No sense in having her start to question why I was so adept at getting out of life-or-death situations largely unscathed.

Let them think it was good luck.

"We'll have someone come back in the morning to take a few photos in the daylight, if you don't mind, so we can file a proper report. It's hard to say right now if the text and the accident are connected, but I think it's pretty clear that you need to stay out of this case. I hope you plan to listen." He shut his little notebook and gave me a stern look that clearly demanded a response.

"My amateur detective days are over, I promise. I don't want anything like this to happen again." While I was being honest about the last part, my curiosity about who was behind this was stronger than ever. My resolve to look over the notes and details of the case far outweighed any self-preservation skills. Besides which, none of the suspects would know if I was just looking at some notes.

I had no intention of doing any more interviews or in-person snooping, that much was true.

But that didn't mean I needed to stop entirely.

If someone wanted me dead, it meant I was getting too close for comfort to the truth. The killer was out there, and they were watching me, and what had once been about clearing my name was now about protecting my life.

Needless to say, I was still very invested in finding Madeline's killer, before they decided to become *my* killer.

Detective Martin returned, her coat damp and short hair glistening from the rain outside, even though I suspected she'd been under the protection of the patio's roof most of the time. "All clear out there. Just make sure you lock your doors and windows, okay?"

As if I wouldn't have thought of that on my own.

"Of course."

"We all good?" she asked Kim.

He nodded, pushing himself up from the chair with a little difficulty. Eudora's chairs were very squishy and great for reading, but they basically swallowed you whole. It could be a real struggle to stand up once they had you in their cushy velvet grasp. "We really appreciate you calling us, Phoebe. I'm sorry for what happened to you tonight, and can assure you that we're going to do everything in our power to figure out who did this to you."

I gave him a small smile and sipped my tea. Rich got up from the sofa and walked the detectives to the door, then came back and hovered in the doorway of the living room like he wasn't sure what he should do next.

"Are you hungry? Do you need more tea?" He was shuffling awkwardly, and the nervous energy radiating off him was endearing. I could tell he wanted to make me feel better but, given the unusual circumstances, didn't know how.

"Want to bring that pizza in here and we can try to salvage what's left of it? Busy Bee pizzas are too good to let it go to waste, even if it does look a bit tragic." I set my tea on the side table next to me, pulling my blanket around me and covering Bob up in the process.

Rich bobbed his head a few times, then disappeared, returning a moment later with the grease-stained Busy Bee pizza box. It still smelled delicious, and while its appearance—half the cheese sliding off and most of the toppings littering the bottom of the box—left a lot to be desired, I suspected the taste wouldn't have been impacted. I did my best to push most of the cheese and toppings back into place and grabbed a piece, plopping it on one of the paper towels Rich had brought along, then took a big bite.

It was mostly cold, but cold pizza was still delicious, and I hadn't realized until that moment how ravenously hungry I was. The shock was probably starting to wear off, and my stomach remembered I hadn't eaten anything since my breakfast sandwich hours earlier.

Rich and I sat in companionable silence, enjoying our room-temperature slices, with the dulcet tones of Bob's contended purring to lighten the atmosphere and drown out any chewing sounds. With Bob on my lap, a frustrating thought occurred to me, and I let out a long groan.

"Are you okay?" Rich was sitting up straight, obviously ready to leap out of his chair to my aid at a moment's notice. I waved at him to sit down, and it took him a moment to obey, but he finally settled once more.

"I just remembered that the container of anchovies I got for Bob at the restaurant are all over the front seat of my car." I let my head fall back onto the sofa, gazing up at the ceiling. "So not only did someone try to kill me, but tomorrow my whole car is going to smell like stinky fish."

Chapter
Twenty-Eight

While being psychic was not one of my many witchy gifts, I was right about one thing. My car absolutely did smell like briny fish.

After a lovely officer named James stopped by my house to take some photos of the damage and attempted to scrape some lingering dark paint from the door that might belong to my attacker, I was finally able to clean.

The auto body shop wouldn't open until the next day, but I didn't see the point in letting the carnage from my dinner sit in the front seat until then. Thankfully, the rain had let up, and while it was still cloudy, it was dry enough for me to head out to the curb in a pair of dingy, battered overalls, my hair pulled back in a silk scarf and a big bucket of soapy water in one hand.

When I opened the passenger door, wilted leaves of Romaine lettuce tumbled to the pavement, bits of bacon still clinging to them. The overwhelming scent of fish and garlic wafted out to greet me a moment later.

"Yikes. Guess I'll be asking the mechanic if he sells air fresheners." There was no one around me, but I'd gotten used to having one-sided conversations thanks to a certain orange tabby. I'd thought about letting Bob out with me, but the ground was still wet, and I didn't want any little muddy paw prints stamped over my beautiful duvet in the bedroom.

It took me about an hour to get all the bits of salad out of my floor mats, and I gave my best effort at getting the grease stains out of my seat. Thankfully, most of the mess had happened when the food sailed off the seat and onto the floor, but a few bits of lettuce had stuck to the fabric, and the dressing had soaked into the gray upholstery.

I used an old trick I'd learned from my mother, which was to coat the stains in Dawn dish soap and let the soap work its magic overnight. I wouldn't wait quite that long, but a few hours should help get the worst of it out. I hoped.

Now that I was sweaty, soapy, and had little bits of fish under my fingernails, I thought a shower was in order. It was Sunday, and I wasn't required at the shop today, though habit made me want to go in. And since my investigation was effectively shelved for the time being, I wasn't going to be driving back to Barneswood to chat up any of the other attendees from the auction. I decided it might be a good idea to distract myself from last night, and from the murder in general, by focusing my attention on the garden beds around my house.

I knew perfectly well that days without rain were going to be few and far between for the duration of the spring and through the summer, so I should take advantage of a rain-free Sunday and get some plants into the empty beds. Eudora's perennials were mostly up now, which gave me a good idea of how many vacancies I had, and it wasn't a small number.

Since I was just going to be getting dirty again, I took only a quick shower to chase off the scent of anchovies and got dressed in my overalls again, adding a battered Seattle Mariners cap over my hair. The look said *yard work*, and I was perfectly okay with that. I didn't need to put on makeup and a dress just to buy annuals.

Before I headed out, I stopped quickly in the shed to see what kind of supplies Eudora had left from the previous year so I knew what I needed to buy. I had picked up quite a few things at the hardware store in Barneswood, but I was sure there would still be things I hadn't thought of.

Eudora had all the tools I would ever need, of course, and also a few mason jars filled with powdered fertilizer blends and a metal canister labeled *Garden Tea*.

I hadn't noticed that one when I'd been digging around for the plywood and pulled it curiously from the shelf. The tin itself was identical to the storage tins in the basement, but when I opened it up, the smell was altogether different. I blinked back tears and the unexpected potency of the scent. It wasn't *bad*, exactly, just a dense, earthy smell I hadn't been anticipating. I glanced into the tin in the low light of the shed's one window and tried to guess what was in it. Dried banana peel, cracked eggshells, dehydrated apple and carrot peels, and an assortment of other kitchen and garden scraps that had been dried out to keep them from rotting.

I glanced at the front of the tin, and under the label was a handwritten note in Eudora's distinctive cursive. *Add a scoop to your watering can, then forget it in the sun for a few hours. Your tomatoes will thank you.*

I ran my fingertips over the label, grateful to still be finding these secret little pieces of her around the house. I felt like there was so much more Eudora here to discover.

I set the canister down by the door so I could find it easily later, then as I was about to step outside, I noticed a pair of garden gloves, bright pink with a floral pattern on them, and so new I assumed they had never been worn. Almost like they'd been left there for me to find.

Ghosts might not be real, but I still looked around the shed with a smile and said, "You sneaky old witch." I took the gloves with me on the way out.

There was a cute seasonal market set up on the end of Main Street, the opposite end from Lansing's Grocery Store. I didn't love the idea of driving my bashed-up car, but it was still running okay and the damage to the door could have been caused by anything. Gossipy neighbors would assume fender bender before attempted murder, thankfully.

I didn't have any other option. Since I was buying flowers, I needed to be able to transport them, and unless I borrowed a car from someone else, this was really the easiest way to do it.

The car smelled a lot better after being washed, and I had to remind myself not to put my purse on the thin coating of dish soap I'd left on the passenger seat. Still, there was the faintest smell of garlic and fish around me, so I rolled my window down on the way.

Saint Theresa's Flowers read a hand-painted sign at the entrance of the cute makeshift market. A little green sign next to it explained that Saint Theresa loved to do the little things in life well and that she was considered the patron saint of flower growers. I wasn't a churchgoing person myself, but I loved learning about the various saints and their patronages. Saint Theresa sounded like she'd be my kind of lady.

Saint Theresa's shop, abbreviated as *Tessie's* on all their bags, was a seasonal pop-up that took over a vacant lot every spring and shut down again in September when the main growing season ended.

Of course, in the Pacific Northwest there were no *official* start and end times to the season, but it certainly got too cold over the winter for a lot of the more delicate annuals, and quite a few of the perennials died back in the colder months, only to return in spring.

I was astonished by how permanent the shop looked, even though I knew it had opened up only a few weeks earlier. There was a sheltered area built from a trailer that had corrugated plastic sheeting to create a long overhead roof. Beneath the roof were open bins of produce, one of the major perks of living on the West coast. It might be May, but there were already cherries, peaches, and other tasty treats piled high in the bins.

I hadn't come for food, but I'd certainly be leaving with some. I was already imagining a fresh cherry scone, or perhaps a vanilla scone with fresh cherry jam. So many wonderful possibilities.

The rest of the lot—fenced in on all sides to keep anyone from wandering off with the goods—was stocked to the nonexistent rafters with plants. There were tall rolling racks loaded with colorful annuals, dreamy green perennials, and every type of fruit and vegetable plant imaginable.

I grabbed a cart and decided that since I didn't know much at all about gardening beyond flowers being pretty, I'd just go with what I thought looked nicest. Keeping in mind the pale-blue shade of Lane End House, I gravitated toward violet and blue hues at first. Then I remembered how Eudora always had bright-pink geraniums in her flowerpots and knew I'd need to get some of those as well.

It took less than half an hour for my cart to be completely loaded. In addition to a surfeit of seasonal flowers, I'd gotten two baskets of cherry tomatoes, a potted cucumber plant, and a hanging strawberry basket. Eudora used to have a giant vegetable garden in her backyard, but as she got a bit older, the maintenance and bending required to keep it up became too much for her and she focused her energy on the flowers instead.

The garden plot was still in the backyard, though largely grown over with weeds and native vegetation. I might consider resuscitating it next spring if I got really bold, but it wasn't my first priority.

I also grabbed a bunch of different herbs, anything that might be good in my teas. There were about fifty different kinds of mint, and limiting myself to a handful was a real chore. I ultimately settled on getting the pineapple, strawberry, chocolate, and mojito varieties. Then a blueberry basil plant stole my focus and found its way into my cart without my permission, but I let it stay.

My focus was so locked on the plants that I didn't even notice I was being watched until a hand tapped on my shoulder.

I yelped, practically jumping out of my skin, and instinctively hid behind my cart, as if someone were going to attack me in broad daylight.

"Whoa, whoa, whoa." Honey took a step back, giving me some distance, a concerned expression on her beautiful face. "Are you okay?"

As I caught my breath and tried to slow my pulse, I offered her a soft smile. "Sorry, you scared me half to death. I must have been off in my own world."

Honey wasn't going to let me get away with that explanation. "No, you looked really scared there for a second. What's going on?"

I cast a quick glance around the small lot to make sure we were alone, then explained to her what had happened last night. I didn't get into too much detail about the funeral, but I gave her the most basic details about the mysterious text and the attack on the highway.

When I was done with my story, Honey looked pale and sick. "Oh my goodness, that's unbelievable." She then moved instantly into problem-solving mode and started piling my cart with more herbs. Rosemary, rue, dill, and almost every pack of sage in sight.

"Am I making an herb garden?" I asked her. "Or a green goddess dressing?"

"Protection, Phoebe. These are all herbs used in protection magic. And I'm coming over after this to put up some wards."

"Honey, I don't know if all of that is necessary."

"Someone tried to kill you." She reached over and tapped the necklace I was wearing, which had been a gift from Eudora. "And you're lucky you had someone watching over you."

"I don't know how much of it was luck."

"Luck and magic are intertwined, babe; there's a lot of luck in any magic you do. So don't assume because your powers helped you that there wasn't a little bit of Eudora in that car looking out for you too."

My hand drifted up to my necklace, which was warm from the heat of my body, and I said a little thank-you to my aunt for whatever help she had offered me in the car last night.

Honey relaxed a bit at the sight of all the sage in my cart.

"I read somewhere online I shouldn't use sage, because it was meant only for Native American practice?" I said, picking up one of the containers.

"That usually refers only to white sage, which is grown by very specific Native American tribes for their own use and is considered sacred. It's also endangered. This is garden sage; they're very different things. We don't stock any white sage at my shop, though if you're ever gifted some from a member of the tribe, you are allowed to use it. Plus you're just putting this in the ground, not smudging with it." She put a sage plant in her own basket. "I like that you're doing your own research. Remember when you're reading about magic online, though, that most of the things you read are more for a neo-pagan audience. Things like white sage being a closed practice are good to know, but I hope you're not expecting to get extra insight into your powers on a Reddit thread. Some things you'll need to learn as you go, I'm afraid."

We wandered around Tessie's a little longer, though I couldn't have fit any more plants in my cart if I tried. As we approached the checkout, I filled a few reusable produce bags with the fresh fruit and grabbed a gorgeous bouquet of flowers that were begging me to bring them into my kitchen.

No lilies, of course, which were incredibly toxic to cats.

Bob, for his part, didn't seem very interested in eating plants or flowers, which I appreciated. But you could never tell what would be the thing to inspire him to chow down, and I didn't want poison to be on offer.

After I paid much more for my plants than I had anticipated, Honey helped me load everything into my car.

"I don't know how to tell you this," she said, obviously trying to keep her tone polite. "But your car smells terrible."

I burst out laughing, wedging a raspberry bush onto the floor of the front seat. "I know. Blame the side order of anchovies, I'm afraid."

Honey wrinkled her nose but didn't ask any further questions.

We headed back to my place, Honey trailing behind me in her cute teal-green convertible, which I was sure had never smelled like fish a day in its existence. Having her with me was much more helpful than I'd expected, as we made quick work of getting all my plants onto the front lawn. It turned out that she was also something of an expert when it came to what went well together and where to put my new flowers.

She made a trip to the shed, returning with an armload of trowels, claws, and a big watering can, then guided me through the best process of planting. First, we put everything where we thought it would go best. And by we, I mean Honey told me where things should go and I gratefully obeyed her every command.

She insisted we place a sage plant at every corner of the house, and near the front and back entrances as well. The little plants, whose leaves looked like they'd been licked by frost, were pretty and smelled gorgeous, so I had no problems with having so many of them around.

Soon the flowerpots lining the front walkway were filled with Eudora's signature pink geraniums, and spiky dracaena. The window boxes had a mix of purple and yellow pansies and cheery yellow and orange marigolds, and the vegetables were in a raised garden bed just outside the back door, where they'd get plenty of sun through the day, and I could easily step out of the kitchen to grab whatever my heart desired.

The work took us a few hours, but when it was all done, the yard looked so bright and alive, it was worth the growing ache in my lower back.

"You're incredible," I gushed to Honey. "I'd still be sitting here wondering where to start if you hadn't come with me."

"The one thing I miss because I have an apartment is not being able to have a big garden. I have a little deck upstairs, but it's not big enough for more than a few planters, sadly. My mom has the most incredible garden. Flowers all over her house, every inch of the yard. And so much produce she has to spend a full month every fall canning what's left. In case it's not obvious, her witchy strength is her green thumb." Honey beamed with pride. "People come from all over to ask for her help with their plants, their gardens, their crops. Her powers can help save someone's entire livelihood."

"She sounds incredible."

Honey nodded, a little sad, but obviously warmed by the thought of her mother. "She really is. I wish I got to see her more, but Alabama is a long way away. And I keep trying to convince her that she should move here, but she loves dry summers and warm winters, and I can't offer her either of those things. Plus she would never want to leave her garden, y'know?"

"I think I can understand that." I looked out over my new yard, amazed at how the extra color made me feel lighter and happier already. I could certainly understand how people became addicted to gardening. "Do you want to come in for lunch?" I asked.

It was closing in on three in the afternoon, my entire morning and much of the day having been devoured by the process of buying and then planting all my new greenery.

"I can't; I should have been back at the shop hours ago, but thankfully I have a part-timer now who can give me some relief on Sundays. Totally sweet girl; I think she's been watching a lot of witchy content on TikTok and is completely in love with crystals and herbs. Not a hereditary witch, but we can't all be so lucky, right?"

The clouds were beginning to loom heavier and darker, and Honey put up the cover of her car before driving off with a wave, leaving me with a newly designed yard, a freshly fixed porch, and not the faintest clue of how to use the rest of my time.

Again, I considered going in to the Earl's Study, but there wasn't much point. We closed at five on Sunday, and there'd been no indication from Daphne that things were so busy she needed any assistance. If I was going to give her more hours and more responsibility, I had to trust that she was capable, and she needed to believe in my trust. Showing up just because I was bored wasn't going to do her confidence any favors.

I headed back into the house, took my second shower of the day, and slipped into my fancy pajamas. Sure, it wasn't evening yet, but with nowhere else to go and nothing demanding my time, I didn't see the problem with lounging in some nice silky pants and a matching button-down top. They were covered in a rich, teal peacock pattern that I liked to think made my blue eyes really pop. At least that's what I'd told myself in an effort to make the rather hefty price tag on them feel more worthwhile.

With no excuses to hold me back and a promise that I wouldn't work on the case, I decided it was high time I try my hand at something I'd been avoiding for far too long: making new batches of Eudora's magical tea blends.

Chapter
Twenty-Nine

Eudora had set up a bit of a homemade apothecary in her basement, with shelves heavily laden with tins of extra tea for the shop as well as glass jars filled with the raw ingredients to craft all her blends. There was a large wooden table in the middle of the storage area, which was currently covered with several big metal mixing bowls, Eudora's recipe binder, and measuring cups. A small sink on the wall gave me an opportunity to rinse things out as needed.

In my months of going through Eudora's things and figuring out just what my inheritance entailed, I'd found a great number of unique, fun knickknacks, plenty of jewelry—some of it even valuable—and a great number of antiques that might have been better called "oddities." She had a taxidermized two-headed duckling, a number of bones kept in glass keepsake boxes, and a whole medical kit from the nineteenth century that looked more like a collection of torture devices than anything helpful.

The other thing I'd discovered was her collection of journals. *Journal* didn't seem like the right word, because these books—all slim and bound in black leather—were not about her day-to-day life or any drama that was occurring in Raven Creek. She didn't make nosy-neighbor notes or track the number of birds that stopped at her feeders. These books were all about her magical work.

She had jotted down hundreds of spells over the years. Ways she'd discovered to keep rust off the ceramics in the sinks and bathtubs, tricks to make it so your bread never went moldy, a ward against door-to-door salesmen. With the last she had noted that if you sprinkled a cup of sugar at your gate, it would allow Girl Scouts to come through with their cookies rather than being put off by the wards.

I had put little Post-it tabs on many of the pages with spells and charms I wanted to try and noted a handful of recipes that might be good, but something had been stopping me from using Eudora's work for my own gain. Honey had told me that witches need to find their own path and that we all have our own individual strengths and weaknesses. I think what I feared most about trying the spells in Eudora's book was that I wouldn't be as good at her brand of magic as she'd been.

I worried I'd never be able to cast a good-luck charm so that anyone who walked by my front gate would have a lovely day. More than anything, though, I was worried that when the special, magical blends of tea at the shop ran out, I'd never be able to duplicate them again.

The Earl's Study offered two very distinct types of tea. One was the normal type that anyone could walk in and buy by the gram or have a cup of while sitting at one of our tables. That was the tea I used in our baking sometimes, and it was certainly the more popular option we offered.

The other type of tea we had was something not everyone knew about, but those who did swore by it, and for good reason: it was legitimately magical. Eudora had crafted a dozen different blends, all of which were stored in the kitchen and available only if someone asked for them directly. There were teas to help bring money and success into your life, teas that would help you find love, teas for health, and teas to provide clarity in making big decisions. While I'd once assumed the love and money tea blends would be the most popular, it was actually Eudora's Count Your Sheep sleeping tea that most people came back for time and time again.

Unlike a normal chamomile, it offered a few extra ingredients, as well as the power of magical intention, all of which helped send the drinker off to dreamland almost immediately. All with the assurance that you wouldn't have any bad dreams. It was popular with new parents, people suffering from anxiety, and anyone who was just having a hard time shutting their brain off at night.

You'd wake in the morning feeling totally refreshed and ready to take on the day. While the teas weren't a cure-all and couldn't banish depression or other mental illnesses, they were a salve that could help someone get through the day.

Obviously, this tea came with a big *use at your own discretion* warning, and Eudora actually had a list of customers who were approved to buy it tucked behind the jar. It was a long list, but I supposed they were customers she trusted to use it only for their own benefit, rather than to knock someone out cold with a nice cup of tea.

I was exceptionally curious as to why a woman named Jeanie Johnson had once been approved but furiously scratched off the list at some point, but unless Eudora had noted the reason for the black-listing in one of her journals, I'd never know.

Since I was down to my last cup or two of Count Your Sheep and I was also an enormous fan of a good night's sleep, I figured it would be the best place to start things with my first batch of magical teas.

I'd sampled every single blend in the shop since taking things over. Not because I wanted to benefit from the magic—every tea also had special instructions to follow, and I didn't take those extra steps—but because I wanted to know how they tasted so I could duplicate them.

At their core, our magical and nonmagical teas were very much the same. They were a blend of herbs, spices, and various tea bases: black, oolong, green, rooibos, white, and matcha. What was added into those bases was what created the distinct flavor profiles of everything we offered.

Herbs also had magical properties, and knowing what those were helped guide the creation of the various magical teas. I was no expert in magical herbology, but thankfully, I didn't need to be. Eudora had written out all her various tea recipes, along with notes for potential adjustments, in her journals.

I found the journal where I'd marked the Count Your Sheep recipe and placed a heavy glass jar on the pages to keep it open. The process would be much the same as blending the normal teas, but the key, as Honey had explained, was intention. The reason Eudora's teas were such a hit was because she spent the creation process imagining success for everyone who drank the tea. For a love tea, she pictured couples walking hand in hand after taking a sip. For money tea, she imagined winning lottery tickets and growing bank balances. She thought only of others and the joy her tea could bring them.

That unselfishness, and her motivation to help, had been so genuine that her teas packed a punch. I was worried perhaps I was too selfish, or too scatterbrained to give the process the attention it needed, and that had kept me from trying for half a year.

Now I wanted to think about anything *other* than me, because my problems, and the current events of my life, were more stress than I wanted to deal with. This seemed like an ideal time to get out of my own head and put my burgeoning powers to good use.

I lit two candles as I stood in front of the table. An orange one, which would help channel success, joy, and creativity; and a black candle, which would help ward off any negativity. I then set about collecting all the ingredients the tea would need.

The herbs were very similar to our Sleepy Time tea: a white tea base, chamomile flowers, lavender buds, and the faintest whisper of dried apple pieces for a little touch of sweetness. But into the Count Your Sheep tea went a little valerian and some sweet blackberry leaves.

The other thing Eudora added to her magical blends was crystals. Since they wouldn't hurt anyone as part of the steeping process and you wouldn't drink them, there was no problem with adding them into the blend; you just needed to warn people to be aware of them.

Into the bowl I sprinkled clear quartz pieces and little bits of purple amethyst. With the amethyst and lavender buds side by side, as well as the cheery white-and-yellow chamomile blossoms, the bowl of tea ingredients looked like a lovely field of flowers on a spring day.

I held my palms near each of the lit candles and cleared my mind of anything involving myself. Instead, I began to picture the people I knew in town. I thought of Imogen smiling with her braids wrapped in silk as she slept; I thought of Amy, her alarm clock set for such earlier hours that every minute of sleep was precious to her; I pictured Rich, coming home from a night spent in his car, dragging his tired body to bed. As I dug my hands into the tea mixture, I pictured all of them falling into a restful, deep slumber that wouldn't be interrupted for hours.

I pictured them waking before their alarms in perfect contentment.

I kept focusing on those images, my eyes closed, as I sifted all the contents of the big metal mixing bowl together, and by the time I was done, it almost felt as if I was coming out of a peaceful sleep myself. Looking down at the mixture I'd created, I saw the little crystals glinting warmly in the candlelight, and the whole thing smelled soothing and wonderful.

It also looked *exactly* like the blend Eudora made.

I filled up the already empty overflow canister with my hope-fully magical creation and put the rest into a Tupperware container to bring to the shop with me the next day. Tonight I'd try a cup for myself just to make sure it worked, but I had high hopes.

If I could make one magical tea properly, maybe there was hope for me yet.

Chapter Thirty

The Count Your Sheep tea worked well.

Almost *too* well.

I had a cup after my dinner, and within fifteen minutes I was facedown on my pillow, not having bothered to pull my duvet all the way around me. I awoke exactly eight hours later, as refreshed as I'd ever felt after a night of sleep, and more than a little proud of myself.

Sure, you could blame part of it on all the hard labor I'd done the day before, between cleaning out my car and planting a whole garden. But I knew better than to dismiss magic when I saw it. I was a toss-and-turn sleeper almost every night, no matter how physically burnt out I was. Last night had been like flipping a switch.

I'd done it.

I tried to keep my excitement restrained, but it was difficult not to do a little victory dance in my kitchen. I'd been avoiding trying the magical tea blends for months, and now it seemed like there had been no reason for me to be so scared of them.

When I got to the Earl's Study, I would take inventory of what remained of the other blends and start working my way through them one by one.

After my usual morning routine—a run, a shower, and donning my best librarian chic ensemble—I gathered Bob into his carrier and headed to the shop. I'd need to leave when Imogen arrived to drop my car off at the mechanic, but thankfully it was still running fine, and the fishy smell was gone. The Dawn soap trick had also done wonders getting the little grease stains off the upholstery. Thank goodness for Mom's cleaning skills.

I let Bob out in the store and gathered up a big bag of the teas I'd noticed were almost empty at the Sugarplum Fairy the last time I'd been in. A lot had happened since the last time I saw Amy, and I wanted to let her know what had been going on.

The little bell over her door chimed as I entered.

"I come bearing gifts," I announced, holding up the bags of tea to show her.

"Oh, awesome, your timing is perfect." She wiped her hands on her apron and unburdened me of my offerings, lining the bags up on the counter. As she pulled each of her glass display jars off the top of her pastry cabinet, I started refilling the jars for her, making sure to mix the existing tea in with the new stuff so the old wasn't just lingering at the bottom of the jar forever.

When I did it at the shop, I always emptied the old into the new mix bowl first so it all incorporated. I liked to think of it as something like the tea version of sourdough, where little bits of the mix might survive year after year after year, always being incorporated into the new blend.

Sourdough could, in theory, live forever. There was even a place called the Sourdough Library, where food scientists tried to store different sourdough starters from around the world. There were some that were over a thousand years old and could still make bread.

I thought it was fascinating, and sort of lovely, that a kitchen item like sourdough could outlive its creator by generations.

When Amy's jars were all full, I slipped the bags back into my purse so I could reuse them later.

"Thanks for the tip about the travel mugs, by the way," she said. "I have a few samples coming in the mail to see if I like them, then we'll start stocking them here as well. I got one that has a metallic holographic foil, which sounded too delightful not to at least *see* what it looked like, right?"

"Holographic foil sounds very right for the Sugarplum Fairy." I laughed. "I can't wait to see them; I'll be the first person in line to buy one."

"Oh, I'll just give you one. Don't be silly."

I shook my head. "I think you give me more than enough at the Amy discounted rate." I laughed again. "Besides, I want to support you. Let me buy one."

She flushed a little, and I could tell she wanted to argue, but finally she said, "Okay, fine. But I'm filling it with a free latte, and you can't stop me."

"Wouldn't dream of it."

"How was your trip up to Barneswood the other day?"

I let out my breath in one long stream. The last time I'd spoken to Amy had been Friday before Rich and I hit the road, and it felt like a million years had passed since then. So much had happened I barely knew where to start.

I quickly gave her the highlights—of talking to Franny, what I'd learned about Keely, of attending the funeral, and then my harrowing experience on the highway coming home Saturday afternoon. I tried to lighten the mood by telling her about my yard, but her mouth was hanging open with a stricken expression glued to her face.

"Someone tried to *kill* you," she squeaked.

"I know, or at least they really wanted to scare me."

There was a small line of tears dotting her eyelashes, and her lower lip trembled. "I can't believe you're being so calm about it. I'd be an absolute wreck." She lifted the divider that split the employee area from the customer section and wrapped me up in a hug. "I'm so glad you're okay."

Amy smelled like sugar and lemon and gave one of the best hugs I'd ever experienced, almost good enough to give Leo a run for his money. I felt comforted, and it made me smile to know how much she cared about me and how much my experience had impacted her.

"Hey." I patted her back gently and she pulled away, swiping at an errant tear that trickled down her cheek. "I'm okay, I promise. I'm too tough for some jerk in an SUV to take out like that. I'm basically a Formula One driver."

That made her laugh, and her spirits seemed to be lifted as she returned to her side of the counter and started making my morning chocolate hazelnut latte. The boxes of my regular delivery were on the counter beside her, and I could see a happy sun drawn in black marker on the top of the box.

When she was done prepping my drink, she put it and the boxes between us and rested her elbows on the counter, putting her chin in her palms thoughtfully. "You know, thinking about everything you said, it's a bit odd that that Keely woman would sell everything, isn't it? If you inherited a fully furnished mansion, stocked to the gills with nice art, jewelry, and all those lovely things, why would you sell everything off?"

"Maybe it wasn't her taste."

Amy hemmed and hawed, then shook her head. "No, to me it sort of sounds like she's liquidating assets, trying to make a quick buck. I wonder if she has major debts or there's someone in her family that needs money. Medical issues, something like that. I think the only reason someone at that age sells off a whole estate is because they want the cash."

I considered this. Part of me had thought that Keely just disliked Mr. Weatherly's family and wanted to make sure there was no way they could get their hands on the physical parts of his estate. But Amy was right: the more obvious thing would be that she just wanted the money.

But for what?

It was no small amount of money, and for someone who seemed to come from wealth, if her car was any indication, I had to wonder what could make her so desperate for cash that she'd sell everything her supposedly beloved former boss had owned.

"That's certainly something to consider," I said.

"Except you're *not* going to consider it, right? After the text, and the car? You're going to leave the investigating to the professionals?"

I sipped my latte.

"I promise I'll stay out of trouble."

She gave me a look that very clearly said she knew I would do no such thing.

Chapter
Thirty-One

I mogen arrived at five minutes before ten, as usual, and except for old Mr. Loughery, there was no one else in the store. I figured I would take the reprieve before the lunch rush and drop my car off at the mechanic.

As I'd never needed to take my car in for any kind of work, it was my first trip to Al's Garage, a squat little building that looked like someone had taken an old double-wide trailer and stuck a garage on one side. When I wandered into the little lobby, though, I knew Al was going to be my kind of person.

Every single window was filled with plants. And there were a lot of windows, because what might have once been a living room had been turned into a proper waiting area, complete with several chairs and a beat-up coffeemaker that had half a pot still in it from the morning.

The plants were incredible, though. There was a gigantic cactus that overwhelmed its terra-cotta planter, and a Christmas cactus in full bloom even though it was the middle of May. There were palms, and more cacti, and a massive fiddle-leaf fig that reached the ceiling. As someone who had killed a fiddle-leaf fig once, I knew how finicky they could be. Mine had died because I moved it ten feet, to the opposite side of a room.

They were very dramatic plants, but Al seemed to have quite the green thumb.

A small man in his late sixties appeared from a back room, adjusting his little half-moon glasses. He wore a navy-blue jumpsuit with a name tag on one side that had *Al* stitched in bright red letters. The man himself.

"Hi, I'm Phoebe Winchester. I left you a message over the weekend about my car?" I hoped he wasn't one of those people who just ignored voice mail messages.

"Ah, yes, the police told me about your situation. They were pretty adamant I collect any extra paint from the door. Just in case." He gave me a quick once-over, I think to assess whether or not I'd been injured in the accident. Seeing that there was nothing worth mentioning on my person, he jerked his chin toward the front door.

"Let's go have a look, then."

Outside, I showed him the driver's side door, and he made a handful of *hmm* and *mm-hmm* noises, bobbing his head with some frequency and adjusting his glasses several times to get a better look at the door. He opened and closed it, peered at some mechanisms inside, and finally said, "Gonna need it a couple days. I'll have to replace the door, gotta see what I can find locally. If I need to order it in, I'll let you take 'er back for the time being, but if I can get a decent one at the junkyard, that'll do."

While I didn't love the idea of a junkyard door, I had to assume he knew what he was doing.

"Paint from the dealer might take a bit, so you might have a mismatched door for a while. Hope ya don't mind."

I shrugged. "I'm not trying to win any beauty contests with it."

"Mm-hmm." He didn't laugh but gave the car a pat on the roof as if to apology to her for my poor attempt at humor. "You're at Eudora's old place, right?"

"Yeah, she was my aunt."

"Mm-hmm. I'll call you when it's ready." And with that, Al headed back inside with my keys, our business here done for the time being.

It was a good thing this was such a small town; otherwise I'd have been pretty put out about him taking my car without offering me a loaner, or even a ride back to the Earl's Study. I kicked myself for not thinking of putting my bike in the trunk. I hiked my purse up on my shoulder and gave thanks to the Washington weather gods that it was such a lovely, rain-free day, because otherwise this would have been a real bummer.

I was a few blocks away from Al's place and almost back to Main Street when an obnoxious honking sound caused me to turn around and see who was behind me. When I did, my heart sank, and I immediately began looking for places to hide.

The little red Honda pulled over to the curb and had barely stopped rolling when Dierdre Miller popped out. Her fake-red hair dye was almost the same color as her car, and she was wearing the biggest faux movie star sunglasses I had ever seen.

"Phoebe Winchester, just the woman I was looking for." Her voice was bright, pretending to be happy to see me, but she and I both knew she wouldn't be on the lookout for me unless she wanted something.

"Dierdre, good morning."

"Playing hooky from work?" she teased.

I looked at her like she'd grown antlers. Dierdre was not in the habit of making jokes, or if she was, she wasn't in the habit of making them with me. Something was definitely fishy here.

"I had to drop my car off at Al's."

"Oh yes, we've all heard about that dreadful *incident*. I'm so relieved you're all right." Her hand went to her chest in an effort to look properly horrified by my near-death experience.

Maybe she was wearing the glasses to help make this little performance more believable.

I also couldn't believe how quickly gossip spread in this town. I'd told a few people, but I doubted it had been Honey, Amy, or Imogen who had told others. The battered car door and the police presence had likely gotten the locals buzzing, and some way or another they'd stumbled over the story. Guess I'd been wrong to assume they wouldn't jump to the most dramatic conclusion.

There wouldn't be a soul in Raven Creek who didn't know about my brush with death by the time the day was done, especially if Dierdre knew. Her work might be selling real estate, but her business was everyone else's.

"The car got the worst of it." I stared at her, and she fidgeted uncomfortably. Part of me wanted to draw this out a bit longer just to make her feel as uneasy as possible, but I needed to get back to the shop and prep for the lunch rush. "Do you need something, Dierdre?"

"Well . . ." She wrung her hands, looking anywhere but at me, fidgeting as if she wanted to say something but couldn't quite get the words right. It wasn't like Dierdre to be at a loss for words, so I savored it for a moment. "You know we've been discussing those alterations to your bookshop."

"Not alterations. There won't be any physical changes to the building. I just want to add a small kennel area where I can host a couple of adoptable cats." I had explained this in depth in my proposal, and also earlier this week at the council meeting, but I wasn't sure how much of what I said was getting through to her. She always made it sound like I was planning to add a new wing to the store. The Earl's Study already took up two stores' worth of space; we didn't need more. We couldn't continue to expand if we wanted to either, because the Sugarplum Fairy was on one side, and the cute plant store The Green Thumb was on our right. They were both good tenants, and thanks to the low fixed rent, they wouldn't be leaving anytime soon.

I just wanted to help find cats a new home, and Dierdre was trying to make it into a shady capitalist endeavor.

I felt like this was about to turn into the same fight we'd been having for months, and I really didn't have the patience or energy for it at the moment.

"Dierdre, if you're just here to tell me no again, I'm sure it can wait until next month. I really do need to get back to the store."

She shook her head, which was surprising enough to make me plant my feet and give her a few more moments of my time.

"No, no. After the meeting we reviewed your proposal again, and as much as it pains me to say it, you've completed all the appropriate paperwork, and the kennels are far enough away from your kitchen to remain health code compliant." She let out a long sigh. "I thought I might as well be the one to tell you that at the next meeting we'll be granting you approval to go ahead with things."

I couldn't help it; my mouth fell open in shock, and I waited one second, then two, for a *but* to come from her, yet nothing did. For almost six months I'd been fighting with them, filling out one set of papers, then filling out another when they decided those weren't the *right* papers, and going to every town council meeting so they could see I was an active and enthusiastic part of the community. They didn't need landlord approvals, because Eudora had owned the shop outright, so now I did as well. I'd done everything to the letter and had begun to think they were going to continue denying me out of spite just because of my history with Dierdre.

She did have a lot of sway with the town council, I had to admit. I thought the mayor sided with her on a lot of things simply to avoid having to argue with her.

Yet here she was, standing in front of me giving me the one thing I wanted most . . . as what? A peace offering? No, she wanted something; otherwise, she would have just waited a month until the next meeting.

"Well, that's wonderful news, Dierdre, thank you. I know the shelter will be thrilled. They're usually overflowing with cats, and I think we can help find homes for some very deserving animals."

She wrinkled up her nose, obviously not very interested in animals or helping them. Not a real shocker.

We stood in silence for a beat. She continued to fidget, so I knew there was more to this, but I wasn't going to drag it out of her. If she wanted something, she was a grown woman; she could ask.

I glanced back at my fitness tracker, which functioned mostly as my watch. It was getting close to eleven, and I *really* needed to be prepping our toast of the day.

I was about to say as much when Dierdre cleared her throat. She threw back her shoulders as if to give herself the illusion of courage and spoke at last.

"I would . . ." She stopped again, chewed on her lip a moment, then restarted. "I would like to rent Owen's old shop."

Of all the things she could have said to me in that moment, this one was at the bottom of the list of what I might have expected. Dierdre was one of the few people who knew about me owning the buildings in town, a secret she actually *had* managed to keep to herself, mostly because telling anyone about it wouldn't hurt me but give me more power than her.

The shoe store next to the plant shop had been vacant for over six months, thanks to the previous owner being locked up for murder and no one in his family stepping in to take over the shop before its lease was up for renewal. And while one or two applicants had requested the space, the council had rejected their requests, deeming their businesses not suitable for Main Street. They'd still found space in town. One was a hemp-themed store, now two doors down from New Moon. The other was a cookie maker, and we had felt that would be too many shops selling baked goods in one stretch. They were now a few steps away from the pet store and had even come to an arrangement to bake and sell dog-friendly biscuits in Charlie's shop. So it had all worked out, and yet the little store remained vacant.

"You want to rent the shop? What for?" She had her own real estate office one block off Main already and couldn't possibly want to pony up the higher rent for a different location, when she should know better than anyone that no one was coming to Main Street to buy houses. Her office was fine where it was.

She shook her head. "No, you see, my nephew is coming to town this summer. Moving here. And I'd like to help him secure a space for his business before he arrives. In speaking to Mountain View, they told me all rental approvals would need to come from their CEO." She gave me a meaningful look, or at least her eyebrows did from over the sunglasses.

"Well, I'm not going to agree until I see a business plan, but what kind of shop would he be opening?"

"He makes soaps and candles, all using natural ingredients, most sourced locally." She whipped out her phone the moment I sounded even remotely interested and handed it to me. I was moderately surprised Dierdre knew what Instagram was, but lo and behold, here was her nephew's page.

Briar and Pine Candle Co.

Their social media was tidy and aesthetic, and they had a huge number of followers. The products all looked cute and well packaged, and while New Moon sold candles, they didn't have anything quite like this.

The old shoe store wasn't a gigantic space, but I knew there was a workroom in the back, somewhere that this nephew would have room to make his wares. I also happened to know that the apartment above the shop had recently been vacated and no one had moved in yet.

"This looks really nice, Dierdre. I'm assuming if you're asking me about it, you've already got the approval of the rest of the council." Sort of shady of her to get that before asking me, but it was classic Dierdre.

"Yes, and I can drop off a copy of the business plan at the Earl's Study this afternoon if you'd like to see it."

"Please." It was one thing to look good on social media, but if I was going to rent prime real estate to this nephew sight unseen, I wanted to make sure he wasn't going to close his doors before Christmas came around. We were a pretty tight community here, and vacancies on Main were rare. I wanted to keep it that way. "And I'm sure you know the apartment is available as well." I raised my eyebrow at her. Obviously, as a real estate agent, she would know about all the local rental opportunities.

"Yes. He'll be staying with me when he arrives, and I'll let him make the decisions on where he wants to move, but I will definitely be mentioning that location to him."

"I hear the landlord is very fair." I offered her my hand, and for a second she flinched, like I might be grabbing at her, but when she settled, she shook my hand gratefully, her palm damp and her grip loose.

"Drop that business plan off, and if it all looks good, I'd be more than happy to rent the space to him. It sounds like a lovely business. But if you don't mind, I really need to get back to the store."

Dierdre nodded several times. "Thank you, Phoebe. I appreciate it."

Words I'd never thought I'd hear come my way from the mouth of Dierdre Miller.

Maybe today *was* going to be a good day.

Chapter Thirty-Two

I didn't have any time to dwell on Dierdre's request, or my car accident. Once I got back to the shop, things were already starting to pick up, with Imogen handling a small line of customers. I immediately ducked into the kitchen to get everything ready for lunch.

I cut several loaves of sourdough into slices. Today's offerings were a plain sourdough with ricotta—blended with local honey—slices of prosciutto, and the fresh peaches I'd gotten from the garden center the previous day. It was all topped with fresh black pepper and had the perfect balance of sweet and savory.

I was particularly proud of the ricotta, because I had started making it myself. One night, after a bit too much Food Network and just the right amount of pinot gris, I'd ordered myself a cheese-making kit off the internet. I'd learned two things very quickly after it arrived: cheese making required a massive amount of high-fat milk, and the flavor of fresh-made cheese was entirely worth the effort.

First I'd tried mozzarella, then had middling results with homemade burrata—I couldn't stretch the mozza thin enough to make the little cheese bags that the fresh curd went into—but I really found my stride with ricotta. So once or twice a week I'd pick up some near-expiry milk and make a new batch of it to serve with our toast.

The ricotta was always a sell-out favorite, especially when people realized the cheese was homemade. I wasn't sure what it was, but adding *homemade* to the description of a typically store-bought ingredient made people go wild for it.

The other option was the newly-perfected cheddar-and-jalapeño loaf, with big chunks of cheddar cheese and slices of pickled jalapeño baked right into the bread. Today we were topping it with thinly sliced turkey and fresh tomato layered with slices of Monterey Jack cheese, which I melted by putting the whole thing under the broiler for a couple of minutes. I had a little bit of the bacon tomato jam left from earlier in the week, so I'd probably top it with a dollop of that as long as it lasted.

The kitchen over lunch smelled incredible from the aroma of toasted bread, melting cheese, and the sweet perfection of sliced tomato. At this point I almost believed fresh black pepper could replace any perfume on the market as my favorite smell.

We whipped through lunch, completely selling out of both options, save for one slice of each, which I'd split in half so Imogen and I could have them. The glass case where we kept our pastries was picked through by one o'clock, with only a few sourdough scones and eclairs left to show.

My featured tea of the day was a lemon, blackberry, and vanilla mix we called Sweet Brambleberry, and the jar was nearly empty. Considering that had been my very first invention on my own and not one of Eudora's recipes, I felt a gleam of pride in my chest that it was so popular.

With traffic slowing down and only me, Imogen, and Mr. Loughery in the shop now, I brought out the plates of leftover toast and put half a slice of each on them, offering one to Imogen. We sat side by side at the counter, very delicately stuffing our faces to appease our rumbling bellies after such a busy ninety minutes.

As we ate, I told her a little about the events of the weekend. She already knew about the car accident. I'd had to explain that so she wouldn't freak out when she saw the car today, but I hadn't told her about what I'd found in Barneswood or what we'd seen at the funeral. I wrapped up by telling her about Amy's theory that Keely had sold all of the Weatherly goods to make quick cash.

Imogen chewed her ricotta toast thoughtfully, waiting until she was done before speaking. "I don't know, Phoebs. Selling a multi-million-dollar estate when you know perfectly well the dude had family members strikes me as high-key petty. Like, that's the sort of thing you do to *hurt* someone, not to make a quick buck. You saw how much individual items were going for in that sale, right? I mean, I wasn't there, but you paid over two grand just for the books. I'm betting the art alone was worth thousands. If she just needed to pay a hospital bill or help someone in her family, she didn't need to go so hard. Selling everything feels super intentional, like she wanted to hurt the remaining Weatherlys. But maybe that's just me. My auntie Jasmine literally sold my uncle Waylon's prize Buick on Craigslist for like fifty bucks after he messed around on her." Imogen shrugged. "It just doesn't seem like it's *only* about the money, if you ask me."

"I don't know what to think, honestly. I've seen the car Keely drives, and her designer clothes; it doesn't seem like she or her family are hurting for money."

"Well, you know rich people. They spend and spend to make everyone know they're rich, but usually they're doing it on credit. That'll catch up to you eventually."

As someone who had managed to get myself wildly into debt on the first credit card I'd ever received because I was eighteen and no one explained what interest was, I definitely knew the pitfalls of credit.

"Wonder if that Franny girl would tell you how much money the estate sale made." Imogen pondered. "Might be interesting to find out how much cash Keely pocketed after the event, even though it was interrupted."

I hadn't considered leveraging my earlier conversation with Franny that way. But we had gotten along pretty well when Rich and I came to visit, and she *had* mentioned that she was now working on the accounting for the company her dad owned. I wondered if a little casual conversation and questioning might get me the information.

"You're kind of a genius," I told Imogen.

"I'm also drop-dead gorgeous, but no one likes to give you credit for being the whole package." She winked at me. "Maybe if I could make food like this, someone would finally marry me." She took another bite of her toast, making a happy little *mmm* sound.

"I've tried it," I reminded her. "I'd rather have the toast."

Chapter
Thirty-Three

I decided to wait until the end of my shift to call Franny, hoping it would also be nearing the end of her day and she might welcome a chat more readily. I knew that if her job was anything like my old desk jobs had been, she would probably relish an excuse to take a short break from her work and help the clock hands get to five a little faster.

I'd looked up the phone number for her father's estate sale business online and tucked myself into the office at the back of the Earl's Study for a little privacy. I could have gone home, but by the time I got there it might have been *too* close to five o'clock and I'd have risked missing her altogether.

The line rang, and a chipper voice picked up. "New Again Estate Sales, where everything old is new again to us, Angie speaking, how can I help you?"

The brightness of her voice could have knocked me off my feet, it was so staggering. Who had that much energy left in them after four o'clock? "Hi, Angie, do you think I could speak to Franny?"

"Oh, sure thing, hon. Mind if I ask who's calling?" Her voice had a decidedly midwestern twang, the dead giveaway being her free-wheeling use of the phrase *hon*.

"My name is Phoebe Winchester. She and I spoke at the Weatherly estate."

"Oh, Ms. Winchester. I believe we have a lot to coordinate shipping to you. Franny handles our accounting, but Bernie is actually responsible for shipping and delivery. I could pass you over to him in a jiff."

While I certainly *did* want Bernie's help coordinating the delivery of all my new books, that couldn't deter me from my main focus. "I do want to talk to Franny first. Maybe I could get her to transfer me to Bernie after."

"You betcha, hon. If she has any problems with the phone, you call me right back and I'll get you taken care of, okay?"

Bless her heart, Angie seemed to care considerably more about getting me connected to the right people than wondering why I was calling. And bonus points for me: it seemed like I might get to kill two birds with one stone on this call. Hurray!

After a few rings to announce my call was being transferred, a familiar voice picked up. "Hello?"

"Hi, Franny, it's Phoebe? We spoke the other day at your house."

"Oh, yes. Hi."

"I know we talked a little about Madeline before, but I actually had a different question today, and since you're the accounting whiz at your company, I figured you would be the best person to talk to about it." This wasn't entirely untrue; her accounting experience would help in terms of what she knew about the funds of the sale, but buttering her up wouldn't hurt either.

"Oh!" Her voice brightened a little, the nervous energy changing to something different, maybe excitement. "Oh, sure, if it's accounting related, I'm your gal. I was worried you were going to ask me more questions about Madeline's death, and after the funeral this weekend, I'm just not ready to talk about that more." She sniffled, and I was terrified I was going to set her off in tears again, so I quickly changed the subject.

"I recently inherited my aunt's estate, her business, her house, and while I'm probably going to keep a lot of it, I sort of wondered how an estate sale would work if I wanted to get rid of quite a few things at once."

"Well, the event you attended at the Weatherly estate was a hybrid sale that was a combination of a standard estate sale and an estate auction. Because of the high value of some of the items in that case, it was deemed worthwhile to offer the auction element to help bundle together certain things to ensure they were all taken. Like your books! By bundling the different units of books, we were able to guarantee that everything would be sold in one lot rather than bits here and there that might need to be taken care of later."

"You mean that it guarantees that the person asking for the auction doesn't need to figure out what to do with the leftover items?"

"Yes, that's right. A more standard estate sale is basically a fancier version of a garage sale. Items are labeled with a specific price, and while bartering sometimes works—if the seller is open to it—you're pretty much expected to pay the asking price. This is great for things like vintage shoes and clothing, art, jewelry, and all that, where people are more inclined to want certain pieces rather than an expensive lot. Which do you think would work best for your aunt's place?"

I'd already forgotten my little fib that I'd used to get this conversation going. "Her place is big, but not as fancy as the Weatherly place, that's for sure. Probably an estate sale, if I decide to go ahead with it. Out of curiosity, if you don't mind me asking, how much money does an estate sale make usually? Like the Weatherly sale, for example."

"It really does depend on the home and the items. We've had small homes, but the former owners were collectors of expensive designer clothing and handbags. Because luxury items actually tend to gain value, a situation like that is different from someone whose loved one was just a bit of a clotheshorse, you know?"

I made a noise of agreement, hoping she'd continue.

"Without naming names, let me look at some of our more recent sales. Oh, here's one near you. You're in Raven Creek, right? Not the same town but nearby. Auction on the full goods of the home made the family about fifty-five thousand dollars. And that was pretty run-of-the-mill. Lots of cool vintage stuff, which helped a lot, but nothing too wildly special. A smaller bungalow in your town made the owners about twenty thousand; definitely less stuff there, but she had a few neat art pieces. Something like the Weatherly estate is much different. When Madeline and I initially reviewed the contents, we estimated that the finished sale would yield about ten million in profits."

I almost choked on the tea I had taken a sip of. "I *beg* your pardon," I coughed out. "Did you say *ten million*? Like, U.S. dollars?"

Franny laughed. "We don't usually take payment in Canadian dollars or that weird crypto stuff, so yes. Good old-fashioned American dollars. Ten million. Now, that's obviously not quite what the sale made, seeing as we only got through a handful of the big lots before . . . well, before things had to be stopped. But because Mr. Weatherly had a half dozen antique cars, some really valuable art, and some other unique things, we believed the contents of the estate to be worth roughly that. Might have gone for more, depending. There was a very small Rothko painting in his art collection; that alone was priced out at a half million, and only that cheap because it was one of his earlier works, and they're simply not as valuable on the market."

I was somewhat surprised, and more than a little impressed, by Franny's incredible knowledge. Had she not been so browbeaten by

Madeline, she probably would have gone on to be an exceptional sales lead.

"How much *did* the Weatherly sale make?" I asked.

"I probably shouldn't say . . ." She paused briefly, considering. I knew it wouldn't take much to push her over the edge and get her to spill. "You know, since we're not yet finished with the sale. The group responsible is still hoping to try again with selling the rest before they put the house on the market. I think the only thing holding them back is the . . . the murder investigation."

Once again, her voice trembled, and I knew it was only a matter of time before the tears began to fall.

"They obviously thought it was worth it to them, if the first attempt went so well."

Franny gathered herself, audibly clearing her throat. "Yes, well. We did make about three million that afternoon alone. Some private bidders were in on the larger items before the afternoon in-person auction began. Many of the cars were sold as well as some more select art pieces." She was back to sounding proud again, which made me wonder for the first time how much commission New Again took home on these sales. It had to be pretty good.

I wondered how much of that Madeline was supposed to have gotten.

Something else Franny had said came bubbling back up to the surface of my mind, and I needed her to clarify. "Franny, you said the *group* that was running the sale. I was under the impression that Mr. Weatherly's estate was solely owned by his assistant?"

"How did you know that?" she asked.

"Oh, I think one of the detectives might have mentioned it to me; I can't remember exactly." Not the best on-my-feet lying I'd ever done. "But is that not the case? Is she not the one requesting the sale?"

"I don't know much about the logistics—I just handled the day-to-day stuff—so she might have outsourced the handling to a different group. It's not that uncommon when people unexpectedly inherit an estate. As I'm sure you know."

She wasn't wrong; I'd let Eudora's lawyers handle almost everything when she died. I didn't know what questions to ask, what to look for, and I certainly hadn't been expecting all the responsibility that went along with being the primary beneficiary of my aunt's estate.

"Yeah, it's a lot. I guess that begs the question, what group *is* handling it?" I realized this might sound too nosy, so I quickly added, "In case they specialize in things like helping with estates and whatnot."

I could hear her typing something, then she said, "They're called Setting Sun Corp, but it looks like they're based out of Fiji. Not sure how much that'll help locally." If it was possible to hear someone shrug their shoulders over the phone, she did it then.

I quickly jotted down the company name. "Thank you so much, Franny. You've been such a huge help."

"You let us know if you want to arrange something for your aunt's estate, okay? We love working out your way. There's this incredible little bakery on Main Street my dad can't get enough of."

"Sugarplum Fairy," I enthused, proud of Amy for her popularity. "Yeah, it's the best. And I will let you know. Could you do me one more big favor?"

"Sure, what is it?"

"Can you transfer me to Bernie?"

Chapter Thirty-Four

B ernie was less enthusiastic about an end-of-day call than Franny had been but was still kind enough to help lock down a day for delivery. The books would arrive on Friday at six o'clock. The weekly Knit and Sip crew was going to have to muddle through with stacks of boxes being brought in around them.

Normally I wouldn't have dreamed of scheduling the delivery for a Friday, but I had a plan in mind. If I could convince—or bribe— Imogen and Daphne to work a little overtime over the weekend, I was positive we could digitize our catalog, starting with the new books, which would give me the base inventory information I needed to look into getting the website up and running.

That way, people in town could email me about preorder items they wanted or simply check online to see if a used book they were keen on was in stock. The system might not be perfect, and I might be out of my mind to think it could be running in two days, but it was worth a shot.

We were about to get into the peak months of tourist season. If I didn't do this now, while our weekends were still nice and slow, we'd be waiting until fall before I got another chance.

I suspected that the promise of some overtime pay, some lattes from Amy, and a few mega-sized pizzas would go a long way toward getting them to help me out. There were literally thousands of books in the collection I'd purchased: three thousand eight hundred and forty-three, to be exact. Bernie had told me. It was going to take up all the free space in our aisles and overflow into my storage downstairs. We would be able to actually get out only a few hundred at a time.

My plan was *not* to do all three thousand plus at once, especially since we wouldn't be able to shelve them. My plan was to catalog everything that was currently on the floor, then add new items to the catalog as we pulled them from the basement storage. That way no one would try to order a book that we had no clue where to find, but we could keep up with new additions.

I hoped that by doing a few new books every week, alongside our standard delivery of new releases, we could manage to keep up with everything.

Perhaps it was a lofty goal, but between the three of us over two days without interruptions, I thought we could probably manage.

I'd spend the rest of the week getting the software set up, and then we could see how easy it was to get books entered. After ensuring I was still getting the books from the auction, I'd ordered a few barcode scanners that were supposed to tie in to the software. I had one that I'd received as part of buying the software initially, and with express shipping, the other two should arrive by Friday as well.

Three people going through the store, cute little barcode scanners going *beep, beep, beep* . . . I had high hopes. Of course, the problem with used books was that often the barcodes didn't read properly—giving the wrong title when scanned—or they were so old they didn't have barcodes at all. In those instances, we would need to scan everything manually, and that's where things would start to eat up more of our time.

I returned to the front of the store, where Imogen was sitting on her stool reading, a cup of tea in a mint-green Earl's Study mug next to her.

"I like the mug advertising," I said.

"Gotta rep the brand." She took a sip, smiling at me.

I had kept with Eudora's traditions in terms of staff benefits. Aside from the usual vacation days and medical that I offered Imogen, there were the discounts. Each employee got one free cup of tea a day, and then any other snacks or tea refills were fifty percent off. If they wanted to purchase tea to take home, that was a forty percent discount, as were used books. New books, simply because of the cost-to-markup ratio, I could only offer a scant twenty percent discount on, but no one seemed to mind. I also didn't care much if Imogen or Daphne borrowed one of the used books to read at the counter during their shift.

The only place I was a bit of a stickler was with new releases, and that was only because our customers expected those books to be *new*. Crisp, unbroken spines, pages untouched by anyone before them. I could understand that, so staff had to purchase a new release if they wanted to read it.

I think as rules went, it was pretty fair all around, and no one had yet complained. Especially since I let them take home any baked items we didn't sell during the shift. There usually weren't a ton, but who was going to turn up their nose at a free fruit tart or Danish?

Likewise, I'd given both Imogen and Daphne freebies of our travel mugs when they arrived, so they each had a ceramic version to use in the store—or at home, I didn't specify—and a travel version.

The ceramic ones were the test prints I'd ordered. I still hadn't committed to getting a batch for the store yet. I wanted to see how the travel mugs sold first.

Imogen left hers at the store, washing it each day and reusing it. I knew she used her travel mug because she was often carrying it when she came in and she left it in the office or kitchen, but the ceramic one was what she used throughout the day.

I preferred the travel mug only because it held more tea.

"What are you reading?" I snooped closer, tilting my head to the side to see the cover of her book.

She lifted it so I could better see a cute, illustrated cover depicting a Black couple embracing. "I'm very deeply in my rom-com phase at the moment and do not want to hear a single word about it." She winked at me.

Romances weren't usually my thing, but we'd sold a metric ton of the book she was holding, and it was definitely making the rounds on social media.

"You'll hear no complaints from me."

"These are really cute. Every one is about a different sister, and they're all plus sized." She patted her own thigh. "Love to see it."

I laughed. "Let me guess, they're all a different main trope, like friends-to-lovers, brother's best friend, fake dating—are those the big three?"

"I can't believe you call yourself a bookseller, forgetting enemies-to-lovers that way." Imogen rolled her eyes in faux disgust. "The disrespect."

"Never again, I promise."

"Shouldn't you be going home?" She set the book back down, open to the place she had left off so as not to forget her place. In the background, I could hear Mr. Loughery snoring. He'd been awake much of the day, so I wasn't too surprised he'd nodded off now. It did mean I wouldn't have a chance to talk to him about the cat I'd seen in Barneswood, though. I'd have to wait until tomorrow.

"I'm just going to knead the sourdough one more time before I go so it rises overnight. Then I promise I'll stop cramping your style."

Since I was already here, I figured I'd get a head start on the morning—especially since I'd be biking in—and get the Earl Grey shortbread prepped as well. The dough took almost no time to get ready, but chilling it overnight would save me that step in the morning. It didn't need a ton of time to cool down, which was why I rarely bothered with doing it the day before, but why not?

As I was slipping the dough into the fridge, I noticed all the berries I'd bought the previous week to try out my iced tea blends. Since iced tea needed time to steep, now was a great time to put two blends together. I filled several tea bags with our Strawberry Fields blend and put them in a pitcher, adding hot water first to really get the most out of the flavor. Once the bags had steeped, I'd fill the pitcher the rest of the way with cold before putting it in the fridge overnight. Then I did the same with our Lemon Meringue blend.

In the morning I'd add the muddled fresh fruit, and we could give them a test drive with our customers. The weather had been so nice lately I expected we'd have strong sales with iced tea, and this would be a perfect opportunity to decide which blends were most popular so we could produce bigger quantities over the summer months.

I was excited to see how we could maximize our foot traffic in the summer as the tourist season really picked up. There were two main seasons in Raven Creek: summer and winter. During the summer, it was a mix of the nearby bird-watching opportunities and the incredible hiking trails. Raven Creek was smack-dab in the middle of some of the most scenic inland hiking in the state, and it brought visitors from hundreds of miles away who wanted something a little different from the metropolitan splash of Seattle.

In the winter, it was our proximity to skiing that helped fill our bed-and-breakfasts and gave those not interested in the slopes a place to spend the day shopping and sightseeing in the nearby areas. We were a stone's throw from Liberty, an old mining ghost town, and the adorable Bavarian-inspired town of Leavenworth was less than an hour away.

Raven Creek's mishmash of European aesthetics and its obsession with seasonal decorating also meant we got people year-round who just wanted to stop in for a day trip. Seattle was just a little over two hours away. Snoqualmie Falls was ninety minutes. We might not be *the* destination, but tourists found us and loved us year after year.

Raven Creek was adorable and picturesque, with the mountains for a backdrop and a local commitment to being a little too invested in the holidays making us somewhat famous, but not so famous that we were overrun like Leavenworth sometimes could be.

It was the perfect balance of busy year-round and slightly unknown that made our town council perfectly happy. They'd just recently added a tag line to the *Welcome to Raven Creek* sign that read *The undiscovered jewel of Washington.*

I'd seen the way things perked up around here close to holidays. Halloween and Christmas had both been a whirlwind, as Imogen explained the expectations of Main Street businesses and even what the local homeowners were encouraged to do. Suddenly the dozens of boxes of seasonal decorations I'd found in Eudora's basement made a lot more sense.

It wasn't just that she enjoyed decorating for the holidays—she did—but it was actually a matter of town pride.

I'd done my best, but Halloween had been lackluster, and Christmas had been pretty good, but I knew I could do better after I'd seen how others in town went all in.

At least over summer it was less about themed decor and more about embracing the season. I already had visions in my head of setting up a *Beach Reads* window display and adding cute beach-themed items inside to really sell it. I still had a couple of months to plan that, as we were currently featuring an *April Showers Bring May Flowers* theme.

Imogen and I had worked hard on the window display, with watering cans hung from the ceiling and fake water made of iridescent cellophane. We'd crafted giant paper flowers, each one with a book in it.

The display had been incredibly popular on Instagram; Daphne had shared a few choice photos with me that we'd been able to reshare on our own page. I was eternally grateful to Daphne for her willingness to take on the social media aspects of the job, because while I did *use* most social media, being an elder millennial, I didn't really know how to run a successful brand for my own business.

Daphne seemed to live for it, so I'd let her go to town.

Some of the other shops on Main had equally creative ideas. Amy's windows were decorated with floating macarons the size of your head in soft pastel shades. She'd attached holographic wings to each of them, making it look as if the macrons were actually little fairies. Next door at the Green Thumb, they had built a lattice forming the letters *SPRING* and had wrapped the whole thing in a variety of climbing plants so the word was spelled out in leaves and dainty little flowers.

I loved how seriously this town took themes.

With the tea steeping in our fridge, the shortbread ready to go for the morning, and a whopping six loaves of sourdough rising in their bowls on the counter, I had to admit it was time to head home for the day. I'd also completely forgotten that I'd be schlepping home on foot.

After calling Bob over, I got him into his carrier, and we hit the road. While it wasn't a long walk by any means, I had gotten accustomed to taking the trip either in the car or on my bike. I'd definitely be using the bike tomorrow, with my car in the shop for heaven only knew how long.

A light mist of rain had started to fall, not enough to soak me but more than enough to deter me from making a stop at the grocery store on my way home. My refill of Heavenly Hash ice cream would need to wait for another day.

Bob let out a plaintive howl from his carrier, and at first I thought it was just because he was being a delicate old soul about getting a little bit damp. Except he continued to do it as we made our way up the hill toward Lane End House.

It wasn't until I was at the end of my block that I realized with a cold sense of dread what had Bob so up in arms. Or paws.

There was an all-too-familiar black SUV parked outside the front of my house.

Chapter
Thirty-Five

O ne near-death experience in a week was quite enough for me, and I had no intention of continuing the rest of the way to my house.

I turned on my heel, Bob still yowling from my backpack, and literally ran all the way back to Lansing's Grocery Store. Once safely inside, I needed to take a moment to catch my breath, because I wasn't used to running with the added weight of Bob and his bag strapped to my back.

Chandra, the evening cashier, glanced over at me with a quizzical expression. "You all right, Phoebe?"

Chandra was Daphne's older sister and had been the first person to be kind to me when I'd shown up in town on my first day living here. I had never forgotten that, and as a result she maintained a special place in my heart.

"I'm fine," I wheezed, not wanting to spook her. "Just running to avoid the rain."

When she returned to scanning the items of another customer, I whipped out my phone and called Rich. The line rang and rang without answer before being picked up by his voice mail.

"Hi, you've reached Rich Lofting. Sorry I can't take your call at the moment, but please leave a message and I'll get back to you.

If this is in regards to a case, please leave your full name and a contact number. I respond to all requests within two business days. Thanks."

"*Rich*," I whispered, doing a poor job to keep my voice down because of the adrenaline spiking in my veins. "The car. It's the car that tried to run me off the road. It's parked in front of my house. I'm at Lansing's; please call me back."

After I hung up, I waited a few seconds before grudgingly realizing there was someone else I needed to call if Rich wasn't answering. I unlocked my phone and found the saved number for Detective Martin.

This time the line rang only twice before being answered, Detective Martin's smooth voice coming through the other end like a comforting hug. "Ms. Winchester, I hope you're not calling to tell me you're in some kind of trouble." There was laughter in her tone, as if she believed it was entirely impossible that I could have gotten myself bogged down in more drama in only forty-eight hours.

Shows what you know, Detective Martin.

When I didn't answer immediately, she spoke again, this time with genuine concern in her voice. "Phoebe, is everything okay?"

"No, not really," I admitted, then explained what I'd seen on my walk home.

"Stay right where you are. I'm just driving back to Raven Creek from Barneswood right now, and I'm fifteen minutes away. I'm going to call the local PD and send a cruiser over to your house. I'm not kidding, Phoebe, stay where you are."

I nodded, even though she couldn't see me, then said, "I will." I had no intention at all of putting myself in the line of danger, especially not after receiving that text message and what had happened on the highway.

Did this have something to do with my earlier call to Franny?

I had a hard time believing Franny would have ratted me out to someone or that she might be the one involved in trying to hurt me, but it seemed odd that only an hour after I'd gotten off the phone with her, someone had come to my house.

Coincidences could and did happen, but it certainly left me wondering, because it was an awfully *big* coincidence. I'd be sure to mention it to the detective when she called me back.

Leo wasn't at the store, it being toward the end of the day, so I couldn't ask him to let me hide out in his office. Still, no one seemed to mind that I was just pacing around in the produce section, checking my phone every three and a half seconds.

It was while I was checking it for the seven hundredth time that the automatic doors opened with a chime and Rich came through. I spotted him immediately and went to him, letting him wrap his arms awkwardly around me, since I was still wearing the bulky cat backpack.

Bob had stopped complaining the moment we'd gotten inside and to safety. "I just got off the phone with Detective Martin; she said you'd already called her. They have someone over at the house now, but the car peeled off just as they were coming up. They didn't give chase, but there's an APB out for the SUV, and they did manage to get a full license plate."

I let out a little breath, as if surprised, somehow, that the police had been able to get that much. Part of me had believed the SUV would have vanished—maybe they'd seen me running away—and by the time the cops got to the house it would be long gone and I'd look like someone who was making up stories about phantom cars.

But they'd seen it, so I hadn't been imagining it.

"Were they able to get a registration from the license plate?" I asked. "Do they know who it was?"

Rich shook his head. "No, Martin said it's not registered to a person but rather a company."

My already cold blood turned to ice. I was afraid to ask the next question, because I didn't want to be right about the answer, but I still had to know.

"Did she say what the company was called?"

Rich held me at arm's length and gave me an uncertain expression. I could tell he didn't want to share the details with me, but when he saw my face, he sighed and relented. "It's called Setting Sun? They have a registered address in Redmond, and Martin has Kim looking into it right now. Why? Does that ring any bells?"

It certainly did, and all of them sounded like alarms.

Chapter
Thirty-Six

I spent well over an hour in my living room with Rich and Detective Martin explaining what I'd seen when I came up the hill, saying I was certain the SUV had been the same one that had tried to run me off the road, and Martin confirmed it did have the same letters and numbers I'd been able to see in the rain. I also filled them in on my conversation with Franny.

I naturally buried the lede by telling them I'd just been calling to arrange delivery for my lot—which was sort of true—and had happened to be chatting with Franny about the Weatherly sale.

For their part, both Rich and Martin pretended to believe my lie rather than lecturing me about continuing on with the investigation even after I'd been threatened. Of all the things I'd done looking for Madeline's killer, making a phone call was hardly the most dangerous.

"It's a bit odd, though, that Franny would tell me about the name of the company and barely two hours later a car registered to that company is sitting in front of my house," I pointed out, hoping Martin hadn't missed the connection.

"I agree, though we can't necessarily lay blame at this point. We're going to have someone pick up Ms. Houseman and question her about it this evening. Given our initial conversations with her, we don't think she had anything to do with Madeline's death, but it's hard to discount the coincidence in this case. Did you speak to anyone else about what you'd learned?"

"No, I've talked to a few close friends about what happened on the weekend but no one else, and none of them would be involved in threatening me, I'm sure of it."

Martin nodded. "We have no reason to suspect any of your friends. But Phoebe, please listen to me, you need to stop looking into this. No phone calls, no internet searches, no carrier pigeons with harmless questions. This isn't just about you being a pain in the butt, which you can be. It's about your safety. Someone very clearly has their eye on you. Take that seriously."

"Trust me, I am."

"I'm going to have an officer watching your place overnight. I'd prefer it if you didn't go out for any morning runs this week, at least until we know what's going on with that SUV and the company that owns it, okay?"

I nodded. No runs. Doors and windows locked. Police parked outside. I was a prisoner in my own home, but I knew it was for the best. If someone wanted to hurt me, I shouldn't make it easy for them.

Detective Martin excused herself, but Rich lingered. "You know, if it would make you feel any better, I could spend the night." He must have heard the way the words sounded or seen the way my eyebrow went up a tick, because he quickly added, "I could sleep on the couch."

I hated to admit it, because I loved to project the appearance of being a strong independent woman who didn't need a man, but I really didn't want to be alone tonight, and having Rich in the house would do ten times more to make me feel secure than having the police officer outside.

"You know, I think I'd like that. But please, there are eight guest bedrooms in this house, including one on the main floor if you want to be close to the doors. The couch is lovely, but it's terrible for your back if you sleep on it, trust me."

"I would not say no to a real bed. Thank you."

Wanting to distract myself from both the events of the evening and the weird excitement of Rich spending the night, I decided to focus on making us dinner instead.

Rich followed me into the kitchen, taking a seat at the little table while Bob curled up in his bed on the hearth. "Do you want me to start a fire?" Rich asked.

Bob, deciding the question was directed at him, said, "Mrow." He then began purring loudly.

"I'll take that as a yes," Rich declared, and set about putting balled-up newspaper and bits of kindling into the big fireplace that sat between the kitchen and sitting room. With everything stacked up neatly, he used a barbecue lighter to get things started, and soon the kitchen began to heat up and the comforting smell of burning firewood filled the air.

Bob continued to purr, his eyes tightly closed and his paws kneading away happily at his cat bed.

"His Royal Bobness is pleased with your offering," I teased.

"Well, we all live to please Bob."

I rifled through the fridge, trying to determine what to make. I wasn't terribly hungry, but it was smart to have a meal, and I certainly couldn't leave Rich unfed if he was going to play the role of my live-in bodyguard for the evening.

I found some shredded chicken and a jar of alfredo pasta sauce. Perfect. Setting one pot of water to boil, I added a hearty pinch of salt, then in a smaller pot combined the chicken and sauce. With some bow-tie pasta in the salted water, I threw in half a bag of frozen peas so they would melt in the boiling water and seasoned the pasta sauce with some extra garlic powder and my favorite seasoning blend.

The whole meal was simple and easy and got rid of some leftovers in my fridge, but it was comfort food through and through, which I needed and I doubted Rich would argue about.

I strained the pasta and added the sauce right into the larger pot, stirring it all together, then topped it off with some parmesan petals and cracked black pepper.

Dividing the pot into two big pasta bowls, I placed one in front of Rich and put the other at the empty space across from him.

"I think today calls for wine," I declared.

"I wouldn't dream of arguing with you."

I headed around the corner into the sitting room, where I'd put a wine rack, and grabbed the first bottle of red I spotted. I wasn't snobby about wine, so I didn't really know which blend went best with pasta, but I imagined any red would pair nicely with our meal. I cracked it open in the kitchen and poured us each a glass.

As I settled into the seat across from him, we clinked our glasses together and took a sip. The wine was lovely, rich and fruity with a nice aftertaste of blackberry. I couldn't usually taste those fruity notes that the label talked about, so I was delighted to pick up on it. I took another sip and smiled.

"You know, I kept hoping you'd ask me for another date. I didn't think I'd need to almost die to get one." As soon as I said it, I felt embarrassed at being so forward and stared into my pasta, my cheeks turning as red as the wine.

"The only reason I didn't ask you out again was because you said you wanted to take it slow. But we never agreed on what *slow* looked like. I was worried you'd think I was being too pushy."

I looked up at him with surprise. "Wait, *you've* been trying to go slow for me? I didn't want to bug you about it because I didn't want to rush *you*."

Rich laughed, a wonderful, warm sound I could feel all the way down in my tummy that made the house feel full and alive in a way it hadn't for quite some time.

"I guess we're both stupid, then." He grinned and took a sip of his wine. "Though I think I could have done better for a date than this."

I feigned offense. "I'm sorry, is my food not date-worthy?"

He rolled his eyes. "That's not what I meant, and you know it. I meant it would have been nice to be able to take you somewhere special. Somewhere that isn't Sweet Peach's. No shade to those burgers. And we could talk about something other than murder. That would be a good date."

"That *would* be a good date," I agreed.

There was a long pause where neither of us spoke, but we also didn't touch our food. "I'd like to take you on that date," he said finally.

I couldn't keep myself from smiling. This night had been terrible, and I'd been genuinely frightened, but all of that seemed very far away now. With Rich sitting at my kitchen table, asking me out on a real date, I felt like I could jump for joy and that nothing bad in the world could happen to me.

But that was probably just wishful thinking.

Chapter
Thirty-Seven

I tossed and turned for hours that night, distracted by both the murder case and knowing that Rich was sleeping in the spare bedroom on the main floor. I think it had been intended as a chef's quarters at one point, because it was just across the hall from the kitchen, but now it served as a cute little spare bedroom, which would be great if I ever had guests.

Guests who weren't just here to make sure no one killed me in the middle of the night, that is.

Finally, around three in the morning I stopped trying to force myself to sleep and pulled my laptop into bed with me. Bob was happily curled up at the foot of the bed, and aside from giving me a bit of a stink eye when I turned the bedside lamp on, he was unmoved by my insomnia.

I opened a search engine and typed in *Setting Sun Corp*, then adding *Fiji* to the search terms, since Franny had mentioned it. I wasn't sure why Fiji in particular was standing out to me, but it was stuck in my memory nevertheless.

There weren't many results to be found in Google. The company didn't have a website and seemed to be only peripherally mentioned in a handful of business dealings, in PDF files that were too dense with legalese and subsections for me to understand.

I decided to try searching *Setting Sun Corp* and *Keely Morgenstern* to see if there was a connection. I wasn't expecting anything to pop up, but to my surprise, there was a hit. It appeared that about three months earlier, Keely Morgenstern had been added to the board of directors of Setting Sun and given the title of their Redmond office manager.

Well.

That was certainly interesting, wasn't it?

The hair at the back of my neck stood on end. Had it been Keely driving the SUV, and Keely who sent me the text telling me to back off? Perhaps she'd seen me at the funeral and decided I was getting too close.

But it seemed odd that Keely would be responsible for an office in Redmond. We weren't exactly *close* to Redmond, the town that was best known for housing the Microsoft campus. It was easily as far from us as Seattle, and definitely not a commutable drive.

Plus, Keely had a regular day job with the Weatherlys. How could she also be holding such a vital role with another corporation?

Unless her role with Setting Sun was in title only.

I continued to poke around, trying to figure out what Setting Sun did and who aside from Keely was involved, but I didn't recognize any of the other names that came up with my searches, and there was nothing to indicate what their business was for.

Since I wasn't a genius hacker, I couldn't dig into bank records or look at what they might be up to; my skills were strictly limited to Google.

I sat back in bed and let out a long sigh, closing my laptop and setting it down next to me. The pieces of the puzzle were all there, and I felt certain I could put them together, but it just wasn't happening.

I replayed the argument I'd overheard Madeline having right before she died.

"*That wasn't our agreement at all. Now you listen to me, we had an understanding, and you can't go back on that now . . . Don't you dare threaten me. I made you. No, this isn't over. You're going to be sorry.*"

I made you.

I *made* you.

What did that mean? At the time I'd assumed it was someone she'd helped professionally, but now I wasn't so sure.

For a moment I wondered if maybe Madeline had been speaking to Keely, if perhaps the conversation had something to do with Keely inheriting the estate. My mind created all sorts of scenarios in which Madeline and Keely had been working hand in hand, but then I remembered the conversation I'd overheard in the Barneswood police station parking lot.

Keely, standing next to her car, angrily speaking to someone about her annoyance at being called to the station so many times.

"*I don't think it's fair, and it's really starting to make me wonder if the money was worth all this trouble . . . Well, you're not the one being questioned in a murder, are you? No, I didn't think so. What did she even say to you on the phone that day? She was absolutely livid with me before the auction started, threatening to call the whole thing off.*"

No, it hadn't been Keely on the phone.

But she and Madeline *had* been planning something together, hadn't they? Keely had been the one to hire Madeline, and Keely was on the board of Setting Sun, the mysterious company that had paid for the estate sale and were apparently the ones reaping the financial gain of millions.

So who was the third person?

The person Keely had been arguing with on the phone was the same person Madeline had argued with right before she died. And if what Keely was saying was true, there was a chance Madeline had been trying to back out of some agreed-upon plan.

I made you.

The words bounced around in my mind, and I pulled my laptop out again, staring at a blank search engine screen.

I made you.

What did that mean?

I searched *Setting Sun Corp* and *Madeline Morrow*, this time *truly* not expecting to find anything. Again, to my shock, there was a hit. In a Washington company registry database, Madeline was listed as the cosigner for Setting Sun Corp. The cosignee was a name I'd seen on the other documents that had popped up: W. Bruckner. No first name, just the initial.

I searched the name along with Setting Sun and found only the original documents I'd found in my first search. No images, no social media presence. Nothing useful.

I tried to search Madeline's and Keely's names together, wondering if perhaps they'd been friends in college or earlier, but nothing came up that put them together. Yet it was obvious they'd known each other before Keely hired the estate company Madeline worked for.

If anything, I was even more frustrated now than I'd been an hour ago when I started searching. I felt achingly close to the truth, but the one missing piece that I needed was evading me.

Who was W. Bruckner?

Chapter
Thirty-Eight

I woke early to find that Rich was still snoring softly in his room. I had hoped to be able to chat with him about my late-night Googling, and likewise hoped he wouldn't get too mad at me about it, but I didn't want to wake him up.

I dressed for work and left a note pinned to the door of the guest room advising Rich of where the coffee was and the toaster if he wanted to heat up some sourdough slices. I told him I'd be at work and wouldn't take any detours on the way.

I would have hung around longer, but the shop needed to be opened regardless of whether or not I was having a crisis, or whether there was a handsome man sleeping in my house. I could have called Imogen in early or told Amy I wouldn't be picking up the baked goods, but I honestly needed the distraction of a normal workday.

Amy was waiting for me when I walked into her café. I'd locked my bike up in front of the Earl's Study, and while I had debated whether or not to bring Bob along with me for the day, I'd ultimately decided I'd feel more comfortable having him in the store, especially if the SUV driver knew where I lived.

I would never forgive myself if I left him at home and something happened to him.

So he was happily in the store, and I was ready to collect some pastries.

Since I knew Amy would be able to sense my mood the second she looked at me, I immediately launched into my story, explaining what had happened the night before.

"Oh, Phoebe, that's so scary. You know I have a spare bedroom if you need somewhere to stay. Bob is welcome too." She patted my hand like a doting grandmother might, and I appreciated it.

There was something about Amy that made me relax. It was a maternal quality, but also a general loveliness that made her a natural person to gravitate toward when something was going wrong in your life.

I only wished she had the ability to answer my questions about the murder, and the mystery surrounding it.

I considered picking her brain about what I'd learned last night while searching for information on Setting Sun but decided against it. There were too many coincidences with the driver of the SUV knowing when I got close to information, and I didn't need to put Amy or anyone else at risk. At this point, I felt comfortable sharing information only with the detectives and with Rich, because I knew they were all professionally trained to take care of themselves.

"I appreciate the offer, Amy, and if it gets any worse, I'll definitely take you up on it. But right now, Rich is keeping an eye on things, and the police have someone at my house, so I think it's probably pretty safe."

"Okay, well, it's an open offer. You come anytime. Promise me."

"Absolutely." I knew if I needed it, I would get similar offers from Imogen and Honey, even though they both lived in one-bedroom homes. Honey obviously had her little apartment, and Imogen had an adorable bungalow a few blocks from the shop. Neither was ideally suited to long-term guests, but I had no doubt they'd both take me in in a heartbeat if necessary.

Was this what it felt like to have real friends? I still wasn't used to it. When I'd been married, all *our* friends had been Blaine's friends, and so he kept them in the divorce, leaving me in the awkward situation of trying to find new friends as an adult.

As it turned out, moving across the state was the key.

Also, having your aunt give your first impression for you didn't hurt. Everyone had loved Eudora, so by extension they loved me.

Amy handed over my boxes and my morning latte, and I headed back to the shop, grateful for the caffeine and also thrilled with my former self for doing so much prep work the night before. I used my time making the shortbread to settle myself in for the morning and get in the right headspace for the day. For Christmas, Honey had gifted me a gorgeous marble mortar-and-pestle set. I think she had anticipated I might use it at home to help my witchy practice, but I'd found better uses for it at the store. Before, I would use a coffee grinder to finely mince tea blends whenever I used them in baking, and while it was fine, it felt a bit impersonal. So after I'd meticulously shaped the cookies—spending a bit more time that was truly necessary—and putting them in the oven to bake, I set about prepping more of the mixture that went into them.

The Earl Grey shortbread used one very obvious ingredient: Earl Grey tea. Specifically, Eudora's signature summer Earl Grey with strawberry. Because I made these cookies every single day, I'd learned it was beneficial to preblend the tea so I didn't need to do it each morning. There was a jar on the counter—nearly empty right now—that contained the blended tea mixture so I could easily add it to the shortbread dough.

I ducked out front, making sure I had my timer with me so I wouldn't leave the current batch in the oven too long, and grabbed a canister of the tea from the shelf, bringing it back into the kitchen with me. I poured a generous scoop into the mortar and pestle, then set about grinding it into a fine powder. The cookies benefited from having decently-sized flecks of the tea in them, but nothing so big it might get suck in your teeth.

While the coffee grinder had been faster, there was something soothing to me about the act of grinding it by hand, feeling the smooth scrape of marble on marble and having to put some actual elbow grease into the process. Some people meditate; I smashed up tea. It also made me think about what Honey had said about Eudora, and how her magic was most powerful when she used her intentions to help others. Even though the Earl Grey I used wasn't a magical blend, I liked to imagine everyone who would taste these cookies would have a better day afterward.

The buzzer went off just as I was pouring the tea into its jar, and I put the sourdough loaves into the oven to begin baking. It was early, but it would take all morning, since I could do only two at a time.

I muddled some fresh strawberries and blended them with a local honey before adding the whole concoction to the Strawberry Fields tea, then sliced up a lemon and added that along with more honey and fresh mint to the Lemon Meringue tea. I jotted them down as iced tea specials on a little blackboard we kept out front, pricing them a little higher than our hot steeped tea because of all the fresh add-ins.

When eight o'clock rolled around, I was a little nervous to open the shop, wondering if my attacker might show up at my workplace. But with Amy next door and the Tanakas in the plant shop on the other side, I highly doubted anyone would try anything funny.

I did double- and triple-check the back door lock before we opened for the day, though, just to give myself a little peace of mind. As it turned out, none of my worry was necessary, and the morning went by quietly, with only a handful of customers. Mr. Loughery arrived shortly before Imogen did, and I noticed him sneak a handful of cat treats out of his pocket and set them on the arm of Bob's chair.

My heart melted.

As soon as Imogen arrived, I headed into the bookstore side of the shop and sat down on the arm of Bob's chair so as not to disturb him. "Mr. Loughery?"

"Oh, Phoebe, you can call me Norman. I think after all this time we can be on a first-name basis."

It felt weirdly informal to call Mr. Loughery by his first name, and I would certainly never *think* of him as a Norman, but if it would make him happy, I'd do it. "Norman, I couldn't help but notice how well you and Bob seem to get along, and you really light up when you're around him."

The old man smiled. "I hope you don't mind me sneaking him some treats. I should have asked first."

I shook my head. "Please, it's not a problem, though I have to confess Bob's vet has implied he is a little overweight, so maybe we should collectively scale back on how *many* treats we give him."

Mr. Loughery chuckled. "I promise, only once in a while. He's my buddy, though. Need to treat him right."

"That's actually sort of what I'm curious about. Have you ever considered getting a cat of your own?"

Mr. Loughery glanced over at Bob, who was loudly chowing down on the little brown snacks he'd been given. "I hadn't before, but spending so much time with him every day, I started noticing that it gets pretty lonely when I get home again at night." He looked wistful, and I knew I had my in.

I told him about the trip Rich and I had taken to Barneswood and my intention of opening a satellite branch of the shelter in my shop—something that was a sure thing now that I had Dierdre's vote—and how I'd seen Frodo the tuxedo cat and immediately thought of Mr. Loughery.

I held out my phone, showing him a picture of the sweet boy, and his expression told me it was immediately love.

"He's been in the shelter for over five years. Apparently black-and-white cats have some of the hardest times getting adopted, especially adult ones."

"Well, he certainly looks lovely, but are you sure I'm not too old to adopt?"

I made a *psh* noise at him. "Norman, come on. You get out every single day and come here like clockwork. That's not the life of a man on his deathbed. I think you and Frodo could spend a lot of very happy years together. And look, if we want to get morbid, I'll promise you this. If anything happens to you, I'll adopt him myself, okay?"

I suspected this was a reason that many seniors talked themselves out of getting a pet late in their lives. They didn't want to saddle anyone with the burden of caring for the pet when they were gone.

I truly believed Mr. Loughery would be around for a long while to come, but I wanted him to know that Frodo would be cared for in the unlikely event he did pass.

Mr. Loughery took my phone again, lowering his glasses to squint at the screen. "And his name is Frodo. My kids just loved reading *The Hobbit* and *Lord of the Rings* when they were younger."

"Seems to me like this match was written in the stars."

He handed back the phone. "You let me think about it, okay? By the time you next go to Barneswood, I'll have an answer for you." As he sat back in his chair he mumbled, "Five years in a shelter." Then he looked over at Bob. "You don't know how lucky you've got it, do you, Bob?"

The orange tabby licked his lips, having devoured all of his snacks, and purred loudly at the pair of us.

"I'll bug you again, I promise," I said.

"Please do."

Chapter
Thirty-Nine

After Imogen and I got through the lunch rush, I got a call from Al over at the autobody shop. He had apparently been able to source a door from the local scrapyard, and while my car would look a bit like Frankenstein's monster for the next couple of weeks, it was back in driving condition.

Leaving Imogen, I walked to the garage, paid an eye-popping amount of money for my now-hideous car, and drove it immediately back to the Earl's Study.

The new door was an orange-brown color that clashed horribly with my navy-blue car, but at least I could close and lock it, and while it looked dreadful, it didn't look like someone had just driven into it.

I parked it behind the store, because otherwise it was sure to stir up commentary from some of our regulars. I'd need to wrestle my bike into the back seat on my way home, but I was relieved to have gotten the car back so quickly.

I decided not to stay late at the shop, as I was ready to head back to my place and see if Rich might be there. I didn't think he would have waited around all day, but I figured he might have come back if his schedule permitted it.

When I parked in front of the house, all the lights were off inside. The police cruiser was still parked on the opposite side of the lane, with a different driver from the one who had been there this morning.

I waved at him, and he gave me a nod as I carried Bob inside the house, deciding I'd fight with the bike in the morning. Twice in one day was simply too much effort for one person to be expected to give.

There was no sign of Rich inside the house, and he hadn't sent me a text all day, but in the kitchen there was a mug and plate in the drain rack, indicating he had enjoyed a little breakfast, which made me smile.

Since he wasn't here for me to bounce ideas off regarding the information I'd received the night before, I grabbed my laptop from my bedroom and settled in on the couch. My initial plan was to do more Googling, but at this point I was completely out of ideas.

Except one.

I opened up Instagram and searched for Keely Morgenstern's account. It was a public profile, with over ten thousand followers, and a quick scroll through her photos showed a very curated life, one of immense privilege. She showed off fancy designer handbags and shoes, all before inheriting the wealth of Mr. Weatherly.

But there were no photos of her and Madeline. No photos of her and the mysterious W. Bruckner—at least not based on the profiles she tagged—and nothing that gave me any hint as to what was actually happening.

I noticed the little bubble around her profile picture was a different color, which indicated she had a temporary post in her Stories. I clicked on it, and it showed her posing in front of the entrance to La Bella Cantina, a restaurant in a little town called Early, between Raven Creek and Barneswood. Early was teeny tiny, but La Bella

Cantina had once been featured on a Netflix food documentary, so people queued up for hours to get a chance to eat there.

It was only a twenty-minute drive from my house.

A voice in the back of my mind screamed at me that this was a terrible idea and I absolutely shouldn't do what I was thinking of doing, but another voice sweetly asked, *What could go wrong at a public place?*

That voice had a point. It was stupid to confront Keely, but it wasn't like she could do something to hurt me if we were at a restaurant, right?

Right?

I decided to throw caution to the wind and take a chance; otherwise it was just going to drive me crazy, and I needed to know the truth. Whatever version of it she was willing to tell me.

Outside the house, the officer rolled down his window when he saw me come out again. "Everything all right, Ms. Winchester?"

"Yeah, all good. I just need to run to grab my dinner. I won't be gone long."

He mulled this over briefly, but obviously there was no regulation restricting me to the house, and he had no real choice but to let me leave.

Twenty minutes later I was parked in front of La Bella Cantina, surprised that there wasn't an enormous line snaking out the door for once. It was getting toward the end of their day, so maybe people had given up on their chances and headed home. I walked into the restaurant, which was brightly colored inside with a bold Day of the Dead theme, including cheerfully painted skulls everywhere, and headed right up to the hostess stand.

"For one?" She glanced behind me as if worried she might be insulting me by asking.

"Actually, I'm looking for a friend. Do you mind if I peek inside quickly?"

"Oh sure, go ahead." The hostess seemed a little relieved to not saddle a server with a brand new one-top at the very end of the night.

I headed past the stand and glanced around the restaurant, feeling my anxiety kick up with every face I passed over that wasn't Keely's, until I spotted a blonde head toward the back of the restaurant, her back to me.

Steeling myself, I grabbed my phone and dialed Rich's number. I didn't wait for him to pick up; instead, I slid the phone into my cardigan pocket and made my way toward the table where Keely was sitting. She was by herself, which gave me the perfect opportunity to slip into the seat across from her.

The look of surprise on her face was worth the price of admission, but her shock quickly faded into a sneer of disdain, and she gave me the iciest once-over I'd ever seen outside a high school bathroom.

"Some people really don't learn," she said coldly.

"I was just wondering if you might be the person I should send the bill to for my car door?" *Ohhh, bold move, Phoebe. Let's see if it pays off.*

"I'm sure I have no idea what you're talking about."

"Really, Keely? Keely Morgenstern, regional operations manager of Setting Sun Corp? The same Setting Sun Corp that owns the car that tried to kill me?" I paused. I hadn't been expecting to come right out and accuse her of this, but now those cards were on the table, and I wanted to see how she would react.

She didn't flinch or show any outward kind of emotion. More importantly, she also didn't sputter any denials or pretend what I was saying was news to her.

"If someone tried to kill you, they didn't do a very good job of it, did they?" She sipped her margarita like this was any old ladies' night. "Good work on the Googling, though. You figured me out. I have a second job." She waved her fingers in a little *I'm so scared* gesture that proved she wasn't at all intimidated by my presence.

"You were poised to make a lot of money from that estate sale, and Mr. Weatherly's estate had you listed as the sole heir. So what I can't figure out is why you'd let a corporation you don't even own benefit from all that money. I'm assuming you knew Madeline was one of the founders?"

Keely choked on her sip of margarita, the green ice splashing onto her cheeks.

That's a no, then.

"The best I can figure out is that someone told you to hire her, right? Said she'd be the best to help you get top dollar on the estate. And you figured she was in it for the commission. Not a bad spot of cash for a ten-million-dollar estate, I'm sure. But I think whatever your partner forgot to mention to you was that they had their own little agreement with Madeline."

Keely stared at me, the emotionless front replaced with something angrier. "Madeline was just the estate agent; you don't know what you're talking about."

"Then what did she and your partner fight about the day of the sale?" Here I had the upper hand, because I'd heard Madeline's half of this conversation and knew the argument had been personal.

"Who says I have a partner? Sounds to me like you've just come up with a pretty farfetched story based on what, a few papers with my name on them? A car registered to a company I work for?" She made a *psh* sound. "You've got nothing."

"I think I'm closer than you'd like to admit, Keely. That's why you sent me that text message telling me to stay out of it."

"I have seen you like *once*. I don't know who you are, but I know you're really starting to get on my nerves."

She was looking around the restaurant, and I feared she might call for someone to kick me out before I got any really concrete evidence that we could use against her.

"Who is W. Bruckner, Keely?"

The seat shifted beside me as another body settled into the faux leather. Before I had a chance to look at our new party member, something hard and metallic feeling was pressed against my ribs beneath the table.

"That would be me."

Chapter Forty

We stayed in the restaurant only long enough for Keely to pay the bill. I still hadn't gotten a good look at W. Bruckner, Keely's partner and the man who currently had a gun pressed to my side. Every time I started to look his way, he prodded me with the weapon and said, "Uh-uh. No peeking."

Once the bill was cleared, he said, "We're going to take a walk, the three of us, and I'm going to answer some of your very annoying questions. Then we're going to get rid of you the same way I got rid of the last person who asked too much."

"Well, I guess at least I got to see the inside of La Bella Cantina before I died," I said grumpily, a little louder than I needed to. No one nearby paid any attention to me, and I had to assume that level of hyperbole was nothing new for the popular eatery.

Keely led the way out to the parking lot and Bruckner stayed beside me, though he had draped his coat over the gun and kept himself locked to my side as we went. I could have screamed, could have tried to make a break for it, but sensing what I was thinking, he leaned over and whispered in my ear, "You do anything stupid and you won't be the only person I put a bullet in tonight, am I clear?"

Glancing around at the other patrons and the waitresses, I couldn't risk him being true to his word.

Outside, the air had gotten colder, and goose bumps exploded over my arms in spite of my cozy cardigan. Keely walked over to a dark SUV, identical to the one I'd seen last night, but the license plate didn't have the letter and number I'd glimpsed on the original. Either they had two identical cars or they'd changed the license plate.

"What happened to the plates?" I asked out loud. "These look different."

"You really are a nosy little snoop, aren't you? Just get into the car."

Keely climbed into the driver's side, and Bruckner pushed me into the back seat, climbing in behind me. With the doors closed and the lights off, he finally stopped caring if I looked at him, which was good, because it was impossible not to in such close quarters.

He was younger than I expected, maybe in his late thirties or early forties. His skin had a dark tan that had wrinkled the skin around his eyes and mouth permanently, but his dark hair remained untouched by age, showing no signs of silver, even in the darkness.

His face looked familiar to me, but I couldn't quite place it at first. Then it hit me not just once, but twice.

"You were at the auction that day. You were one of the servers." I could picture him so clearly it was like being back in the house all over again, which was when the *other* realization hit me.

I'd seen his face somewhere else but hadn't made the connection, because I hadn't been thinking about some random waiter carrying champagne flutes around.

It had been in a newspaper article, one of the ones I'd dug up in my deep dive into the Weatherly family history.

"Oh my *God*," I breathed out, unable to believe what I was seeing. "You're Warren Weatherly."

The only son that Weatherly Sr. had apparently had any love for, who had died in a sailing accident while taking a boat from Fiji to Hawaii.

Except he had probably never left Fiji.

Because he was alive and well, sitting next to me, with a very real gun pointed in my direction. There had never been a W. Bruckner. This whole thing had been manipulated by Warren Weatherly himself.

"Start driving, Keely." He never took his eyes off me, and the gun looked relaxed and natural in his hands. I didn't have very high hopes of my ability to get it away from him or execute my other brief idea, which had been to do a tuck and roll out of the car.

Warren looked incredibly calm, like he could sit there all day with a gun pointed at me and it wouldn't bother him a lick.

"I have to admit, you were the last person I expected to be behind all of this."

"Well, obviously, because Warren Weatherly is dead. How could he possibly have anything to do with it?"

"Very clever. I guess I just don't understand the point of it all."

"Then you're missing the obvious, aren't you? The *point* is the money."

"That money would have all gone to you if your father had known you were alive, though. He only ever wanted to give it to you. Faking all this was so unnecessary."

"You have no idea what goes on behind closed doors in families, Ms. Winchester. My father was very clear before I left on my last trip to Fiji that his expectations for me were different than the life I was living. He wanted me to run the family business and give up on my passions, and told me in no uncertain terms that if I went to Fiji, he would remove me from his will and he would no longer have a son. I went to Fiji, and he called and told me he was a man of his word and that I was no longer welcome in his home or his life."

"That's not the story he told your family. He told everyone else that the estate would *only* ever go to you and no one else had been deserving."

"Then I guess he decided no one was deserving at all. Wanted to take it all to the grave with him. But I met Keely and found out she was from my hometown, and I made her a proposition. I could help her get close to my father, be his nearest and dearest. I told her everything she needed to know about him, his likes, his dislikes, his quirks. Soon enough she was indispensable to him, and there was no question at all of who he would leave his fortune to."

"Where did Madeline come in?"

"Well, I tried it with Madeline first, was going to have her become Father's assistant, but she got greedy and took on a job with the estate firm. Visions of dollar signs for those commissions, you know. But she had already helped me open the shell company, so I knew I had to stay on good terms with her because she knew a little *too* much."

"Like who you were."

"Yes, and admittedly, she also helped set me up financially so I could support myself until the old man finally kicked the bucket."

I glanced up into the rearview mirror and caught a glimpse of Keely's tense, furious expression. She obviously hadn't known how connected Warren and Madeline had been, and finding out she had been the second choice to run his con had to sting a little.

"So that's why you told Keely to hire Madeline. The commission would help you pay her back what you owed her and then some, and you would get all the money from the estate that you believed you had coming to you."

"Like you said, it *should* have been mine, but my father was a cruel and petty man, and loved nothing more than ruining the lives of those around him. But he sure did like Keely. He must have seen himself in her." He cast a cruel smile up to the front seat, and it was clear there was no great deal of fondness between these two.

Funny. I had assumed it must have been a love affair that drove her to help him, but at this point I was positive it was all about the money and nothing more. For some reason, that made it even worse to me.

"Why did you kill Madeline?" If he was pressing a gun to my ribs, I wanted an answer to the most obvious question of them all. "I overheard her arguing with someone on the phone that day. I assume that had to be you."

"Then you must know why I had to kill her. She was holding her knowledge over me, asking for more than just the commission. She didn't stick to her end of the bargain and was threatening to give it all away. You obviously know I was there that day. She was ready to tell everyone the whole truth if I didn't agree to pay her more, and frankly, I don't appreciate it when people get greedy."

The irony of that statement was not lost on me.

"So you killed her."

"She didn't give me much choice, did she?"

"I would argue there's probably always a better choice than murder, but perhaps that has something to do with the situation I currently find myself in." I gestured toward the gun, unable to believe I was saying it all so calmly. "It was you in the car that night on the highway, I take it."

He smiled, a feral, predatory smirk. "You were just getting too close. You almost saw me at the funeral, and if you'd remembered me from the auction, it would have been done right then and there. If you'd been smart, you would have listened to that message I had Keely send you. Now look at you."

"Yeah, I'm seeing the error of my ways, trust me."

Car lights passed going the opposite direction, but otherwise it was completely dark outside now. Aside from the rare overhead light that helped drivers not get lost, I couldn't even see Warren's face anymore.

"So what now?" I asked.

"Well, now we need to kill you, I'm afraid."

"I figured that much out. I meant for you two. Since I'm not long for this world, maybe you'll humor me."

"We had a bit of delay with the sale, but once that wrinkle is smoothed over, we'll finish selling off the estate, and then Ms. Morgenstern and I can go our separate ways, with all the wealth afforded to us by this little endeavor."

"Uh-huh, yeah. See, here's the problem I see with that. Keely, do you really think that the guy who was willing to kill Madeline over her share in the money wouldn't do the same to you? He had it all put in the Setting Sun accounts, right, the accounts that you're connected to, sure, but that he owns? So, is there anything from stopping him removing you from those? Or even deciding you're too much of a liability like Madeline was? Think about it for a second; do you really think you're walking away from this with millions?"

"Shut up," Warren snarled.

"I think I hit a nerve."

"Keely knows I'd never do that to her."

"Mmm, does she, though? If I were her, I wouldn't be so sure." I wasn't sure if Warren could feel it, but the SUV had begun to slow. This time when I looked into the rearview mirror, Keely was looking back at me. "Pretty sure once that sale is complete, he's done with you. Right now, you're not a murderer. You didn't know he was going to kill Madeline, right? But you know what he's planning to do to me."

"Shut *up*." This time he lashed out, bringing the gun down hard. It was dark, though, and he didn't get a good angle on it; instead of hitting me in the back of the skull, the butt of the pistol glanced off the side of my head, mostly catching my ear.

It still hurt like the dickens, but I didn't lose consciousness. Still, there were pretty cartoon songbirds spinning around my head, blue and red ones lighting up the interior of the car.

"Son of a—"

I guess Warren saw them too.

As Keely pulled the SUV over to the corner of the highway, the last thing I saw before slumping onto the floor of the car was Detective Martin approaching the side of the car with her weapon drawn, very calmly insisting that Keely get out of the car.

From somewhere in the pocket of my cardigan, I faintly heard Rich's voice saying, "You're going to be okay. We're coming for you."

Chapter
Forty-One

Four days later

B ob jumped from one tower of boxes up to another, until he was positioned atop the tallest stack in the store, lording over all of us in his ginger-and-white tabby glory.

"Mreow," he crowed triumphantly.

"Yes, you're the king of the castle. Good boy." I gave him some chin scritches as I passed, and he closed his eyes, purring with delight.

The store was an absolute disaster. There were literally hundreds of small boxes covering every single inch of available space. I scratched absent-mindedly at the bandage over my ear, annoyed that it was so itchy. I'd needed three stitches in my forehead and two in my ear thanks to Warren's misdirected blow, but I had to be thankful it wasn't the concussion I probably would have gotten if he'd hit me where he intended.

Everything had happened so quickly in the SUV that night I hadn't been able to panic, which meant my powers hadn't kicked in. I was a bit miffed, only because I felt like having magical time-stopping ability would have come in really handy when I was being hauled into the back of a getaway car, but apparently my powers seemed to decide on their own when I got to use that particular gift.

Daphne stood in the archway between the tea shop and the bookstore, sipping my bribery latte and assessing the carnage. She hadn't been here the previous night when the boxes arrived, so this was her first time seeing just how ludicrous it all looked. There was a vacant circle of space around the fireplace and a path leading from there to the register, but that was it in terms of open floor.

The Knit and Sip ladies had *not* been deterred by the presence of so many boxes. They were very dedicated to their Friday night gossip sessions, it seemed.

Now that it was just me, Daphne, and Imogen, I couldn't believe we'd also managed to wedge six old ladies in here the previous night. That had probably been a fire code violation of some kind.

Our front door had a sign taped up reading *Closed For Inventory*, but if someone were to peek through the window right now, they would assume we were moving.

"This is . . . a lot." Daphne was wearing grubby jeans, at my suggestion, and an oversized BTS T-shirt hanging off one shoulder. Her curly blonde hair was pulled up on the top of her head in a messy bun.

"Yeah, but remember, we're not doing inventory on all these boxes right now," I said, hoping it would help make the task less intimidating.

"No, we just need to do all the books on the *shelves*," Imogen interjected, sweeping into the room in the cutest velour joggers I'd ever seen and a Gucci T-shirt I suspected might actually be real. Daphne groaned.

I was wearing my denim overalls and a Chicago Museum of Science and Industry T-shirt. My hair was pulled back into a high ponytail, because otherwise I'd sweat to death, but I was glad only

Daphne and Imogen were here to see the bandages on the one side of my head. I was also eternally grateful that Warren had managed to hit me in such a way that I hadn't needed to have my hair shaved for the stitches.

Small favors and all that.

Bob was now curled up on the tallest box, happy as a clam in the warm morning light that poured in from outside.

"Well, boss," Imogen prompted. "Where do we want to start?"

I glanced around the room, feeling a little lost and hopeless, wishing I had even the faintest idea. "Why don't we keep the stacks by the fireplace up here? That way we can scan those at the end and sit while we do it. Everything else we can take to the basement. I don't want to worry about what's in each box or we'll be here for a month. Just one box at a time, right? We'll take turns on the stairs."

Daphne gave me a funny look. "No offense, Phoebe, but I think you should probably avoid doing a lot of heavy lifting right now?" Her gaze was locked on my forehead.

"Yeah, normally I wouldn't be giving out any free passes, but this time you're lucky," Imogen said. "Daphne and I will move the boxes. You get started scanning."

I had missed two days of work thanks to my trip to the hospital and subsequent visits with the police after I was released. There had been *many* lectures, both from the detectives and from Rich, but they had collectively agreed that my quick thinking at the restaurant had helped bring in the killer.

Me loudly complaining about the restaurant and mentioning the changed license plates had helped them narrow down where I was and what car they were looking for, which was how the cops had managed to intervene so quickly.

And Rich, a smarty-pants of his own, had recorded the incoming conversation. While it had been muffled thanks to my sweater, it was very clear that Keely and Warren had admitted their parts. Warren's even being alive was a big shocker to the whole family, of course, but certainly went a long way toward explaining what had happened.

Warren was probably going to spend a lot of time in prison thanks to his confession, but Keely had hired a good lawyer, and as I'd pointed out to her in the car, she hadn't actually helped kill anyone.

She'd probably get tagged with some accessory charges—I wasn't feeling very forgiving about her part in my kidnapping—but at the end of the day, she'd go to a rich-person prison for a year or two, then get to live out her life in peace.

Technically, she'd still inherited the estate, though I'd heard from Rich that Riley and the Weatherly clan were planning to contest that on the grounds that she had manipulated and lied to Mr. Weatherly. I wasn't sure it would go in their favor, but the whole thing was bound to be in the courts for many months to come.

What had already been sold at auction remained a legal sale—millions in goods now with their new owners. Including my hundreds of boxes of books.

Daphne and Imogen formed a two-person assembly line, where Imogen would get the boxes to the top of the stairs and Daphne would take them the rest of the way down. While they worked, I grabbed a tablet and a scanner and set about scanning our in-stock inventory.

Hours passed, pizzas were ordered, and as we were sitting down to enjoy a break with pepperoni and pop, a gentle tapping called my attention to the door.

"You guys eat. I'll take care of it." I brushed my dusty hands on my overalls and went to the door, cracking it open to tell our would-be customer they'd need to come back another day.

Mr. Loughery was standing outside, wearing a newsboy cap, a light jacket draped over his shoulders. But he didn't have a book in his hands.

"Mr. Lough . . . Norman, we're actually closed for the weekend, I'm so sorry."

"Oh, I know, my dear; you told me yesterday you would be. I might be wrinkled, but my noggin still works okay." He tapped the side of his head. "I came by for another reason, and I didn't want to wait until Monday. Worried I might lose my nerve, you know?"

I gave him a quizzical look, opening the door a little wider. Bob appeared next to me and looked up at Mr. Loughery, giving him a gentle "Breow" in greeting.

"'Ello to you too, Bob. No treats today, I'm afraid."

Bob licked his paws to show there were no hard feelings.

"That's actually why I've come," Mr. Loughery continued. "I've thought about it—about Frodo, that is. And I think I'd very much like to adopt him."

Tears sprang to my eyes unexpectedly, and I pressed my hand to my chest, trying to calm my joyously tripping heart.

"Norman, that's wonderful news. I'll arrange everything with the shelter. You're going to be our first adopter for the new adoption center."

"Can I make a little suggestion, if that's the case?"

I nodded. "Of course."

"I think you oughta call it *Bob's*. Since he's the reason I decided to say yes." He tipped he cap at me and headed back down the street, a little slow but very steady.

I looked down at my cat and smiled.

"I think that's a great idea."

Recipes

Easiest Sourdough Starter

Multiple cups whole wheat flour
Water, cool but not cold (this can also depend on your home
temperature; if you're having trouble getting your sourdough
to activate, your home might be too cool, in which case try
lukewarm water instead)

Final yield: About 1½ cups active starter

Sourdough feels like kitchen witchcraft. You take two totally shelf-stable ingredients, then turn them into a living thing. It's mad science, but it's also a relatively easy process.

To start your sourdough journey, get a clear, nonreactive container like glass (this makes it much easier to see the progress your starter is making). Make sure it's big enough to provide plenty of room to grow; at least 1 quart is ideal. Designate a place on your kitchen counter that doesn't get too much direct light and doesn't experience too much temperature fluctuation (so keep it away from your stove or from any windows or doors).

To begin, mix 1 cup flour and ½ cup water until no dry flour remains. Cover the container loosely and let it sit for a day. The next day, discard half of your starter and again add 1 cup flour and ½ cup water, blending until combined. Wait 24 hours.

This process can feel a bit wasteful, but once the starter has successfully activated, you will be able to use the discard in other recipes.

On day three, things should start to look a bit like a science experiment. The starter may be actively bubbling, it will likely have increased in volume, and it should start having a noticeably yeasty or sour smell to it. It's time to start feeding it more frequently. Every 12 hours, remove ½ cup of the starter and discard the rest. To this starter, continue to add 1 cup whole wheat flour and ½ cup water, stirring to combine completely. This process is known as "feeding" the starter, and you will continue to feed the starter twice a day for three more days.

By the time you get to day six, you should be seeing a bunch of bubbles and the "sour" scent will be much more noticeable. If you have achieved this, congrats—you now have an active sourdough starter. Give it one last feeding, and then you can go into maintenance mode.

No bubbles? Continue to feed it twice a day until you do see them. Don't worry; this process can take anywhere from one to three weeks. Just keep going until you see the bubbles and the starter seems to be doubling in volume.

If you have successfully achieved bubbles, you can now transfer the starter to a more permanent storage container (glass definitely works best). If your container has a cap, do not screw it airtight but leave it loose. Most home cooks will store their starter in the fridge, where it will be just fine being fed once a week. If you are a more frequent baker (like Phoebe), you can keep your starter on the counter and feed it daily.

If you store it in the fridge, bring the active starter to room temperature for two to four hours before you bake to make sure it's at its best.

If you plan to need more than ½ to 1 cup of starter, you can give the starter an extra feeding the day before you plan to bake but without discarding any starter; this will give you enough extra for your recipe.

Sourdough starter can be kept and used indefinitely as long as it continues to smell good and stays bubbly. As Phoebe notes in the book, starters have remained active for decades and even centuries if well cared for, and you can even dry out your starter if you'll be gone on an extended vacation and rehydrate it later.

This base recipe will get you your own unique starter and is a great base for many of the recipes you'll find at the Earl's Study.

Cheddar-Jalapeño Sourdough Bread

½ cup active sourdough starter, such as Easiest Sourdough Starter
1½ cups water
⅓ cup whole wheat flour
3¾ cups bread flour
2 teaspoons sea salt
¼ cup chopped pickled jalapeño (feel free to use more if you like it
    spicy)
1 cup cubed old cheddar (you can use ½ cup shredded cheddar, but
    the cubes are more aesthetically visible in the loaf and have a
    more obvious taste)

Makes 1 loaf

Bring your recently fed starter to room temperature for two to four hours before you begin baking.

Add 1 cup of water to the starter and stir to combine, then add both types of flour. You can mix this with a stand mixer, but since the dough is quite sticky at this point, it may be easier to mix by hand. Once all ingredients are combined and a shaggy dough is formed, let the dough sit for one hour.

Add salt to the remaining water, then pour the liquid into the resting dough. Mix again until fully combined, then allow to sit for one more hour.

Now begin repeated kneading of the dough, about every 30 to 40 minutes. Begin to stretch and knead the dough before re-forming it into a ball. You will do this three times in your mixing bowl.

During the second kneading, add the jalapeños and cheese, and continue to stretch and knead until the pieces are completely incorporated into your dough. Repeat the kneading process a third time, then form your final loaf. Flour your work surface, then put your dough down and gently shape it into a ball, ensuring there are no obvious seams or gaps. (A bench scraper can be very useful during this process, as it can help lift the dough more easily off your counter.)

Let the dough rest in a floured bowl or a floured proving basket if you have one. Then let the dough sit untouched for about three hours. The dough should increase in size but not double.

Get a Dutch oven ready by placing it in the oven and heating it to 500 degrees.

Now you can get creative. Place your shaped dough onto a piece of parchment paper, then use a lame (if you don't have one, any sharp knife will work) to score the top of the loaf. The standard cut is one long single slice across the top, which keeps the loaf from overexpanding in the oven, but you can use a lame to cut intricate and beautiful patterns into the surface of your loaf. You can also dust the top of your loaf with flour, which will give it a slightly powdered finish when it comes out of the oven.

Remove the Dutch oven from the hot oven, then use the parchment paper to lift and place your loaf into it. Reduce heat to 450 degrees and bake covered for about 30 minutes. Remove the lid and bake another 20 minutes or until the loaf is a nice golden-brown color, though some may prefer to cook it to a darker brown.

Let cool completely before serving.

Phoebe tops her slices with thinly sliced turkey, fresh tomato, and a slice of Monterey Jack cheese, then places them under the broiler for 2 to 3 minutes until the cheese is melted.

Homemade Ricotta Cheese

8 cups whole milk (not ultrapasteurized)
½ teaspoon salt
3 tablespoons fresh lemon juice (white vinegar will also work as the
    acid here)

Makes roughly 2 cups of ricotta

This recipe works best in a nonreactive bowl, so if you have glass mixing bowls, get them out! Before you start, line a strainer with cheesecloth that has been folded over three times and place the strainer over
your bowl. You are now ready to begin!

Heat milk over medium heat. Add salt and stir; use a wooden spoon
for this if you have one, and be careful not to let the milk sit too long,
as it may burn. A thermometer is best for this, as you will want to
heat the milk to 185 degrees (simmering but never boiling).

Reduce heat to low and add lemon juice (or vinegar).

Stir until you begin to notice the milk part separating into curds (sol-
ids) and whey (liquid) and appreciate that you now know what Little
Miss Muffet was eating when the spider showed up, but also wonder
why on earth this was her snack of choice.

Remove from heat and let stand covered for 15 to 20 minutes.

Once cooled, ladle the ricotta into your waiting cheesecloth and strain. You can strain lightly if you want a creamier finish (like if you plan to put it on toast) or strain more thoroughly to get a firmer ricotta you can use in cheesecake or lasagna.

Enjoy immediately, as it will not keep in the fridge for long.

Note: You can also buy cheese kits, as Phoebe did, from most major online retailers or local cheesemakers that will help you make your first batch if you want to try multiple kinds of cheese, but this nontraditional ricotta is genuinely a three-ingredient wonder, no special tools needs aside from cheesecloth.

Why is this nontraditional? Real ricotta is traditionally made from the leftover whey of other cheese products, so this version is not a truly "traditional" ricotta recipe, but certainly an easier one if you don't happen to have leftover whey on hand.

Amy's Breakfast Hand Pies

2 sheets puff pastry (cold but not frozen)
Stuffing ingredients of choice (see below)
Flour to dust work surface

Bacon, Egg, and Cheese Stuffing:
1½ cups scrambled eggs at room temperature
3–4 slices cooked bacon (crispier is better)
½ cup shredded cheddar cheese
Salt and pepper to taste

Crab, Chive, and Goat Cheese Stuffing:
1 can crabmeat, drained
1 cup crumbled goat cheese (or 1 log soft goat cheese)
3 tablespoons finely chopped chives
1 teaspoon Old Bay seasoning
Salt and pepper to taste

Each recipe yields 6 hand pies

Preheat oven to 400 degrees.

Lightly flour your work surface. Take cold puff pastry dough and unfold onto work surface, then cut both sheets into six equal rectangles. This should give you twelve total rectangles.

Place six of the puff pastry rectangles onto a parchment-lined baking sheet.

In a medium-sized bowl, combine all stuffing ingredients.

Leaving about a ½-inch border, put a sixth of your stuffing of choice onto each rectangle. Then using water, wet the edges and place the reserved rectangles on top. Use a fork to crimp the edges until the hand pies are sealed, then cut a small ½-inch slit in the top of each pie.

Bake for 20 to 25 minutes depending on desired color. Let cool for about 10 minutes before serving.

Note: These are basically adult Pop-Tarts, so you can really have an endless number of filling options. Try these to start, then let your imagination run wild.

Peach's Signature Butter Smash Burger

2 sticks unsalted butter
3 pounds ground beef, preferably chuck
1 tablespoon seasoning salt
½ teaspoon celery salt
Pepper
8 slices American cheddar
8 brioche buns

For serving: caramelized onions, crispy bacon, pickles (sliced lengthwise), chili (optional), other condiments to personal preference

Makes 8 burgers

Grate the unsalted butter using a box grater.

In a large bowl, combine the beef and butter and mix with your hands until well combined. Do not overmix, as the butter will begin to melt the more you handle it. Generously season your meat mixture with seasoning salt, celery salt, and pepper.

Shape into eight big balls. Yes, that's right—balls, not patties. Don't worry; trust the process.

Place balls on a baking sheet or in a metal bowl and put in the fridge until right before you cook.

For a true Peach's experience, you will cook these burgers on the stovetop, unless you have a griddle option for your barbecue grill. Heat a cast-iron skillet or your griddle to super-high heat, then take your burger balls out of the fridge. Working with three to four burgers at a time, depending on the size of your work area, let the balls sit for 3 to 4 minutes, and then comes the fun part. Flatten your burgers as much as you can. You can use a spatula, a burger press, or even another clean skillet, but get them as flat as you can.

Cook for 3 to 4 minutes more before flipping. Add the cheese slices and cool 1 to 2 minutes more.

While the cheese melts, you can quickly add butter to your brioche buns and broil them for 1 to 2 minutes with the interior facing up until they are just golden brown inside.

Assemble your burger and enjoy immediately. Napkins are required.

Note: Peach's chili is a chili con carne with no beans and a slightly sweet finish, thanks to brown sugar added during cooking. Your favorite chili will work just fine if you want to go for a loaded burger, and the burger is also wonderful with no chili at all. Do what your heart tells you.

An additional note on the buns: While the buns as written in the book have an onion crust on them, these may prove difficult to source unless you make them yourself. Any brioche bun will work for this recipe.

Acknowledgments

First and foremost, I want to thank every single person who read *Something Wicked*. Your support and enthusiasm for the first book in this series far exceeded any of my expectations, and because of you Phoebe and Bob's adventures get to continue. Thank you a million times over. I hope this series keeps charming you, because I love writing it.

Next, I have to thank my incredible editor, Melissa Rechter, for believing in this story and believing in me. My gratitude to you is endless. And likewise to the entire staff at Crooked Lane Books, who continually champion me and my work and are just genuinely the best people to work with.

I have to thank every one of my friends—my chosen family—for the way you rallied around me and these books. After a decade in publishing, I was sure you'd be sick of being my cheerleaders, but you showed up for me like *Something Wicked* was the first book I'd ever written. You made this whole process feel fun and exciting again. Thank you.

Special thanks to Darby Robinson, my podcast cohost, for all the wonderful insider tips on local PNW snacks and general Washington information. For anyone who actually caught that "Tim" chips reference in the first chapters, I owe it to Darby.

And last but not least, thanks to my past self for spending so darned much money on tea. Guess it's finally paying off.

About the Author

GRETCHEN RUE lives in the Canadian prairies, which affords her ample time to read during six months of winter. She plays cat mom to seven mostly indifferent fur children, and plant mom to roughly 100 very demanding flora. When she isn't sipping tea and working on her next novel, she enjoys swimming, hiking, and watching baseball.